The Sun
is
Bright

Also by Susan Hubert

FICTION

Sabi Star

Sunrising – Book 1 of the Sunrising Series

The Full Moon Rises at Sunset – Book 3 of the Sunrising Series

The Sun
is
Bright

A Novel

SUSAN HUBERT

Cover design - Duncan Watson

Main front cover photograph of the Matobo - Frankie Kay

Photograph of Staffordshire bull terrier – Frances Randell

Photograph of Aloe aculeata (otherwise known as a Red Hot Poker) – Gavin Stephens

*This book is dedicated to
Margaret Montgomery*

Cast of Characters

The Craigs

Isabella b 1877 married in 1900 to Anthony b 1873 d 1905
Oliver b 1905 married in 1933 to Emily d 1943
Amanda b 1940

Sunrising Staff

Gonda Zulu – the butler
Patience Zulu – the maid and Gonda's daughter
Kefi Nyoni – the cook
Admire Mpofu - the chauffeur

Brightside Staff

Miss Harrison, known as Harry – the governess
Prince Zulu – the cook and Gonda's son
Agnes Sibanda – the maid
Bhutu Nyathi – the stable hand

The Brookes

Celia b 1874 married in 1906 to Sir James b 1862
Timothy b 1907 married in 1935 to Serena b 1914
Tim and Serena's children:

                    Martin b 1935
                    Valerie b 1936
                    John b 1939
                    Beatrice b 1940

Patricia b 1909
Graham b 1917

Sunlands Staff

At Brooke House

Tuppence Moyo – the cook
Jesus Ndlovu - the gardener
Champion Nkala – the stable hand
Daphne Wolhunter– the nurse
At the Cottages
Isaiah Ndebele – the gardener
Amen Shumba – the gardener at the second cottage

The Sandersons

Peter married to Ella
Lillian, known as Lily
Obvious Ncube- the gardener

The Tates

Toby b 1893 married in 1918 to Pamela

Others

Mrs Jenkins -boarding house owner
Priscilla Clark - Lily Sanderson's best friend
Barbara Fletcher - Serena Brooke's best friend
Cyril and Julia Manning - proprietors of the Matopos Hotel
Barnaby Weir – the son of Isabella's best friend, Muriel Weir

Chapter 1

Bulawayo 1947

THE front door opened as Lily Sanderson leaned her bicycle against the veranda pillar of the boarding house where she stayed. Mrs Jenkins appeared in the doorway, an apron over her dress, a spoon in her hand, flour smeared across her cheek.

'You're back,' she snapped. 'Come quick. Your mother is on the telephone. It's the third time she's phoned in the last half hour, and it's annoying when I'm trying to make a pie for dinner.'

'I'm sorry, Mrs Jenkins. I had to take the standard twos for extra reading after school,' Lily murmured as she hurried into the hallway. The receiver was lying on the hall table, also covered in flour. Lily snatched it up, hearing the usual static in the background and wondering if a stranger was listening in on their call. 'Anyone there?' she asked.

'Yes, Lillian, it's your mother.'

'Anyone else?'

'Of course not,' her mother said, but Lily heard the click of another telephone being put down.

'Is something wrong, Mum? Mrs Jenkins said you keep phoning.' She lowered her voice and cupped her hand over the mouthpiece, whispering. 'You shouldn't do that, Mum. Mrs Jenkins doesn't like it.'

'Oh, rubbish, I'm sure she doesn't mind. However, you are back now, so we can talk. Your father and I are both well, thank you, but I want to speak to you about something else, about recent developments here. As you know, the Royal Family are visiting and I need you home this weekend to help me plan for this.'

'Mum,' Lily sighed. 'What on earth are you talking about? Everyone in Southern Rhodesia is making plans for their visit. The whole country is looking forward to it.'

'I know, but I'm not talking about their visit in general; I'm talking about them coming to our house. To our house, Lillian.'

Lily hesitated, absorbing this news. 'Goodness… But why? And when?'

'On the fourteenth of April. An *Indaba* is being arranged out here in the Matopos for the King to meet the chiefs. As Assistant Native Commissioner your dad is involved with the organization of this event.'

'Yes, I know.'

'Well, after the *Indaba,* tea will be served, and then the King, Queen and Princesses are using our house to freshen up, before going to see Rhodes's grave. They were to use the Wright's house, as he's the Native Commissioner, but Mrs Wright isn't well, so now they're using ours. Oh dear, there is so much that needs to be done before this place is fit for them. Please, please, come home this weekend so we can discuss everything.'

'But it's only February, weeks before the royal visit. I'm busy with marking and lesson plans this weekend, and I want to make some charts for my classroom walls. Teaching is difficult when you first start, even though I spent the last two years at teacher training college.'

'I know, I know.'

No you don't, Lily thought.

'But I need you this weekend,' her mother wailed. 'Your dad is travelling to town tomorrow. He can collect you after school. You can bring your work back and I will help with your charts and whatnot. The builders are coming on Monday, and plumbers and electricians too, and I want to go through everything with you before they get here. You are so good at visualising things.'

'Plumbers and electricians too? Goodness, our house is going to have a complete makeover.'

'It is. Electricity is to be installed in the office so they can have a sound system at the *Indaba*,' her mother continued. 'You know, microphones and speakers, to save people from yelling when they're making their speeches. Your dad asked if they can run a wire across here while they're about it, which means we will have electricity in this house at last.'

'What a difference that will make. It's so much easier turning on electric lights than fiddling with lamps and candles the whole time.'

'Yes. And besides this, basins, with hot and cold water, are to be fitted in all our bedrooms also.'

'Oh Mum, that is wonderful.'

'But I haven't told you the best news of all,' her mother said, then paused for emphasis.

'What?'

'We are having a water closet installed.'

'A water closet?'

'Yes'

'That is brilliant news.'

'We can't have the Royal Family using our smelly old long drop, can we?'

Lily laughed. 'No. Of course not.'

'So will you come home tomorrow, Lillian? You will be such a help.'

'Yes, Mum. I'll see you in the afternoon.'

After saying goodbye Lily wiped the flour from the receiver and replaced it, then went outside to retrieve her bicycle. She pushed it through the hall and up the stairs to her bedroom, leaning it against the wall in the corner at the foot of her bed. She shared the room with her best friend, Priscilla Clark, and each side of the room reflected their personalities. Lily's bed was neatly made, with nothing but a small cushion on it for decoration, while Priscilla's was scattered with dresses, cardigans, belts and scarves, discarded as she sought the perfect outfit for work that morning. But Lily ignored this mess as she walked to the window and looked out at the power station being built on the opposite side of Lobengula Street. She loved watching its development; the construction of six enormous cooling towers and the massive furnaces which would soon generate electricity for the town and surrounding areas. As she surveyed this progress, her thoughts returned to the impending royal visit, and her heart swelled with excitement. After all the years of war, the terrible news of men she knew being killed, the shortages and the rationing, it seemed that things were finally turning around.

*

The hill on which the Matopos Hotel is built is steep, so Peter Sanderson stopped his Model T Ford Tourer at the bottom to make a U-turn. This meant driving back and forth a number of times as the steering was heavy and the road narrow. Once he was facing the way he had come he grated the gear into reverse again, turned in his seat to look out of the small back window and pressed his foot hard on the accelerator. The engine revved ever louder as he drove up the hill backwards, just getting to the top with smoke billowing from the exhaust. Every time he did this he felt like an idiot, but his car was old and not designed to go up steep hills.

After reversing into the flat parking area at the side of the hotel and up to the tree where he always left his car, he picked up his hat and climbed out, straightening his tie as he walked towards the hotel. The hotel was little more than a small bungalow perched on top of the hill, but Julia had done wonders with the garden and this had transformed the place, he thought, as he made for the steps leading to the front door.

'Peter, how lovely to see you so early on a Friday morning,' Julia Manning said, from where she stood on the top step, just outside the door. She jerked her head inwards, and rolled her eyes, mouthing, 'I am not alone.' She was as smartly turned out as ever, with her hair pulled into a perfect bun, wearing stockings, and elegant shoes. 'Come in, come in, I'm sure my husband will be delighted to see you.'

'Morning Julia. Um, I see. Mm. Very well.' He straightened his tie again. 'I, um, I thought I would drop in on my way to town, um, to chat to your husband.'

'Always a pleasure. Please, come this way. Cyril is still having his breakfast.' She hurried ahead of him down a narrow passage, which opened into the dining room. Peter could not help but admire the black seams of her stockings and the way they went straight up the back of her shapely calves, disappearing under her skirt. He took off his hat and followed her, wondering what he would say to Cyril Manning.

'Morning Peter,' Cyril said, patting his mouth with his napkin and standing up. 'You're lucky to catch me. I had planned to be in town long before now. I like to get there before the heat of the day. But I have an upset gut this morning. Must've been something I ate, can't think what, because Julia is fine. Anyway, I'm having a piece of toast and marmalade to settle things, and then I'll be on my way. How can I help you?'

'Maybe I should come back another day, Cyril, when you are stronger?'

'No, not at all. You are here now. How about a cup of tea? Julia, can you ring for another pot?'

'No Cyril, this one is still fresh and only half drunk. Think of the poor people in Europe. We can't waste anything.' She poured Peter a cup as he sat down. He put his hat on the empty chair next to him and stared out of the window.

'Such a splendid view of the dam from here, Cyril.' he said, crossing his legs and reaching into his shirt pocket for a packet of cigarettes. He offered one to each of the Mannings and then patted his pockets, feeling for his matches.

'That's better,' he said drawing on his cigarette, after reaching over with a match for the Mannings to light theirs, as smoke wafted around them.'

'And how is Lily?' asked Julia, waving the smoke from her face. 'Is she settling in at Milton Junior?'

'Yes, she appears to be, thank you. She's teaching the standard two class. Early days yet, as she's only been there for four weeks, but so far so good.' He noticed the way Julia's red lipstick made a perfect puckered shape of her mouth on the end of her cigarette. He forced his eyes back on Cyril.

'So Peter, what did you want to discuss?' Cyril asked.

Peter drew on his cigarette again, turned his head towards the window as he exhaled, then ground his cigarette into the ashtray. 'Well, I'm on my way to town and thought I'd stop by to find out how your preparations are going for the royal visit?'

'Of course. It's only eight weeks away I believe.'

'That's correct.' Peter said. 'The organising committee has now decided the Royal Family will come to our house to change after the *Indaba.*'

'Oh really, I thought they were going to the Wrights.' Cyril said.

'They were, but have you not heard the unfortunate news?'

'No.'

'Poor Mrs Wright has cancer.'

'How awful,' Julia gasped. 'After what she went through with their son being killed in the war and all that. Oh, dear me, how worrying for them.'

'It is. She won't be able to cope with the preparations involved with the royal visit, so the Royal Family are going to use our house now, instead of theirs.'

'Well, that shouldn't be a problem,' Cyril said. 'Your house is right next to where the *Indaba* is taking place.'

'Not a problem for you or me, Cyril, but my wife is already getting herself into a total twist about it. She had a sleepless night last night worrying about everything, despite my telling her the Native Department is going to upgrade our house. We are to have a water closet as well as electricity and other plumbing.'

'Oh how wonderful to have a proper toilet at last, and to not have to use a long drop,' Julia said.

'Yes, but this is not stopping Ella from fretting,'

'I'm sure she will feel better once all the work is done,' Julia said.

'As for us,' Cyril interrupted. 'We don't have the funds for any renovations here. With all the post-war shortages, we will have to make do with what we have.'

'I'm doing what I can to make the garden as pretty as possible,' Julia said. 'I've hired two extra gardeners, and they've been working like Trojans making the garden look good, just in case the royal party drops in here to admire the view of the dam, or whatever.'

'I doubt they will have time for that. They have such a tight schedule. But there's nothing wrong with being prepared, just in case.' Peter smiled at Julia.

'That's how I see it.' Julia said.

'And what about hotel bookings? Have any of the invited guests contacted you about staying here around that time?' Peter asked.

'We've just had the one booking so far,' Cyril said. 'You know Isabella Craig was commissioned to do a painting of Rhodes's grave?'

'I do, and I'm not surprised. She is such a talented artist.'

'She is. Her painting is being presented at the *Indaba,* and her son, Oliver Craig, phoned to book himself and his mother in to stay here for two nights. He's bringing her to the function, and he said they may as well make an outing of it as the old girl will be too tired to drive back after all the excitement.'

'So it's just the two of them so far?'

'Yes, but I'm sure we will have more bookings.'

'Well, if you don't mind, I'd like you to update me on how this goes, in case I need to book some of the VIPs in here. I believe there is going to be a large contingent from Salisbury, and some of them may need billeting.'

'Between Julia and me, we will keep you posted,' Cyril said.

'Thank you. I would appreciate that,' Peter replied. He picked up his hat. 'I had better be on my way. I have a fair amount to do in town before I collect Lily after school. She is coming home for the weekend.'

'I won't be long behind you,' Cyril said. 'That piece of toast might just have done the trick. Maybe I will bump into you in town later, Peter. Please see our guest out, Julia.'

Chapter 2

OLIVER Craig opened the passenger door of his Chevrolet Coupe Imp and laid the painting on the seat. He pushed the brown paper bag of groceries onto the floor and made sure the painting was secure. It would be a disaster if he harmed it. There was no time for his mother to paint another one now, with the royal visit just weeks away. He wished someone else would take responsibility for the painting until they presented it to the Royal Family. But as usual, Isabella insisted on seeing the painting in its frame. She is such a perfectionist, he thought, she has to check everything.

He opened the driver's door, slid into the car, and wound the window down. He had parked in the shade of a tree in the parking spaces in the centre of the road outside the framing shop, but it was still scorching hot in the car. He climbed out again, took off his jacket, loosened his tie, and undid his top button. After throwing the jacket into the back, he felt for his cigarettes in his shirt pocket. He lit one, tossing the match into the dirt surrounding the tree, and slid back into the driver's seat. Starting the motor, he turned right out of the parking place, did a U-turn at the end of the centre parking bays, and headed north down Fife Street. He wanted to get the painting to Sunrising so that he could stop worrying about damaging it.

9

Everything looks so different, he thought, as he drove along Athlone Road, past the cemetery. Everywhere he looked, new homes were being built. So different from when he grew up at Sunrising, when he and his mother considered themselves living "out of town". Now, houses were being built right up to its gates, to accommodate all the people arriving from Europe, escaping the aftermath of the war. He could not blame them. If he lived in Europe, he would want to get away too. It was still far too depressing. After all the time he spent in Italy, ducking and diving from the Germans, he had also had enough of Europe for a while.

Sunrising is a big enough property that once you're in it, you don't notice all the building outside, he reflected, as he turned into the gate and drove up the drive, parking in the tree's shade beside the old fish pond. His mother's maid, Patience, opened the front door as he was walking up the steps onto the veranda.

'Good morning, Sir,' she said, a broad smile spreading over her brown face. 'We have not seen you for some weeks.'

'Morning Patience. I've been busy on the farm and haven't been to town since my last visit here,' he said.

'And the *picannini* missus? How is she?'

'Well, thank you. And your father? Where is he?' Oliver asked.

'He is in the kitchen, Sir. Today is the day silver is cleaned, and he is making sure the kitchen boy does it properly.'

'And where is my mother?'

'In her studio, Sir.'

Oliver smiled. 'Nothing much changes around here. I will go and find her there.'

He walked across the drive to the old stables, above which was his mother's studio. The stables had been converted into a garage before the war, and Isabella's Rover was parked in it. It looked shiny and newly polished, in contrast to the dusty tractor next to it. Isabella had the Rover sent out from England just before the war, but it still appeared brand new.

Oliver climbed the stairs to the studio. From the door he saw his mother in an armchair next to the window, fast asleep. Her dog, Eddie, was lying on the floor next to her, his ears pricked up, ever alert. He jumped up and ran across the room when he recognized Oliver. Oliver bent and patted his head, pushing him away as he was about to leap up. Isabella was not good at instilling discipline in her dogs. He looked at his mother again, with her head dropped forward and her mouth slightly open. Strands of her greying hair, which was usually pinned up in a bun, fell across her face and she was snoring. She is starting to look old, poor dear, he thought as he stared at her, wondering if he should wake her or not. Just as he determined he would, her eyes sprang open and a look of confusion flashed across her face. Her hands flew to her hair. She pushed the loose strands back and patted them into her bun.

'Darling,' she said. 'What on earth are you doing here?'

'I collected your painting from Naakes, and I've brought it for you to see. You told me you wanted to check it again after they had framed it.'

'Of course, yes. I do need to see it. If it is not how I want it, there is still time to have it reframed. Thank you. Darling, for bringing it.'

'Pleasure. It's a good excuse to drop in and see you.'

'It is always lovely to have you here. Is Amanda with you?'

'No, she had lessons this morning.'

'Of course. Hopefully I will see her again soon.'

'You will. She misses you.'

'And I her, but it is much better she is living with you now. How are the two of you getting along?'

'Things are still strained between us, Mama.'

'I am afraid it will take time. We all have to be patient.' Isabella struggled as she pulled herself up from the deep armchair. 'Let us go to the veranda now for some tea, and you can show me the painting there. Where is it?'

'I left it in my car.'

'Oh my, I hope it is not too hot. I would hate the paint to crack.'

'No, Mama, I parked in the shade next to the fish pond. It's fine. I will fetch it and meet you on the veranda.'

*

Oliver arrived back at the farm just as the sun was setting. He parked his Chevrolet in the garage, hauled his jacket from the back and, as he walked to the house, a sense of dread seeped through him, as if it was being injected into his veins. He had been back from the war for over a year now but he was still uneasy in his own home. He walked through the hall and into the drawing room and made straight for the drinks table, pouring himself a stiff whisky. He took this onto the veranda. The view over the farm from there always relaxed him. Prince came through, carrying a tray on which lay his mail. Ah, yes, the mailbag was delivered that day. He glanced at the tray with distaste. He still had an aversion to mail, in case it contained bad news.

'Good evening, Sir,' Prince said.

'Good evening, Prince. Is everything in order?'

'It is. There is also a letter from Mrs Brooke, Sir.'

He noticed Serena's large, flamboyant writing on the envelope at the top of the pile. He would look at it shortly. 'And Missus Amanda? Where is she?'

'I believe she is at the Brooke's house, Sir.'

'Maybe that is what this letter is about,' he said, feeling immediately brighter, 'Thank you, Prince. That will be all.'

Prince hovered.

'Yes, Prince?'

'Will Missus Amanda be joining us for dinner?'

'Let me see.'

He picked the letter knife off the tray and cut Serena's envelope open, unfolded the paper and started reading. It was as he expected. Amanda had spent the afternoon with her cousins, and Cousin Beatrice had asked if she could spend the night.

'No, Prince. It will just be me for dinner.'

'Very well Sir.'

Oliver settled into his chair, rolling his tongue around a sip of his whisky, savouring the taste, relieved he would not have to spend an awkward evening trying to make conversation with his daughter. The female members of his family had predicted that the two of them would enjoy each other's company by now, but this was not the case. If they both had their way they would never eat together. Amanda would have dinner either with the Brookes, or with Harry in the schoolroom, and he would dine alone in the dining room.

He finished his whisky and moved to the drawing room to pour himself a second. Prince had set out the hurricane lamps in their usual positions, and he breathed in the oily smoke they emitted. He found the smell comforting. It was small details like this that he had missed so much in the years he had lost in Italy. His homesickness only started after the Germans captured him. Although they had not always been busy in Egypt and Libya, there was a purpose to their days then. But once he had been captured and sent to Italy, where they moved him from one camp to the next, all sense of purpose disappeared. In the camps they just existed, wondering for how long they would be there. Now and then one of his fellow POWs tried to escape. Oliver shuddered as he thought of the time his friend Cranmore tried; how he was recaptured and shot and his body hung on the prison fence for two weeks, as a reminder to anyone else who was thinking of doing the same.

Stop! He told himself. He needed to keep busy so that his mind would not wander. He took his whisky and went into his study, to do some work before dinner. The phone rang, three short rings followed by one long, his number on the party line. He picked up the receiver.

'Oliver, it's me,' said his cousin-in-law, Serena.

'Good evening, Serena. Thank you for the note. It's fine for Amanda to stay the night with you. I was about to phone to tell you this.'

'Good, I did not think it would be a problem. She brought her pyjamas and toothbrush, just in case. Clever rascal.'

'I'm not surprised. She loves being with your lot.'

'Well, she's always welcome. They had such fun this afternoon. They made themselves a fort in that enormous fig tree behind our house. You know the one, near our garage?'

'Yes, the Ficus capensis.'

'Well, it's ideal for making a treehouse.'

'No snakes nor spiders?'

'No, not with all of them running around making their usual commotion. Martin is going to be furious when he gets back from school and discovers they have done it without him, but the girls were desperate and Jesus was his ever willing self and assisted them, in other words, he did everything. But I guess it makes a pleasant change from gardening.'

'I'm sure.'

'It was either that or going off to the river for a swim. But I'm always so afraid of crocodiles, I will not let them go near that river unless one of us is with them.'

'Quite. And how were their lessons this morning?'

'Fine, although I need to talk to you about this. However, not now. I'll have the children tucked up straight after supper and will send Amanda home after breakfast tomorrow if you like.

'Well, tomorrow is Saturday so there won't be any lessons. I don't mind if she wants to stay for the morning and carry on playing with her cousins.'

'Oh, that is kind of you. Would you like to come for lunch then, and you can take her home afterwards? It'll just be us for lunch. Us and the old folks too, of course. You didn't bring Aunt Isabella back to the farm for the weekend, did you?'

'No. She's arranged a luncheon party at Sunrising tomorrow. The old Fletchers and the Weirs.'

'I'm now wondering if we should invite some other people here tomorrow. I worry about you. You don't socialise enough.'

'Serena, please. No.'

"Oh, alright then. We will see you tomorrow at twelve-thirty.'

He put the telephone down, looking at the wedding photograph of Serena and Tim on the bookcase next to his desk, taken outside St. John's Cathedral in Rhodes Street. Stunning Serena, handsome Tim; reported in The Chronicle as Bulawayo's "Beautiful couple". He sighed. Everything had changed so much for all of them since then. He, coming back from the war to a daughter he didn't know, Tim with his debilitating condition.

It's little wonder I am depressed so often, Oliver thought.

Chapter 3

IF they did not have afternoon activities, Lily and Priscilla went to Borrow Street swimming pool after school finished at one o'clock. Priscilla taught at Coghlan School, and, as both Coghlan and Milton schools are on the same road as the swimming bath, it was a short bicycle ride to get there. Mrs. Jenkins packed sandwiches for their lunch, and they ate these while relaxing on the lawned terraces surrounding the huge pool. Before eating her lunch, Lily always swam, at least ten lengths, which she worked out was over a mile. She considered this good exercise and always felt better afterwards. Priscilla was not so keen. She preferred to sit on her towel, leaning against the trunk of the palm tree at the far end of the pool, and observing everyone there. This palm tree afforded a superb view of the entire area. Also, the shade under the palm was dappled at this time of the day so she could enjoy tanning in her new two-piece bathing suit. She loved the tan it gave her; a delicious looking brown stripe from above her belly button to below her breasts. She thought it looked sexy, although she was the only person to see it, of course, when she was changing or having a bath. She sighed and reached for her packet of sandwiches.

The town council had planted gum trees behind the palm when the swimming pool was built in 1927. These were a good size now, and, on boiling hot days, when the partial shade of the palm tree was inadequate, Priscilla would spread her towel under the gums. But not today. Today she was under the palm and her eyes were riveted to the diving boards, which were close to where she was sitting. Usually people using the diving boards did not interest her, as most just jumped into the pool from the lowest one, often holding their noses, which she thought looked stupid. But today someone was diving from the highest board.

'Look at him. He's incredible,' Priscilla said as Lily came up the terraces to join her under the palm tree, water still glistening and dripping off her slender body. Lily looked around. She unclipped her bathing cap strap and pulled it off, running her fingers through her short, dark hair, patting down the curls as she picked up her towel to dry herself.

'Who?'

'Him,' Priscilla said, pointing to the boards. 'Do you know who he is? I have never seen him here before.'

As if he knew he was being watched, the man walked to the end of the board, jumped once, twice, and launched himself off the end, his legs pushed together, his arms stretched beyond his head, his body arching through the air towards the sparkling water. He glided into the water with the smallest of splashes.

'Goodness, I almost feel I should clap,' Lily said.

'That is the third time he's done it. You didn't notice him before because you were too busy chatting to Margaret in the shallow end.' Priscilla's blue eyes widened. 'Look Lily. I believe he's going to do it again.'

Both girls watched as he climbed the stairs to the top board. His bathing suit was bright yellow, tight-fitting with a thin black belt around his slim waist.

'I bet he's new from England,' Priscilla said.

'As every second person here is "new from England" that's not saying much,' Lily responded.

'True. I wonder if he is a professional diver.'

'I doubt it as there won't have been any opportunities to dive professionally these last few years, what with the war going on.'

'A skydiver, perhaps? Maybe he used to dive out of planes. Over France, or Germany, or Italy. To spy. Maybe that is what he did during the war, and that is why he's so good at diving now.'

'You let your imagination run wild, Priscilla dear. Why don't you ask him who he is and what he accomplished during the war before you fantasise anymore about him?'

'I can't do that. Don't be so silly.'

Lily opened her pack of sandwiches and took one out, peering at it. 'Boring old egg again,' she muttered. 'I do so wish these shortages would ease up.'

Priscilla had no interest in talking about their sandwiches. 'Now look,' she said, watching the man in the yellow swimsuit pick up his towel and make for the change rooms. 'I think he's leaving. How disappointing. I'm never going to know who he is.'

'We can come back here every day until we see him again. And then you can contrive a way to meet him. You're good at that.'

'Ha!'

'It's true. But enough of him, I've got some serious matters I need to talk to you about.'

'Oh yes?'

'Mr Weir, my headmaster, asked me if I want to move into the hostel next term and I said yes.'

Priscilla's face fell. 'Oh no. I don't want you to leave Mrs Jenkins's boarding house. I love sharing a room with you. You don't complain about the mess I make, or when I snore and grunt.'

Lily smiled. 'I have learnt to be very accepting of everyone's idiosyncrasies. With a mother like mine, I have no choice. I don't want to leave the boarding house either. Mrs Jenkins can be a dragon, and it's a pain having to keep our bicycles in our bedroom, but I do enjoy being there with you. However, moving into the hostel will mean I earn more money. They will pay me extra for hostel duties, and I won't have board and lodging expenses.'

'Well, that's a plus.'

'Yes. I could do with the extra cash at this stage in my life.'

Thin lines played across Priscilla's forehead as she thought of something else. 'Your move next term won't change our holiday plans, will it?'

'No, not at all.'

'Good, because my godmother is expecting us in Beira on the twenty-fourth of April. All we need to do is pay for our train tickets and we're set.'

'I'm counting the days,' Lily said.

'Me too. I've never been to Portuguese East Africa. It's going to be such fun. Sand, sea and, um, let me think.' Priscilla paused.

'We can go to the harbour to watch the ships coming and going,' Lily suggested.

'Oh yes. And my godmother says they hold a tea dance at the Grand Hotel every afternoon.'

'How wonderful. So there is a Grand Hotel there too. I wonder if every town in Africa has one.' Lily laughed.

'I doubt it. But, like Bulawayo, my godmother says there is a Grand Hotel in Beira, and they have a resident band that plays at their tea dances, which start at three o'clock every afternoon. Of course, she won't be able to come with us, what with her job at Shell and all that, but she said we can catch a taxi from her flat.'

'I can't wait,' Lily said. 'Life is exciting these days, isn't it? First, we have the royal visit to look forward to, and afterwards, our trip to Beira.'

'But the royal visit is going to be so much more exciting for you than for me,' Priscilla said. 'I'm only going to be one of the thousands, in the welcoming crowd on Main Street when they first arrive, and then at the garden party in the park. And worse still, I will have lots of flag-waving Coghlan schoolchildren to look after, so it's not going to be fun. Unlike you, who will have the Royal Family in your home. I can't tell you how envious I am.'

'It's not as if I will be there. The Royals are going to have the use of our house, but we're not allowed anywhere near the place.'

'I know, but still. Just the thought of them being in your house, in your bedroom, it's so exciting. And you will see them close up at the tea party after their *Indaba* with the chiefs.'

'I'm not sure. I will help at one of the tables, but it'll be one of the "minor tables", which means none of the Royal Family will be anywhere near me.'

*

Lily planned to catch the train back to the Matopos the weekend before the royal visit. Her father was so busy preparing for this occasion, she did not wish to disturb his plans by asking him to collect her after school. Besides, she enjoyed train trips. She had travelled by train to Salisbury a few weekends earlier with the senior tennis team, to play a match against St. George's College. It had been a splendid adventure, despite having to oversee eight excited young schoolboys. She shared a compartment with three other women, with the boys in the two compartments on either side of hers. Whenever she heard them laughing and yelling, she banged on their doors then barged into their compartment and reprimanded them. However, in between, she managed to sneak off to the dining car for a relaxing cup of tea. She loved sitting at a table there, appreciating the crisp, white table cloth, the vase of flowers on the table, and **RR**, the insignia for Rhodesia Railways, written on every piece of crockery and cutlery she used. She even ordered a piece of banana bread to have with her tea, and wished she could have dinner there too, but her finances did not stretch to this and she had to make do with the unexciting bully beef sandwiches Mrs Jenkins made for her trip.

The train journey from Bulawayo to the siding close to her parents' house, in the foothills of the Matopos, only took an hour. Lily did not ask Mrs Jenkins for sandwiches this time, but ate lunch instead at the boarding house before she left; an uninspiring meal of boiled beef and dry potatoes. Afterwards, she walked to the station and, despite being just two blocks away, it was difficult this time because she had packed as much as possible into her suitcase. She did this because she was moving out of the boarding house soon, and she needed to have removed everything by then. However, as she hauled her heavy suitcase up the road, she thought it was a mistake to have packed so much in it this time. Her main worry was that the dress Mrs Jenkins had made for her to wear to the tea party would be crushed.

Mrs Jenkins was not her first-choice seamstress, but when she was serving breakfast one morning, she overheard Lily telling Priscilla she needed to have a dress made for the royal visit. Mrs Jenkins offered to do it, explaining that she had been a seamstress before she married. Lily knew life was difficult for Mrs Jenkins, with Mr Jenkins having died during the war. He left her with little more than his pension, making it necessary for her to open the boarding house. So, when she showed such interest in making a dress, Lily did not have the heart to say no, and what a pleasant surprise this turned out to be. Priscilla's aunt, who was French, had received a newspaper from France with an article in it about the latest fashion trends by the new designer, Christian Dior. He introduced what he termed a "New Look"; a softer style to the boxy-looking clothes they had worn in the war years. Priscilla and Lily pored over the photographs in the newspaper; the below mid-calf, full skirts, pointed busts, small waists, and rounded shoulders. Lily showed the newspaper photographs to Mrs Jenkins, who said, "No problem, I can design and make something along these lines." And she did.

The conductor noticed Lily struggling with her heavy suitcase when the train stopped at the Matopos siding. He helped her offload it, putting it on the dusty ground next to the tracks and looking up and down the railway siding to see if there was anyone around to help her. There was no one; just grass, trees and big rock hills known as *dwalas,* beyond. The only sign of life was the tweeting of birds.

'Don't worry,' Lily said. 'I live only half a mile down the road. I'm sure I can manage from here.'

The conductor looked sceptical, but at that moment the whistle blew and a jet of steam blasted from the funnel.

'I'm afraid I can't leave the siding as we will be moving off shortly,' he said.

'You don't have to concern yourself about me. If the worst comes to the worst I will get someone from my father's office to help me.'

She picked up the suitcase, pretending it was easy, and started walking down the dirt road, determined to keep going until she was out of sight of the siding. This took a great deal of effort and she wished, yet again, that she had not packed so much. She focused on reaching a shady fig tree further along the road before stopping. When she got to it, she dropped her suitcase on the ground with relief, the thick leather creaking with indignation as it hit the dirt. She was now just two hundred yards from her parents' gate, with the entrance to her father's work buildings on the opposite side of the road. Behind these buildings, she could see a huge marquee, erected for the *Indaba* with the chiefs. Just two days to go before all this, she thought. How lucky

I am to be a part of it. She was about to continue when she heard a man's voice.

'Good afternoon, Madam.'

She jumped, not realizing anyone else was around. But now she saw Obvious, her parents' gardener, standing nearby in the long grass.

'Goodness Obvious, you gave me a fright. Where on earth did you come from?'

'They sent me to siding to fetch mailbag.' He stepped onto the road and she saw he was carrying a thick canvas bag with the words

Native Department. Matopos District

written on the side. 'Everyone at office is busy, so they ask me,' he said.

'But I didn't see you at the siding.'

'I took shortcut through bush.'

'Of course.'

'Let me take suitcase, Madam. I carry it to house.'

'Thank you. Give me the mail bag and I'll drop it at the office. I can say hello to my father at the same time.'

They walked the short distance down the road together, Obvious carrying the suitcase with enviable ease.

'Thank you so much. That suitcase was far too heavy for me,' Lily said when they got to the gates. 'Leave it on the veranda and I'll take it inside when I get there.'

She was at the office for less time than she expected because no one was there. The marquee was erected away from the office, and she could see everyone bustling about busily like ants. She did not need to disturb them, so she left the mail bag and a note on her father's desk and walked over the dirt road to her home.

'Hi, Mum,' she called, as she approached the house, seeing her mother on the veranda staring at her suitcase.

Her mother glanced up, a look of horror on her face. 'What, what is this?' she stammered, pointing at the suitcase, her finger trembling.

'My suitcase, of course.'

'Lillian, you should have just brought an overnight bag. What is in there, and where are you expecting to put it?'

'Goodness Mum, it's only my clothes and stuff. I wanted to bring as much back as I could this time, as it's the end of the term and I need to move out of Mrs Jenkins's place.'

'Well, you shouldn't have. We gave this house a thorough spring clean in preparation for the Royal Family, and there is nowhere to put your clothes and suitcase.'

'I will unpack the clothes and put them in my cupboard, and the suitcase in the garden shed. I can't believe the Royal Family are going to be snooping around our house, opening our cupboards, when all they are doing is using it to change after tea?'

The worried look on Ella's face lifted. 'I suppose you're right. But please Lillian, you must not leave anything lying around and do put everything away neatly. You never know. They may just open a cupboard or two,'

Lily laughed. 'Of course Mummy dear. And how about a hello hug? I haven't seen you for a few weeks.'

'Mm, I could have done with you here, helping me prepare for all this.'

'I know, but Priscilla and I went to the cinema last weekend to see "The Harvey Girls", with Judy Garland. We have been waiting to see that film for ages, and we did not want to miss it. It's a musical, and we loved it.'

'Mm.'

'However, I'm home now; ready to assist you with any last-minute preparations that still need to be done.'

'The first thing you can do is help me pack for the two nights we will stay at the Matopos Hotel,' her mother said.

Chapter 4

OLIVER drove his mother's Rover out to the Matopos instead of his Chevrolet. In his opinion, she did not use her Rover enough, pottering to town and back once or twice a week. It could do with a long journey, "to blow out the cobwebs," he told her.

'Are we nearly there?' Isabella asked, not for the first time on their short journey

'Another five miles, Mama,' Oliver answered. 'Keep your eyes pinned to the bush. Maybe we will see some game.'

He shifted down a gear as they climbed an incline, and changed up again as they made it to the top and the road flattened out.

'Stop, Darling stop. Over there. Some zebra and wildebeest.' The leather seat creaked as Isabella turned to glimpse the animals again.

Oliver braked, and the car came to a halt.

'Back Darling. Go back. This is too far.'

'I stopped as quickly as I could, Mama.'

'Yes, but you still need to go back.'

'I'm not certain I can reverse easily on these narrow tar strips, but let me try.' He twisted in his seat to look out of the back window as he put the car into reverse gear. 'At least the sides of the roads are well gravelled so we won't worry about sharp drop-offs puncturing your tyres,' he said, feeling a jerk as the back wheels left the tarred strip for a moment.

Isabella wasn't listening. She was too intent on seeing the animals again. 'There, there they are.' She pointed to the now fast-retreating zebra and wildebeest. 'Oh dear, I think the car made too much noise.' The wildebeest continued running, but a group of zebra stopped and turned around to stare at them. 'Look, Darling. How lovely they are.'

'Yes. And all in such good condition.'

'But when are zebra not in excellent condition? They are always happy and healthy-looking.'

'True.'

They gazed at them for a few minutes longer.

'Well, I think we should get on,' Oliver said. 'We want to reach the hotel in time to have lunch and a nap and then take a tour of the place where the function is being held. Best be prepared, so we know what to expect tomorrow.'

'That sounds like a good idea, thank you Darling.'

A short while later they turned off the main strip road and onto the dirt road towards the hotel. This led round a corner and up a sharp incline. Oliver stopped the car.

'I hope your old girl can manage this hill, Mama. It looks steep.'

'I am certain she will cope just fine,' Isabella answered.

Oliver laughed, knowing his mother had never driven her car. 'I hope you are right.' He put the car into reverse gear and drove the twenty yards back to the corner. 'I think we need a bit of a run-up,' he said, before changing into first gear and pressing his foot hard on the accelerator, making a dash towards the hill. The car lost speed and revved ever louder as it climbed the slope, but they reached the top.

Oliver pulled up the hand brake. He and Isabella looked at each other and smiled. 'That was a close call,' he said.

'I never doubted my old girl for a minute,' Isabella replied, tapping the dashboard in front of her.

They were both still laughing as they drove into the empty hotel car park.

*

The sun was setting when Oliver and Isabella attempted the steep hill up to the Matopos Hotel for a second time later that afternoon, after visiting the venue for the royal function.

'It seems easier, now we know what to expect,' Oliver declared, reaching the top with relative ease this time. He drove into the same parking bay they used earlier. 'Why don't we go to the veranda for a sundowner Mama? I'm sure there will be an excellent view of the dam from there.' He walked around the car to open the passenger door for her.

'Yes. Good idea.' Isabella threaded her arm through the strap of her handbag and eased herself out of the car. Oliver closed the door behind her. 'What a beautiful garden they have,' she said, walking on a path between two beds of flowering cannas, round the side of the hotel towards the veranda. She got to a flight of stone steps leading up to the veranda and stopped to admire the view. 'Oh my, how lovely the dam looks in the evening light.'

A waiter appeared at the top of the steps, his starched white uniform and metal tray gleaming in the warm evening sun.

'Ah, just the man. What would you like to drink Mama?' Oliver asked as the waiter came down the steps towards them.

'I think I would like a dry martini,' Isabella said to the waiter. He looked confused. 'Perhaps you do not stock dry martini?'

'No, Madam.'

'Never mind, I will have a gin and tonic instead then.'

'Make that two, thank you.' Oliver said, then pointed to a table and chairs in the garden. 'Let's sit there, instead of the veranda, Mama. I think the view may be better.'

'Yes, it is such a lovely balmy evening. We must make the most of being outside.' Oliver pulled out a chair for her and she sat down. 'It has been a long day. I shall sleep well tonight.' She looked out towards the dam. 'Your father's life changed forever when he first came here to the Matopos,' she said.

Oliver glanced up at the hotel, surprised.

'No, not to this hotel, Darling, it was not built then, although the dam was. Rhodes had the dam wall constructed sometime around the turn of the century. And a furrow. Now let me see, where is it?' She twisted in her chair to look eastwards. 'There.' She pointed to a long scar cutting into the side of a hill. 'Do you see it? Rhodes had that furrow dug after they built the dam wall so that water from further up the hill could drain into the dam. He was an innovative man, I'll give him that. Not that I cared much for him myself.'

Oliver reached for his cigarettes and lit one. 'How did Father's life change, Mama, when he came out here? No one has ever mentioned that he was involved in this dam construction or the furrow.'

'Oh no. Not at all. No, no. It was to do with getting to know James Brooke. Their initial meeting was at a drinks party in Bulawayo, a drinks party held by a Mrs Heyman. She used to arrange such lovely parties, did Mrs Heyman.' Isabella sighed. 'But I digress. Your father and James met again at Rhodes's funeral, out here in the Matopos in 1902. They got to know each other well. The night before the funeral they camped at the base of a hill called Ififi, and your father made an impression on James. James decided after this that he would invite him to join his business as a partner. The rest is history, as they say.'

'So your life changed after this encounter too?'

'Yes. Although, of course, I was not at the funeral. No women could attend. But yes, James changed both our lives. First for the better, and then for the worse when your father died. Not that James could have helped that. And then for the better again.'

The waiter arrived with their drinks.

'Thank you,' Oliver said, taking the glasses from the tray and setting them down on the table in front of them. He turned back to the waiter. 'What time will you serve dinner?'

'From seven o'clock, Sir.'

Oliver looked at his watch. 'Good, we have plenty of time to relax and enjoy our evening.'

Isabella sipped her gin. 'Oh my, I am lucky to see so much around me that I find inspiring. This sunset, for instance. How I would love to be painting it now.'

'The Native Commissioner and his staff seemed impressed with the painting you did for the Royal Family.'

'Yes.'

Oliver threw his cigarette butt into the flower bed. 'So are you nervous at the prospect of presenting it to them tomorrow?'

'A little, but I will do my best not to show it. The Assistant Native Commissioner's wife seemed an anxious woman. Did you notice?'

'No, I did not.'

'Fluttering and fretting. She is lucky to have that lovely daughter of hers helping her and calming her. What a beautiful young lady she is. Did you catch her name?'

'No.'

Their conversation was interrupted by the sound of a car revving as it came up the hill.

'Well I never, speak of the devil. It is the Assistant Native Commissioner and his family,' Isabella said. 'But how strange. Look,

Oliver, they are driving up the hill backwards. Why on earth are they doing that?'

Oliver paused for a moment. 'It's an old Model T Ford. The engine probably isn't strong enough to go up steep inclines in first gear, but as reverse is a lower gear, it will make the engine more powerful.'

'Dear, dear. It does looks odd, don't you think?'

They could not stop themselves from chuckling at the sight of the Sandersons reversing up the hill. Mrs Sanderson and Lily staring through the front windscreen, down the hill, while Mr Sanderson was turned and facing the back, so he could see where he was going through the small rear window. They disappeared into the car park behind the hotel.

'Too, too funny,' Isabella declared, taking another sip of her gin.

*

The same waiter who served their drinks earlier showed Isabella and Oliver to their table in the dining room for dinner. There was no one else there.

'How odd,' Isabella said. 'I would have thought there would be many people staying here tonight, it being so close to where the event is being held tomorrow.'

'The hotel will be brim-full tomorrow,' Julia Manning interrupted, walking into the room through the door from the kitchen and overhearing Isabella's remark.

'Good evening, Mrs Manning,' Isabella said.

Oliver made to stand up, the scraping of his chair echoing in the quiet dining room.

'Please don't Mr Craig,' Mrs Manning said, gesturing with her hand for him to remain seated. 'But yes, we're going to be chock-a-block tomorrow, which I am delighted about, as I will hear first-hand news about the royal event.'

'You will not be there?' Isabella asked.

'Sadly not. Only invited guests can attend. However, I was at the Native Department offices this afternoon, dropping off some cakes and scones for the tea, so I know what it looks like. It's so exciting. Do you perhaps have your painting here, Mrs Craig? I would love to see it.'

'No. My son took it to the Native Affairs office in town last week, and they brought it out to the Matopos Office.' Isabella smiled at Julia.

'Well, I am positive it is splendid. I have always admired your work.

'Thank you.'

'Now, let me give you the menus, and I'll be back in a jiffy to take your order. May I recommend the bream? Caught fresh today from the dam below us.' Mrs Manning was distracted as the Sandersons walked in and sat at a table on the opposite side of the room. 'Let me attend to them,' she said.

Peter Sanderson nodded to the Craigs, and they smiled back.

'A little awkward, don't you think,' Isabella murmured, looking at Oliver over the top of her menu.

Oliver raised an eyebrow.

'Just us and them in this dining room, I mean. I feel we need to talk in whispers so we don't disturb each other.'

The Sandersons must have felt the same because, as they were finishing their meal, Peter Sanderson came over to their table. 'Mrs. Craig, Mr. Craig, good evening. We would be delighted if you would join us for coffee on the veranda. It seems odd with only us and you staying here, trying not to disturb each other.'

'That is what I was saying to my son,' Isabella said, leaning down to find her handbag at her feet. 'Thank you, we would love to join you for coffee.'

Peter helped her with her chair and led her onto the veranda. 'May I introduce you to my wife, Ella, and my daughter Lily?'

'Very pleased to meet you.' Isabella said, easing herself into a metal veranda chair and putting her handbag at her feet again. 'We saw you earlier, but you both looked far too busy to see us.'

'Oh, but we did,' Lily said. She blushed and looked away. 'Shall I pour the coffee, Dad?'

'Yes please.'

'My son agreed to bring me to the Matopos a day early,' Isabella explained. 'I am getting far too old to be gadding around. We thought I would rest better here than at home, where I would worry about the journey. It is just a quick hop and skip to the event tomorrow.'

'And you?' Oliver asked. 'Why are you staying here when you live right there, where the event is taking place?'

'The Royal Family are going to use our house to change, before and after the *Indaba*,' Peter explained. 'The place has been turned upside down in preparation for them. There was some concern that we may mess things up if we stayed the night. So we're staying here instead, and tomorrow night also, in case the house is needed by them again.'

'Is it necessary?' Oliver asked. 'Surely the Royal Family don't expect such perfection. It's not as if they will be in your house for long.'

'That is what I thought,' Lily said, 'but everyone on the organising committee was adamant that we shouldn't stay there.'

'We've been preparing our house for weeks,' Peter continued. 'We've had a water closet put in, and basins with hot and cold running water in all the bedrooms.'

'This sounds splendid and is something we need to do with our houses on the farm,' Oliver said.

'We even had electricity installed. I can give you the name of the contractors we used if you like,' Peter said.

'Thank you. I would appreciate that.'

'And can you do it at Sunrising too, Darling, if it's not too expensive?' Isabella asked.

'Yes, Mama. It will be a great deal easier and cheaper at Sunrising, as there is so much building going on in your area already.'

'Building houses for all the people coming out from England and Europe to live in our country,' Isabella explained to the Sandersons. 'I live north of Bulawayo, where hundreds of new houses are being erected. Many out of mud, you may be interested to hear. I have a big, old, brick house and I feel fortunate when I see all these small mud bungalows being built for the new immigrants. Not that they are as rough as the pole and *dagga* huts we lived in when we first came to Bulawayo in 1900, mind you.'

'I didn't know you ever lived in a mud hut, Mama. I cannot imagine it.' Oliver could not resist teasing his mother.

'Well it wasn't exactly me who lived in a mud hut, Darling, but most other people did. Your father certainly did. I was lucky enough to live in a corrugated iron house when I first came to Rhodesia.' She took a sip of her coffee. 'But going back to the mud houses that are being built now; you would hardly know they were made of mud, and they look like they will last for many years. Not like the pole and *dagga* huts that the settlers of my era built, or that the Africans still build to this day.'

'Well, they will have to last. With the boom that is going on now, I don't think anyone will have time to build more substantial residences for a while,' Peter said. 'There is just not enough accommodation for everyone moving to Rhodesia right now. Can't blame them for wanting to get away from Europe.'

'Maybe you could turn your house into a residential hotel,' Ella suggested. 'You say it's big.'

Isabella sipped her coffee.

'Mama would find it difficult having strangers living in her home,' Oliver said. 'She's lived there for over forty years and it's her sanctuary.'

'I am not sure about that, Darling. It's just that the idea has never occurred to me before.'

'I must tell you something hilarious that happened today, as we were about to leave,' Lily said, sensing the need to change what seemed to be a touchy subject. 'Not a square inch of our house was left out in the big clean-up exercise. To the extent that every single book was taken out of the bookcases so that they could all be dusted. After this, the books were replaced from the biggest to the smallest. Well, thank goodness I decided I needed a book to read while I am here because I went to the bookcase to choose one, and you will never guess what I discovered?' She paused. 'All the books had been put back into the bookcases upside down.'

'Oh no,' Isabella laughed.

'It was too funny,' Lily said. 'There we were, aiming for perfection. Imagine if we hadn't noticed, and one of the Royal Family had.'

'It was anything but funny,' Ella said with a smack of her lips. 'It was a nightmare having to take all the books out and put them back again, the right way up, just as we were about to leave. That's why we arrived here so late.'

'Oh Mum, you did find it amusing, and even laughed, once we finished.'

'It was more out of relief than amusement, Lillian.'

Chapter 5

LILY'S eyes clouded with tears when she glimpsed the Royal Family for the first time. She tilted her face upwards in an attempt not to sniff, sucking in her bottom lip, and feeling for the small lace handkerchief in her handbag to dab her eyes and nose. She had not expected to be emotional, but they were so impressive, she could not help it. King George VI, resplendent in his white naval uniform, with white shoes and cap, a sash over his left shoulder, his many medals glistening on his left breast, a gold braided lanyard over his right shoulder. Queen Elizabeth, elegant in her cream skirt and embroidered blouse, under a long-sleeved cream jacket, open at the front to reveal strings of pearls around her neck; her cream hat worn to the right side of her head, shielding her eyes from the sun. She finished her outfit with long white gloves and a clutch bag, tucked under her left arm when she walked. This fascinated Lily. Keeping the bag there occupied her left arm, while her right arm was free to shake the hands of all her well-wishers. Brilliant.

And then there were the two beautiful princesses. Both wearing suits with pleated skirts, shorter than their mother's, and long-sleeved jackets. Princess Elizabeth wore pearls also, with her jacket closing at her waist in a neat bow, while Princess Margaret's jacket looked more formal, buttoned up to her neck. It pleased Lily to notice that the light, flowery hat Princess Elizabeth wore was not dissimilar to the hat Mrs Jenkins had made for her. How clever Mrs Jenkins is, she reflected yet again. She lifted her hand and pushed her hat further back on her head, to position it just as Princess Elizabeth had hers. But then she worried someone may have noticed what she did. She glanced around to see if anyone had been watching her, and was relieved that all eyes were on the Royal Family. Lily looked at Princess Margaret again. So beautiful, but with a whimsical, almost sad look about her; surely she had nothing to be sad about? Princess Margaret's hat was more formal than her sister's; with a small peak. Both princesses carried neat handbags with short straps draped over their left arms when they were walking, and both wore short, white gloves. Their outfits captivated Lily. She could not help comparing them to her own. She decided she was not unhappy with her dress in comparison, but she so wished she had gone to Haddon and Sly to buy herself a pair of kid gloves like theirs. What a lovely touch that would have been. She noticed that all three royal women were wearing brooches on their left lapel. I must buy one when I can afford it, she resolved, glancing at her mother sitting next to her. Ella wore no jewellery, other than her wedding band, or anything fashionable, and had not made an effort to spruce herself up even for this occasion. She said she was too busy preparing everything for the Royal Family, to doll herself up.

Lily turned her attention back to the Queen and princesses, who were being presented with flowers. They held these in their left hands while they walked to their tables at the tea party.

The only person who might rival the royal women with their attire, Lily felt, was Mrs. Craig. She may be near seventy, but how elegant she looked in her cream, gauzy, almost floor-length dress and her wide-brimmed hat, also worn to the right side of her head.

And like the Queen, she wore long, white gloves and strands of pearls around her neck.

Lily could see both Mrs Craig and Oliver standing near the front. She could just make out wisps of grey in Oliver's brown hair. He was looking smart in a dark suit with a white shirt and, she noticed earlier, a striped tie. She wondered if it was his regimental tie, which made her speculate about what regiment he was in and what he had done during the war. He was so thin. Maybe this had something to do with what he experienced. She knew about the terrible concentration camps in Poland and Germany. Had he been in an awful camp too?

Lily brought her mind back to the present, and what was going on around her. The Royal Family stopped in front of the Craigs, and Mr Beck, the Chief Native Commissioner, introduced them. Lily could see Mrs Craig curtsey and Oliver nod his head while some discussion took place.

Lily contemplated the Craigs again. How elegant they both were. She reflected on their meeting the night before, and their gracious manners. The way Oliver called his mother, 'Mama', and she called him, 'Darling' all the time. Lily could not help but consider herself ordinary compared to them.

*

The Matopos Hotel was a jolly place the night after the *Indaba*, as the royal visit was deemed a success, and everyone involved now dissected and savoured the occasion. The King, inspecting the Guard of Honour of the Rhodesian African Rifles; hundreds of soldiers standing in perfect lines, backs straight, chests out, feet together, rifles pointed to the ground, formal and disciplined; in contrast to the thousands of African schoolchildren who were cheering and singing. The Native Department bussed some of the children in; but many had walked from mission schools, often a good many miles away.

The chiefs looked dignified in their uniforms of office. Many of them also walked great distances to get there. Their efforts were rewarded with a sumptuous traditional meal afterwards of *sadza* and stew. Ten Impala had been shot for the pot.

For the first time in a long while, no one worried about the need to save food to send to Europe.

It was the same at the Matopos Hotel that night. The guests may have enjoyed a magnificent spread at the tea party earlier, but the Mannings still laid on an impressive cold buffet at their hotel; cold chicken, baby potatoes, beetroot, green salad, and fresh baked rolls. Cyril Manning even brought out a pack of real butter. He melted some of it over the potatoes with parsley, and the rest was served with the rolls. Tonight was not a night to worry about the suffering in Europe, and the constant need to cut back on food so that they could send it there. Tonight was a night to celebrate, to look forward to a world that was healing.

Peter Sanderson was one of the loudest and most jovial at the gathering in the bar. Although Lily knew he had been under a lot of pressure, preparing for the event, she wished he would be a little less raucous. He stood at the bar counter in the smoke-filled room, cigarette in one hand, beer in the other, stubbing out his cigarette and taking a bite of his roll, talking in an animated fashion to the circle around him. Lily sat with her mother at a table in the corner of the bar. She could sense her mother's displeasure. She wished she could get up and leave her but felt obliged to stay so that Ella was not alone.

'You can't blame him, Mum, he's had a great deal to sort out in the last few months,' Lily said.

'That goes for all of us.' Ella's voice was low and her face blank.

Another roar of laughter came from the group at the bar. Julia Manning was behind the counter, looking smart in a black dress and a single string of pearls. Peter handed his empty beer glass to her, and she took it, smiling at him and nodding. She filled it and put it back in front of him, before refilling someone else's glass.

'I'm going to bed,' Ella said, standing up. 'Please let your father know. Are you coming too?'

Lily was not in the least tired. 'If you don't mind, I will stay awhile. I'll see you in the morning.' Her mother bent to kiss her and then slunk out of the bar.

With her mother gone, Lily seemed a little spare, sitting at the table in the corner by herself. She looked around, trying to decide what to do. She did not want to join her father's crowd at the bar, but knew she should tell him about her mother.

Her father's mouth dropped when she mentioned it. 'Oh well, that sounds like her,' he said. 'Never mind, what can I get you to drink? Do you know everyone here?' Lily shook her head. 'Everyone, this is my lovely daughter, Lillian.'

Lily smiled, but felt awkward. She only knew Julia Manning. 'How about some of my homemade lemonade, Lily?' Julia asked.

'That sounds delicious. Yes, please.'

Her father put his arm around her shoulders and pulled her against him. He smelt of beer and cigarettes.

'Dad, if you don't mind, I'll go off too,' she said.

'All right, Sweetheart, if you must.'

She took her glass and left the group, no one noticing that she was going.

She still did not want to go to bed so decided she would sit in the garden instead and enjoy the view. The moon was almost full and cast a silvery light over the dam. She remembered the bench she had seen a little way down the hill, tucked behind one of Julia's lovely flower beds, overlooking the dam. She made her way towards it, walking around a big flower bed, filled with snapdragons. As she continued down the hill, she stopped dead. There, sitting on the bench, smoking a cigarette, was Oliver Craig, his back to her, facing the dam. She was about to retreat when he turned around.

'Ah, hello,' he said, getting to his feet.

'I'm, I'm sorry,' she stuttered. 'I'm sorry to disturb you, um, Mr Craig.'

'Not at all, this is a public place. You are just as entitled to be here as I am. The moon makes everything look rather mysterious.'

'Yes, I think it's beautiful. That is why I came out here too.'

'Well, you are very welcome to join me. It would seem odd if we were each enjoying the evening in separate places in this garden. A repeat of last night, almost.' Lily nodded and blushed. Oliver shifted to the other end of the bench and Lily sat down.

'Do you smoke?' he asked. 'Would you like a cigarette?'

'No thank you, Mr Craig.'

'Please, call me Oliver. Mr Craig sounds too formal on such a night. I smoke far too much,' he said, inhaling deeply. 'A terrible habit I picked up during the war. I need to stop one day, I suppose.'

Lily wanted to ask him what he did during the war, but considered it may seem forward.

'My mother went to bed as soon as she could,' he continued, 'and I had no appetite for the festivities in the bar.'

'Me neither.' Lily took a sip of her lemonade. Oliver flicked his cigarette into the flower bed behind them and picked up his glass.

'I'm enjoying a quiet whisky. I even brought a hip flask to replenish it when I finish this.' He lifted his glass and looked at the moon through it. The golden liquor had taken on a grey hew. 'Cheers,' he said. 'Today was a success.'

'Oh yes.'

'What are you drinking?'

'Homemade lemonade.'

A smile played on Oliver's lips. 'Would you like a splash of whisky in it?'

'No, it's fine as it is, thank you.' Silence swept between them and Lily wracked her brain for something to say. 'Um, your mother did very well, presenting her painting to the Royal Family,' she said

'Oh yes, my mother always does well. She's the mistress of good etiquette.'

'Her painting is lovely.'

'Thank you. I will tell her you like it.'

'She's very talented.'

'She has painted my entire life. I cannot remember a time when she did not paint.' He sipped his whisky. 'And tell me, what do you do?'

'I'm a school teacher. I started teaching at Milton Junior recently. This year.'

'How interesting, I attended REPS, but only for standard six and seven as a boarder.'

'I'm going to be living in the hostel next term, as a hostel mistress.'

'Mm, I wonder how you will like it. Nasty little boys all over the place. I did not enjoy it much. I hated not having my space. Mind you, it was a good thing. It prepared me for the experiences I had during the war.'

Again Lily wished she could ask him what he did, but felt too embarrassed to pry.

'Before REPS, I had a governess, a Miss Harrison, whom I called Harry,' he continued. 'She still lives in my home to this day.'

Lily's eyes widened. 'A governess? Is that what people did in those days?'

He laughed. 'Not so much, but you make it sound like it was centuries ago. I suppose I must seem ancient to you.'

'Oh no, that is not what I meant at all. I, I just meant, I never knew of anyone else having a governess.'

'Well, she was not trained as a governess. She was self-taught. She needed to earn her keep when she first came to Rhodesia, as a single woman at the turn of the century, and so she accepted a position as a governess, first with the Greaves family in Nyamandhlovu, and then with us.'

'Oh, I know the Greaves. My dad used to be the Native Commissioner at Nyamandhlovu before his posting here. We used to go out to their farm a lot, but I can't remember there ever being a governess.'

'Well, that is because Harry had come to us years before. They did not employ another governess after her. And we have just had one. Harry. She did such an excellent job, it got to the stage where we never wanted to be without her. She became part of our family.'

'How lovely for her.'

'Yes, for all of us. And you, did you train as a teacher?'

'Oh yes, I went to Teacher Training College in Grahamstown, in South Africa, for two years. 1945 and 46. If it had not been for the war, I would have gone to England to do my training earlier.'

'Bloody war.'

'Yes. The last batch of teachers who were sent from here for teacher training got stuck in England for a while when the war first broke out. They must have been scared when they eventually sailed back to South Africa, with the war going on and a chance of their ship being torpedoed at any minute.'

'I trust this did not happen to a ship-load of newly trained Rhodesian teachers?'

'No, I don't believe it did. Thank goodness.'

'And how did you get to Grahamstown when you were there in 45 and 46?'

'We travelled by train. Twice a year. We used to come back home for Christmas and in June. The first few times I enjoyed the journey, but then it became tedious. It's a long way to Grahamstown, you know. It used to take us two full days to get there.'

Oliver drained his glass, then opened his hip flask to replenish it.

'I think I need a bit of ice and water in this. I'll nip up to the bar to get a jug.'

'I should go, Mr. Craig, I mean, um....'

'Please, don't go just yet. I want to hear more about your teacher training, and what Milton Junior is like these days. I'm so enjoying talking to you. Stay longer. I'll be back in a moment.'

Lily sat on the bench staring at the dam. The moon cast a shimmering silver light onto the water, in contrast to the dark, shadowy bushes and trees surrounding it She sighed, relishing the night. She looked into the sky. There were only a few stars visible because the moon was so bright, but at least she could distinguish the Southern Cross, her ever-faithful constellation in the southern sky. As she looked at it, she did what she always did. In her mind she drew the perpendicular bisector of the two pointer stars and ran an imaginary line to where this met the imaginary line joining the longest points of the cross. The place where these imaginary lines meet shows south. She pondered where this was in relation to the hotel. Her house? No, it was further west. REPS School? Yes. It was south of the hotel, behind the hill.

Lily's musings were interrupted by the murmur of a man nearby. She thought it was Mr Craig returning with his jug of iced water, saying something to her on his way down the path, and she was just about to ask him to repeat himself when a woman giggled. Lily stiffened. Should she jump up and reveal herself, or hope that whoever it was would move on? But then she heard:

'Oh, Peter, I've been longing to have you to myself all evening,' followed by a lot of scuffling.

Lily froze.

'Me too, honey. Come, come to me, come closer. I can't wait a minute longer.'

Lily bit her lip.

'There, let's go a little further down the hill, my darling. Oh how wonderful it is to be alone with you in my garden.'

'And a beautiful garden it is too, Julia, honey, but not as beautiful as you. Quick, let me unbutton your dress.'

Lily cringed. The cannas in a flower bed nearby rustled as her father and Mrs Manning pushed into them. Lily looked around in desperation, wanting to get away, but did not know how to, without revealing herself. What could she do? Her embarrassment immobilised her, when all she wanted was to run away and hide. Somehow she managed to slide around on the end of the bench, and she glanced up the path. Her heart sank further. There, standing in the path, holding his jug of water, was Oliver Craig. He must have heard what was going on in the flower bed too. She did not think the situation could get worse.

A giggle came from the bed of flowering cannas.

Lily closed her eyes and took a deep breath. But then she felt Oliver Craig next to her, putting one hand over her mouth and the other on her shoulder, pulling her from the bench and pushing her towards the path. She stumbled up the steps to the veranda, but the lights were shining and they could hear people talking in the bar. Oliver hesitated. He shook his head and nodded towards the dark car park, directing her towards this. When they got there, he guided her to his mother's car, parked under a tree on the opposite side of the gravel space. He opened the passenger door, pushed her into the seat, and closed it, before going round to the driver's door and getting in.

'You are in shock, and you need time to recover. I thought it best not to go onto the veranda because we would have been walking into the light, and your father might have seen us. I think that would be even more embarrassing for you, at this stage. And then there are all the people still in the bar. The party is in full swing and you don't want to meet any of them right now, do you?'

Lily shook her head.

'That's why I've brought you here.'

Lily rubbed her hand along the soft leather seat. She was shaking.

Oliver dug into the pocket of his jacket and brought out his hip flask. 'Here, drink some of this. It will soothe you. I had it filled up when I went to the bar to get the water.' He put the silver flask into Lily's hand. She stared at it as if it was a foreign object she could not identify.

'Take a swig, Lily.'

She took a gulp. The liquid burned in her mouth and down her throat. She had another. A warmth spread through her body.

'Oh boy,' she murmured. She stared out through the windscreen in front of her. 'What a terrible thing to discover.' She took another sip of whisky and shuddered. 'And in such an embarrassing way.'

'You had no suspicions?'

'Never.' She took one more sip from the hip flask and then handed it back to him.

'I don't want any more, thank you.'

'These things happen all the time if that is any comfort to you.'

She shook her head. What must he think of them, she thought? Her sullen, drab mother, her father romping in flower beds with the wife of the hotel proprietor.

They sat in silence for a long while. What could they say? Lily loved both her parents, and the thought of what her father was doing right then, with Mrs Manning, in the flower bed, made her stomach churn. She felt her eyes fill with tears. That was the last thing she wanted, to cry, but the more she tried to stop herself the more the tears started flowing. Like earlier in the day, she lifted her head to stop them from spilling but then gave up as her tears turned into sobs. She felt Oliver lean across her and open the glove pocket in front of her. He took out a cloth and gave it to her.

'Oh boy,' she said again, taking it and blowing her nose. 'I don't know how I will ever be able to face either of my parents again. What on earth am I going to do?' She wiped her face, pulling herself together again.

'Do you have any brothers or sisters?' he tentatively asked when she stopped crying.

'No, I'm an only child. They had another little boy when I was two, but he died. My mother was never the same after his death, my father told me. I have always been closer to my dad than my mother, but this will change from now onwards.'

'That will be sad. I've never had a father and never stopped wishing I did.'

She glanced at him. 'Oh? What happened?'

'He died a few days before I was born.'

'Oh no, oh goodness. How terrible. How awful for you and your mother.'

'Yes. So you need to work on repairing your relationship with your father because you only get one father in your lifetime.'

They fell silent again.

'Give it a day or two and then consider talking to him' Oliver finally said. 'Tell him you've found out about his affair.'

She shrank at the idea of this.

'Not right now. Wait a while.'

'I'm going to Beira with a friend next week, but I don't know if I can talk to him before I leave. However, he can't go on behaving like a, like a, oh gosh......' she did not know how to describe what she thought of her father's behaviour. 'The funny thing is, I have always liked Julia Manning' she continued. 'She's so friendly, and I have always admired how pretty she looks and how smartly she dresses. Well, now I know why. To catch unsuspecting men like my father. I never want to see her again in my life, ever.'

'Did Mr Manning go away during the war, do you know?'

'Yes, he did.'

'And your father?'

'No, his job was an essential service, so he stayed here.'

'So maybe this affair has been going on for some time. '

'Do you think?'

'The war damaged many people's lives. And I'm not just talking about people being killed. I'm talking about families being separated for many, many years, not knowing when they would see each other again. If ever. Countless people turned to others for comfort because of this.'

'Yes, it's true, but my father has to change. It will kill my mother if she finds out. She already suffers from depression. Finding out about this would be the end for her.'

'I'm glad to hear you are sounding more determined. That's the spirit.'

'I wish I had not drawn you into any of this.'

'Don't worry. It will go no further than me.'

'That's not what I meant. I, well, um…'

'I'm 41 years old and have been through a war, so I expect and accept the numerous difficulties life throws at us. I know it's hard for you because you have not had to cope with too many awkward situations, I assume.'

'Yes, you're right.'

'Well, I believe you will deal with this one, as you appear to have a strong character.'

'Thank you.'

'Maybe you should go off to bed now.' He paused. 'I think you should slip into the hotel first, and I will follow. If any of the partygoers see us coming in from the dark together, they may jump to unnecessary conclusions.'

Lily blushed yet again and fumbled for the door handle. 'Well, thank you again, Mr Craig, for all your help.'

'Please Lily, call me Oliver. I know I'm a lot older than you, but after what we have been through tonight, I think we should call ourselves friends.'

'Thank you.' She slid out of the door, closing it behind her, and ran towards the steps up to the open front door of the hotel, relieved there was no one around as she darted through the reception and down the passage to her room.

*

The next morning, her mother knocked on her door to ask her if she was ready for breakfast.

'I'm not feeling well, Mum. You go without me,' she called from her bed, her voice croaky.

Her mother tried the handle and found it locked.

'Let me in, Lillian. What is the matter with you?' She tried the handle again. 'Let me in.'

Lily dragged herself out of bed, glancing in the mirror as she walked past the dressing table to unlock the door. She had swollen eyes and a puffy face.

'Goodness, Lillian. Whatever is the matter with you? Have you been crying?'

'No, Mum. I'm not well, too much excitement yesterday. Give me some time and I'm sure I will feel better soon.'

'You and your father both. He also said he doesn't want to come to breakfast. Heaven only knows what time he came in. I did not switch on the light to look at my watch, but it was very late. Thankfully we have twin beds in our room so he did not come too close to me. And this morning he turned his back and faced the wall, saying he's too tired to get up.'

Lily shuddered.

'Oh well, I suppose I will go to breakfast on my own. I will bring you a cup of tea when I come back. I'm sure that will make you better.'

'Thank you, Mum.'

Lily also rolled over to face the wall. What a terrible night it had been. How would she be able to look her father in the eye and pretend nothing had changed? What would she say to him when she told him she knew?

Her thoughts turned to Oliver Craig, and how kind and understanding he had been. But she hoped she would never see him again.

Chapter 6

SERENA Brooke sat at her desk writing a list of everything she needed to do in town the next day. Thankfully tomorrow is Tuesday, she thought, and I can get away. She was feeling flat after all the excitement of the previous week. It had been so exhilarating; travelling to town early in morning to be in time to watch the Royal Family's arrival; the reception at Government House that evening; staying the night by herself at Sunrising so she could have a second full day in town to do her shopping; and then having another, unexpected, night at Sunrising. If only her life were always this way.

But no. They had a strict rule in their family that they only travelled to town one day a week unless there was an emergency. She noted there were many emergencies when it came to the farm, but if she tried to go to town on any other day than her prescribed Tuesday, her plans were met with distinct disapproval. The Brookes were so proper; they always behaved as they should. Even her children were becoming like this, except John. The only other person who broke the Brooke mould was her brother-in-law, Graham.

Her heart fluttered at the thought of him. How surprising to meet him again after his six years away, and to feel so differently about him. She had missed him and worried about him a great deal more than she expected when he left for the war, but she never for a moment thought it would get to this. She glanced at the photograph in the silver frame on her desk; Tim and her on their wedding day, Oliver, as Tim's best man, standing next to him, and Graham standing next to her. He was a mere teenager then. This frame had initially contained a wedding photograph of just her and Tim, but she changed it to this one a few years ago; after the Germans captured Oliver in the desert, and Graham was shot down over Germany. Both men had been back in Rhodesia for over a year now, but she never felt compelled to change the photograph. Especially not now.

Serena stared at her list again, then wrote the order of her day in town tomorrow. A visit to the hairdresser to start off with. She ran her free hand through her thick, shoulder length hair as she wrote this. It felt as grimy as it looked, and no wonder. Her previous appointment was over a week ago, to prepare for the royal festivities. After the hairdresser, she would meet her friend Barbara Fletcher for tea at the Doulton Tea Room, as they always did.

Her mind started to wander again. How she enjoyed her day in town, a much-needed break from life on the farm. She no longer found the farm exciting, the way she had when she first married Tim. The thousands of acres of wild African bush; a beautiful home overlooking a section of river with an oxbow lake; the many staff and bedrooms making it easy to have friends to stay for weekend parties; long horseback rides; picnics on the banks of the river; games of tennis on their clay court. None of this held much appeal anymore. Everything was so different from those halcyon days when she and Tim first married.

'Mummy, Mummy, come quick.' The yells of her youngest child shook Serena from her musings. 'Hurry Mummy. Come very quickly.'

Now what, Serena thought, scraping her chair back and running to the veranda where the yelling was coming from.

'There is a snake, Mummy. A very, very, very big snake. It slid behind that trunk.' Beatrice pointed to the wooden trunk against the wall.

Serena shuddered.

'Why have you called me? You know I hate snakes more than anything. Why haven't you shouted for Jesus? Goodness gracious, Beatrice. You know I can't deal with snakes.'

'John has gone to find Jesus, Mummy.'

'Even more reason that you should not have called me.'

John came running up the steps onto the veranda, followed by the stick-wielding Jesus. 'Is it still there? Were you keeping your eye on it so it didn't go off and hide somewhere else Bea?' John yelled.

'Oh yes.'

'I can't take any more of this,' Serena said, desperate for the snake to be killed. 'Just *blala ena nyoka sure sure* Jesus.'

'*Yebo* Madam,' he replied.

Serena escaped through the front door and into the house, trying to ignore the scraping sound of the trunk being pulled out, Beatrice's squealing, Jesus's shouting, and the stick being banged on the floor.

She knocked on her husband, Tim's study door, and opened it without waiting for him to answer.

'Oh, Oliver,' she said as she walked into the room. 'I didn't know you were here. You sneaked in quietly.' Oliver stood up, but her husband did not raise an eye in her direction.

'What's the commotion?' Oliver asked.

'Another snake.'

'Ah, well they should start hibernating soon, with winter coming.'

'I can't wait,' Serena said.

Oliver smiled. 'You didn't hear me arrive because I rode here and left my horse in the stables. The royal visit has given me a new lease on life. No more driving around the farm in my car. From now on, I will endeavour to ride everywhere on horseback.'

'Well done. I suppose it will be better for you, as long as you lose no more weight. You are still far too thin.' She noticed the tea tray on the table in front of Oliver. 'Good, I see they've brought toast with the tea. Make sure you eat all of it.'

'Yes, Serena,' Oliver tipped his fingers to his forehead in a mock salute.

She laughed. 'I came in to ask you if you want me to do anything for you in town tomorrow, Tim dear,' she continued.

Tim glanced up at her, his face blank. 'Um, no, not that I can think of right now.' His attention returned to the map laid out on his desk.

'What are you two plotting?'

'Not plotting anything. Just discussing some last-minute changes before we build the dam wall.' Oliver said.

'It's going to be built here,' Tim said, pointing to a section of the Umguza River, downstream from where the other river on the property ran into it.

Serena peered at the map. 'How exciting.'

'It will be,' Oliver said. 'We're looking forward to expanding our dairy. It has always been difficult, not being able to grow crops all year round for fodder.' He moved and stood in front of the desk, leaning forward to point out a place on the map. 'We're working to clear this area to put in fields for our crops. It's flat and not far from the dam. We intend building an irrigation scheme, with a canal to bring the water from the dam to the fields.'

'What an incredible amount of work you have ahead of you.'

'Yes, but this country, and indeed the entire world, needs development like this now. Europe is still in a mess, and here we are, with all this fertile, virgin soil. We must use it properly, and we can if we have water,' Oliver said.

'So are you going to stop the beef cattle and just do dairy?'

'Not at all. We will keep the beef herd, in the north, away from the dam. We have plans to improve our beef herd too.'

'Please Olly, we need to get back to business,' Tim interrupted.

'I'll tell you our other plans another time, Serena,' Oliver said.

'Just one more thing, Oliver,' Serena said. 'Amanda is welcome to come here as often as she wants during the school holidays.'

'Thank you, that's kind. However, I would like it if Beatrice and John came regularly to my house too. That is another of my resolutions; to make Amanda feel more content at home.'

'Yes, that would be good. Well, how about I send John and Bea across tomorrow morning? Champion can bring them in the cart like he does when they…,'

'Serena, do you mind,' Tim interrupted again. 'We were in the middle of an important conversation when you came in. Please let us get back to it.'

Serena glanced at Oliver, sucking in her cheeks. She hated the way her husband dismissed her like this. She wanted to say something but did not want to start a fight in front of Oliver. 'All right then dear. I will leave you to get on with your important "men talk". Bye Oliver, I'll send the children to you tomorrow.'

She returned to her desk to continue her list for town. How lucky they are, she thought, to have a project like that. She wished she could find something to fulfil her, but in the twelve years she'd been on the farm nothing ever sparked any genuine interest. It's a shame I am not more like my wonderful, ever-industrious mother-in-law, she thought sarcastically.

*

'It shocked me that Tim didn't come to the party at Government House,' Barbara Fletcher said as she poured tea for herself and Serena. They were sitting in the corner of the Doulton Tea Room.

Serena straightened the crochet doily, ruffled by Barbara moving the tray when she poured the tea. 'I keep telling you how difficult Tim is. Maybe you will believe me now.'

'Don't worry. I have always believed you. But this was such a special occasion. It's not every day we get to meet the King and Queen of England.'

'True. I would not have missed it for the world. But not my dear Timothy. He never leaves his study these days. The only person he sees a lot of is Oliver, who visits him most mornings.'

'It's hard for him, being disabled like he is.'

'To be honest, I have given up being sorry for him. I was for years, but now all his moping around and feeling sorry for himself just annoys me. When I consider what other people experienced during the war, he has quite a lot going for him. Okay, the polio almost ended his life, and it was terrible that he got it. I know he can't walk and he's in a lot of pain much of the time, but, he does still have a life. He has his parents, he has his wife, he has four lovely children, he has a comfortable home, he has a private nurse at his beck and call, to give him massages and soothe him whenever he needs.'

Barbara spread the cream onto her scone and took a bite. 'Mm, these are delicious,' she said, wanting to change the subject

'You've still got cream on your top lip,' Serena said, pointing to her lip to show where.

Barbara dabbed her napkin where she hoped the cream was. She did not want to smudge her lipstick, although some of it did still come off.

'That's better,' Serena said.

'It's decadent of us, eating these delicious scones when there is such a need to send food from here to Europe,' Barbara said.

'I'm sure two tiny scones won't change anything for all the people who require food there.' Serena bit into her own scone. 'And even this makes me resentful of Tim,' she said. 'He's never, ever had to go without anything his whole life. We hardly knew there was a war going on, on our farm, if the truth is told.'

'Now you are exaggerating, Serena. Of course the war disrupted your life. I mean, it was worrying when both Graham and Oliver were taken prisoner. And look at Oliver now. He's as thin as a bean pole.

'Yes, it has been hard for him, with poor Emily dying while he was away. And those Italian prisoner of war camps were no picnic, that's for sure. Followed by all the years he had to lie low, to survive in hostile Italy after he escaped from his prison.'

'Fascinating, does he ever talk about it?'

'Not to us. And or course his relationship with Amanda is still awkward.'

'That's a shame.'

'Yes.'

'But Graham has bounced back well enough.'

Serena's heart skipped a beat. She took another bite of her scone before answering, chewing it slowly while she regained her composure. 'He has,' she said. 'It's because he's the youngest and most pampered child, which has made him self-assured. Not even a German soldier could break his belief in himself. Oh no.....' she glared at her plate. 'Don't look now, but my sister-in-law has just arrived.' However, they both did glance towards the entrance where Patricia Brooke was standing talking to the proprietor, Miss Doulton, partly obscured by the Aspidistra which grew in a large brass pot next to the door. 'She's the last person I want to talk to,' Serena said.

'Do not turn around or make eye contact with anyone else but me, and maybe she won't see us here.'

Barbara stared at Serena, trying to keep a straight face. 'You make me laugh. There are so many strangers in this tea room; I doubt she will notice us in this corner. The lace curtains in the windows make it pretty dark in here.'

'Mm, but she has eyes like a hawk.'

'Permission to drink my tea?'

Serena could not help but smile. 'Of course, appear natural.' She sipped her own tea.

'Darlings, how lovely to see you,' Patricia called from halfway across the room, smiling at the patrons sitting at other tables as she walked towards Barbara and Serena in the corner.

'Damn,' Serena murmured under her breath, before saying: 'Goodness gracious, Patricia, I would not have expected you to come here for tea.'

'No, well I don't; I am always too busy, as you know. But Penelope Weir invited me this morning to discuss something important. Hello Barbara, and how are we today?'

'In good form, thank you.'

'Excellent.' Patricia stood next to their table, looking around the tearoom. 'I do like this grey, rattan furniture. I must ask Miss Doulton where she got it from. Very tasteful.'

'Her scones are delicious too,' Barbara said.

'Have you seen Penelope anywhere?'

'No. Not that we've been looking,' Serena said.

'So many strange faces' Patricia sighed. 'Not a person I recognise, other than you two, of course. I'm not sure I like all these foreigners flooding into our country from Europe.'

'Now, now Patricia, think what they went through during the war,' Serena said. 'You need to be more charitable. And besides, they are bringing expertise, expertise that will help the country develop and grow. Consider the progress already. The new power station with all those huge cooling towers, for instance. What a difference this will make.'

Patricia made a face but reluctantly agreed. 'I suppose you are right. Oh, there Penelope is. She's just arrived. I had better join her. Well goodbye then, you two. See you soon Serena.'

'Oh yes,' Serena said, raising a delicate eyebrow at Barbara as Patricia weaved her way back through the tables, nodding to the people sitting at them. 'Look at her. She acts like the Queen herself, or at least a princess.'

'Well, she was born with a silver spoon, as were all the Brookes, and you too Serena dear.'

Chapter 7

A SENSE of relief gripped Oliver as he and Amanda drove into town, thankful they would be busy for the next few days. He glanced at his daughter. She was slumped in the passenger seat, leaning against the door, staring out of the window. He assumed she could not see much. She was still so small; her eye level was only just above the bottom of the window, when she slouched like that. He wondered what she was thinking. Probably counting the minutes until the journey ended and she would no longer be in a confined space with him.

'We're close now,' he said as he slowed down to turn into the road towards Sunrising. 'It's a while since you've been to Granny's house, look at all the new homes that are being built around it.'

Amanda continued to stare out of the window saying nothing.

'Quite different from when you were living here, isn't it?'

Again, no response. He gave up. No one could force two people to be at ease with each other, just because they were father and daughter. Their situation would be repeated countless times because of the war. No, his situation was not unique, although things would have been better if Emily were still alive. She would have helped bridge the gap.

He slowed down again, and the minute he turned into his mother's gate he felt better. The familiarity of the place soothed him. Sunrising would always have a special piece of his heart, as much as he loved the farm too. The slashed grass under tall trees, turning brown now with the end of the rains, the house glowing in the sunlight at the top of the drive, the open shutters, as if on guard at each door, the veranda like a wide skirt, spreading out from the house.

Isabella appeared on the front veranda, dressed as always in a long, off-white skirt and blouse, her dog at her heels. Oliver parked his car under the tree near the fishpond where he always parked it, and, even before he switched off the engine, Amanda sprung to life, grabbing the door handle, wrenching the door open, and dashing across the drive and up the steps, into her grandmother's open arms. She buried herself in the folds of her skirt. Isabella hugged her until Amanda pulled away to bend down and stroke the dog.

Oliver sighed. He closed his door and walked around the car to close the passenger door his daughter had left open.

'Darling,' Isabella said as he reached the steps leading up to the veranda from the drive. 'It is so lovely to see you and Amanda, and even better you are both staying the night. I was trying to remember the last time you stayed here, Amanda, and I believe it was over Christmas and New Year. Such a long time ago.'

'I wanted to come before now, Granny, but we have been very busy with our lessons.'

'Just as it should be. I would not have it any other way.'

'But, at least you came to the farm twice,' Amanda said.

'True. Now, let us all go to the veranda for a cup of tea and some of Kefi's special shortbread.'

Oliver glanced at his watch. 'I can't be long. I have a lot of meetings to get to in town. Graham is joining me for luncheon at the Club, so I will only return late this afternoon.'

'That is fine. There are all sorts of things I want to show Amanda, so I am delighted we can spend time together.' Isabella smiled at Amanda as she spoke.

Gonda arrived with the tray of tea and shortbread.

'Ah Gonda. *Sivugile. Kanjan Wena*?' Oliver asked.

'Very well. *Siyabonga.* And the *picanini* missus?'

'We're both fine.'

'I brought you something from Prince,' Amanda said. 'He gave it to me to give to you. It's in my bag, but I will come to the kitchen later.'

Gonda beamed, his face breaking into a multitude of wrinkles. 'Thank you, Missus.' He turned to Isabella. 'Do you need anything else, Madam?'

'No thank you, Gonda.' She leant forward to pour the tea. 'So what are all these meetings about, Darling?'

'We have many plans for developing the farm, Mama. When I say we, I mean James, Tim, and I. As you know, we have been mulling things over for many years, and now we're going to start doing what we can.'

'How wonderful.'

'Yes. And because of Tim and James's disabilities, most of the running around and meeting people falls on me.'

Isabella's mouth dropped. 'Has James taken a turn?'

'No Mama, you would have been the first to know if he had, but he's frail and nothing will ever change that. But this does not stop him from showing great interest in whatever we're doing on the farm.'

'No, he will be interested until his dying day. And Graham?'

'Mm. He's another story, but, as a shareholder, we're obliged to involve him. That's why I'm meeting him later.'

*

There were just a few cars parked on 8th Avenue near the Bulawayo Club, so Oliver parked his car under the flamboyant tree right outside. He reached for his jacket on the passenger seat and put it on, before closing the driver's door. He felt for his packet of cigarettes in his shirt pocket, and, leaning against the bonnet, he lit one. He relaxed for a few minutes, to appreciate his surroundings. The view of the High Court, majestic-looking at the top of the road, facing the town, the copper dome turned green by sun and rain, in sharp contrast to the clear, blue, autumn sky. He directed his attention to the Club itself which was another beautiful building, three stories high, with a veranda on the ground floor, and a balcony on the first floor. These were separated by high gleaming arches. Taking another drag of his cigarette, he dropped the butt on the tar, and stubbed it out with his shoe, kicking it into the sand around the flamboyant tree. He sprang up the steps onto the veranda, almost slipping on the polished red floor. He stopped to straighten his tie and then walked through the tall wooden door into the wood-panelled entrance hall. The concierge, who was sitting at a desk in the wooden reception booth, stood up.

'Good afternoon, Mr Craig. You are early today. However, we will soon fill up for lunch.'

'I can imagine. I'll go through to the bar for a drink while I wait for my cousin to arrive. Please tell Flight Lieutenant Brooke where I am when he gets here.'

'Of course, Mr Craig.'

Oliver walked through the atrium, separating the hall from the bar. Old Mr Worthington was sitting at one table reading a newspaper. The wood-panelled walls, extensive wooden bar counter, polished parquet floors, and padded leather chairs muffled most sounds in the room, but Worthington turned one corner of his newspaper down to see who had arrived when Oliver greeted the bartender.

'Afternoon Craig,' Worthington said from across the room.

'Afternoon Worthington. You well?'

'Never better.'

Oliver had no desire to converse with Mr Worthington, so he sat at a table on the opposite side of the bar, opened his briefcase, and took out some papers. The waiter brought his gin and tonic, with a slice of lemon floating on top of the ice, the glass misty from the cold.

'Just what I need. Thank you. Put it on my account.'

'Yes, Sir. Can I bring you the lunch menu?'

'Yes please.'

He glanced at the menu, and continued reading his papers, trying not to allow new patrons wandering into the bar for a pre-lunch drink to distract him. The room was soon a murmur of conversations, as the surrounding tables filled up, but he heard his cousin's voice as soon as he walked into the hall, greeting the concierge in his usual robust manner.

Why does Graham always appear to be so noticeable? Oliver asked himself, as he so often did, and then answered it in his mind. Because he's a spoilt, overindulged, last child of two parents who could give him everything he wanted, and did. Even his mother often remarked that she could never understand why his aunt and uncle had allowed this. They had been so much stricter with their first two children.

Oliver took another sip of his gin and braced himself for his cousin's entrance. He could hear him laughing with someone in the atrium, and then at the door of the bar.

'Here you are, Oliver, buried away in the corner,' Graham said, as the waiter pulled back a chair for him to sit down. 'What are you drinking? G and T? Yes, I could kill for one of those too.' Graham looked smart in his blue RAF uniform. He put his cap on the low table in front of him and ran his fingers through his greased dark hair. 'And how is darling Aunt Isabella? Ma told me you and Amanda are staying with her tonight.'

'Yes, we are. She's well, thank you.'

'And her friend, the good doctor Goldsmith. Seen anything of him recently?'

Oliver took a sip of his drink. Typical Graham, he thought. Everyone else was discreet when referring to Stephen Goldsmith and his age-old friendship with Isabella, but not Graham. Oh no, he had to blurt out what he thought.

'No, I have not seen him.'

'I did. He was at the royal function at Government House. I was a little surprised, him being Jewish, and all that. But I guess they considered it courteous to invite him, after what his race went through during the war.' Oliver could feel himself wincing at Graham's insensitive words, but Graham did not notice. 'The good doctor told me Isabella was not there because she was staying the night at the Matopos Hotel with you, before she presented her painting to the Royal Family the next day.'

'Exactly.' Oliver did not elaborate.

'So my lovely aunt can now include "By Royal Appointment" when referring to her paintings.'

'I doubt she's considered this.'

'But look at you, Oliver; with all those papers spread out on the table. You look studious.'

'Mm. I'm going through some numbers. The CONEX man I met this morning gave them to me.'

'Of course. Conservation and Extension Services. To do with the dam we're going to build on the farm, I assume.'

Oliver raised an eyebrow. 'What do you mean by "we" Graham? I've been in comms with them since December last year so that we can get it started before winter, while the river is low. I've brought the engineer and dam builder out to check likely sites. Tim and I have been through their feasibility studies, their lists of costs, and worked out where we're going to get the equipment and how we're going to pay for it. I can't figure out which part of these plans has involved you.' As he said this, it amused him to see that Graham blushed. This did not happen often.

'Well, um, yes. I suppose I should say, um well, dammit, I have shares in the farm too, as you know.'

'That's true, and that's why I'm meeting you for lunch today; to tell you we're ready to build soon.'

'Excellent. This must delight father. He's always said that the only way we will ever get ahead with farming is to dam the rivers.'

'Exactly.' Oliver said.

'Well, good work, Oliver.'

'Thanks.'

Graham looked pensive. He took a long sip of his drink, as he felt for his cigarettes, which he kept in a neat, leather case. Opening this, he offered one to Oliver, and then took one for himself, closed the case, and tapped his cigarette on the leather. His lighter was in his jacket pocket and he lit his cigarette, before tossing the lighter to Oliver. 'So what still needs doing?'

'Not a lot more. We will use tractors and a dam scoop hired from CONEX to build the actual wall. They'll be bringing these out next week, I believe. We have most of the cement and stone needed to build the spillway. We're almost ready to start.'

'This all sounds most exciting. Now may be the time for me to hand in my resignation from the RAF and move back to the farm.' This took Oliver by surprise. Graham showed no genuine interest in the farm. Surely he did not want to live there? 'I would hate you to leave me out, while you two are getting on with this project, and all the opportunities that it will open up for us,' Graham continued.

'But you always disliked farm life,' Oliver said.

'Absolute rubbish. I love it.'

'Then, why did you not follow Tim and me to Cirencester? Why did you not want to learn how to farm, as we did? You always give the impression that the life of a farmer is too dull for you.'

'That's not true. Okay, I have enjoyed pursuing other interests and I'm glad I learnt to fly. Although I did not consider it at the time, I'm also glad the Nazis shot me down over Germany in 1940 and I spent the rest of the war as a POW. If this hadn't happened, I probably would not be sitting here now, talking to you. And yes, I've enjoyed working at the RAF base here in Bulawayo and living in town. I needed a busy social life after all those years of imprisonment, meeting lots of different people; going to dances, parties, dinners. If you ask me, you could do with some of this too, instead of burying yourself on the farm.'

'Not so easy, with a daughter to consider.'

'Understandable. But anyway, as I was saying, I enjoy the social life, living in town, and I will keep the flat in Main Street, still, so I can spend time in town when I feel like it. But I have long known that I don't want to spend the rest of my life in the RAF, and now is the time to come home. I have made a lot of friends, I can invite them to the farm when I need company and don't want to come into town.'

Oliver did not know how to respond. He and Tim were close and worked well together. The idea of having Graham there too, butting in on their plans, filled him with dread. It was the last thing Oliver wanted, and he knew Tim would feel the same way. But what could they do? The farm was as much Graham's home as it was theirs.

*

Oliver found Isabella and Amanda still on the veranda when he arrived back at Sunrising later. Stephen Goldsmith was also there, but more surprising, a puppy sat on Amanda's knee. Isabella's dog lay on the floor next to her, staring up at the puppy.

'Hello Oliver,' Stephen said, getting up and shaking his hand.

'Hello, Stephen. How are you?'

'Not too bad, thank you.'

'And what have we here? 'Oliver said, pointing at the puppy.

'Amanda's birthday present,' Isabella said. 'Stephen found him for me. I have wanted to give Amanda a dog for a long time.'

'Shouldn't you have consulted me first, Mama?'

Isabella smiled. 'No Darling, because you would have said no. Just like when I suggested you get a dog for yourself when you first came home. I still think you need one, but, until you decide this for yourself, Amanda might as well have one of her own. You like him, don't you Poppet.'

Amanda stroked the puppy and rubbed his ears. 'I love him, Granny.' The puppy responded by nibbling her hand.

Isabella's dog could resist no longer. He jumped up at the puppy, but Isabella pushed him down.

'No, Eddie. Down. Don't be a naughty boy. You sit here next to me.' She laid her hand on his head. 'Would you like some tea, Darling?'

'Yes please Mama.' Oliver settled into the armchair opposite her. 'So what are you going to call this puppy?'

'Well, I have been explaining to Amanda how I have had Staffordshire bull terriers ever since I got my first one in 1905, and how I name them in alphabetical order.'

'Granny says her first one was Archie, her second was Bertie, her third was Charlie, then Danny was the fourth, and this one is Eddie,' Amanda said.

'So we are trying to choose a name starting with "F".' Isabella said. 'Amanda came up with Freddie, but this may get muddled up with Eddie. I do not want my Edward here getting confused.' She patted her dog's head.

'But as you call him Edward most of the time, Mama, how will another dog named Freddie confuse him?'

'I do not call him Edward that much, Darling, I often call him Eddie.' She stroked the dog's head again as he jumped up and settled himself beside her.

Oliver smiled, shaking his head. 'You and your dogs, Mama.'

'Yes, they have always been important to me.'

'I've thought of a good name,' Amanda murmured. 'How about Frank?'

'Oh Darling, that is an excellent name for him. He is going to be such a handsome dog. Frank will be a most suitable name. How clever of you.'

'Thank goodness that's settled.' Stephen laughed.

'You will stay for supper, won't you Stephen? It will be early tonight, on account of Amanda. A pre-birthday supper, for her.'

'Don't spoil her, Mama,' Oliver said.

'Of course I won't. But we only turn seven once, and so it must be celebrated.'

'But you are coming out to the farm to celebrate the actual day. How many times does it need to be celebrated?'

'It seems twice, from the way Isabella is behaving.' Stephen chuckled. 'And thank you yes, I will stay for supper now.'

'How about you join us on the farm this week, Stephen? Oliver suggested. 'You could drive Mama out. She wants to stay for three or four nights.'

'I cannot get away from my practice for that long. Another time, for a shorter period, perhaps.'

Oliver smiled. He doubted this would happen. For all the years Stephen Goldsmith had been a friend of his mother's, he had never once been out to the farm.

But this was about to change.

Gonda appeared at the door leading from the drawing room onto the veranda.

'Telephone, Mr Oliver. It is your cousin, Mr Timothy Brooke, who wants to speak with you.'

Oliver raised an eyebrow. 'Mm. I wonder if he's arranged more meetings for tomorrow before I go back to the farm. Excuse me please.'

He walked through the drawing room, across the hall and into his mother's study. He picked up the receiver and cleared his throat, but before he could say a word out Tim started talking.

'Olly, is that you?'

'Yes. What's up?'

'It's Father. He's taken a turn and is in a bad way. You need to contact a doctor and bring him out here.'

'Oh my God. What's happened? He didn't seem any worse than usual when I saw him yesterday.'

'Even this morning, when Daphne took me to see him, he was his usual self but, I don't know. Something happened later. He's terrible now. To be honest, I don't think he's going to last much longer. Ma is frantic with worry.'

'I can imagine. Well, Stephen Goldsmith is here. Shall I ask him to come out?'

'Yes, please do.'

'Right. I'll ask him if he can leave as soon as possible.' Oliver looked at his watch. 'It's five-fifteen now. If he's agreeable, he'll be able to get there by, mm, maybe by seven.'

'Okay. We will manage until then.'

'Good.'

'Oh, and Olly, I think you need to bring Aunt Isabella here too. Ma will need her.'

'Yes, yes. I'm know Mama will want to be with her sister. I will only telephone you if there is any change of plan. Otherwise, expect us this evening.'

Tim cut off, and as Oliver replaced his receiver, he noticed his hand was shaking. He closed his eyes, took a deep breath, and strode back to the veranda. They were talking about the puppy again.

'Mama, Stephen, I have very worrying news.'

They looked at him.

'It's James. He took a turn this afternoon, and he's not good.'

'What? What do you mean?' Isabella gasped.

'I can't say. Tim said James is in a bad way and asked if Stephen can go out there as soon as possible.'

'Did Tim tell you what happened and what his symptoms are?' Stephen asked.

'No.'

'Let me telephone him back, so I know what to take.'

Amanda, who was still sitting next to Isabella, with the puppy on her knee, started chewing her fingernail. She had developed this habit, whenever anything worried her, back in 1943, after her mother died. Isabella noticed what she was doing and stroked her bare arm. 'Try not to worry, Darling. Dr Goldsmith will do his best for Uncle James.'

'Tim has asked that we all join him as soon as we can, Mama,' Oliver said. 'I think they will need us.'

'Oh yes, of course.' She turned back to Amanda. 'We will need to postpone your special birthday dinner, but as it is only your birthday next week, this is not too serious. Why don't you go to the kitchen and ask Kefi to put your birthday cake into a tin? We will take it out to the farm. Here, give Frank to me while you go.'

Stephen returned to the veranda. 'Right then. I need to go back to my surgery to get my medical bag, and then I will go home to pack. I will drive straight to the farm. How long will it take for me to get there, Oliver?'

'From your house in Suburbs, about an hour in your Wolseley. Do you know the route?'

'No, I don't.'

'It's pretty simple. Drive out on the Victoria Falls road for twenty-five miles. You will go over two low-level bridges. The turnoff to the farm is five miles beyond the second bridge, on the right. You will see the signpost. After turning onto the dirt road to the farm, drive for a mile until the road forks. Take the right-hand fork and go another mile, passing two roads to the left. Take the third road to the left, which is the driveway to James and Celia's house. Do you want me to write this down?'

'No, it sounds pretty clear to me.' Stephen looked at his watch. 'Well, I had better be off then. I don't enjoy driving in the dark these days. My eyes aren't what they used to be.'

'Thank you for doing this, Stephen,' Oliver said. 'It will be a great comfort to all of us having you there. We will be behind you on the road if you get stuck or lost and need us.'

Isabella pulled herself to her feet. 'Yes, oh yes. Thank you so much, Stephen. I will go and pack now too, for at least ten days, Oliver, so I am there for Amanda's birthday next week. Oh, deary me. I do hope he is not too bad,' she mumbled as she rushed off the veranda.

Chapter 8

JAMES Brooke died the following morning. 'A miraculous relief that it was so quick,' his family said afterwards. Stephen's diagnosis was that he had a massive stroke the previous day. He would have had no quality of life if he had survived.

His immediate family was with him during the last few hours of his life. Celia, Isabella, Tim, Patricia, Graham, and Oliver. It was a harrowing time for all of them, watching the life drain from him; his breath becoming more drawn, the death rattle starting; Stephen feeling his pulse and rubbing his feet.

Isabella thought she could see his spirit leaving his body. She watched his face as it turned lifeless, like a wax doll. The features were still his, yet she could see when his soul left him.

She rose from the chair she had been sitting on next to his bed, stroked his forehead and kissed it once, then left the room, Eddie following her while the others stayed behind. She escaped into the garden and found a wall to the side of the house where she could sit unobserved. She collapsed on the wall, her shoulders slumped, her head bowed, and she sobbed. Eddie looked at her and tried to jump up, but she pushed him down and stroked his head.

After a long time she stopped sobbing and fumbled for a handkerchief in her pocket. She took it out, wiped her eyes, then blew her nose.

She was both numb and empty. James Brooke; such an influence in her life for over forty years. Her best friend, in a funny sort of way. If it had not been for him, she would have gone back to England in 1905, after her husband, Anthony died. But James signed Sunrising over to her, and that sealed her fate. She loved this house from the first day she set eyes on it. Elegant Sunrising, designed, built and named by James Brooke. It epitomised everything he had been to her. These thoughts brought tears to her eyes, and she swallowed hard to prevent herself from sobbing again. She needed to be strong for Celia. Sitting around moping would help no one.

'Come, Edward, let us get moving. Being busy will help us cope better with our loss.'

James and Celia's house was close to Tim and Serena's, half a mile apart on the portion of the farm known as Sunlands. Both were built of sandstone from the quarry on the farm, and both had thatched roofs. James built the bigger of these two houses, Brooke House, before he and Celia married in 1906. He brought a stonemason out from England to oversee how it was built, and this man passed his skill on to the people who helped him. There were always several talented stonemasons in the area after this. When Tim and Serena became engaged in 1935 the second, smaller house was built by these local stonemasons, and James and Celia moved into this, while Tim and Serena moved into Brooke House after they married.

Oliver's homestead was quite separate from these two houses, on the section of the farm known as Brightside, three miles away. This house was built for Isabella back in 1907, at James and Celia's insistence. At first Isabella, Oliver, and Oliver's nanny, Harry, stayed in it for brief periods whenever they visited the farm. But these visits lengthened, and they would stay for the whole of every school holiday, as Oliver grew up and showed such interest in farming. Later, they built a small cottage for Harry, consisting of two conjoined rondavels, beyond the kitchen garden, so she had a place of her own. Then, when Oliver returned from Cirencester Agricultural College with his English wife, Emily, Isabella's farmhouse became their home, while Isabella spent most of her time back at Sunrising.

Isabella resolved she would walk to Brightside now, pack her things, and get Bhutu, Oliver's stable hand, to bring her back to Celia's in a cart. She wanted to stay with Celia for the next few days while they came to terms with their loss. She met Isaiah, Celia's gardener, as she was walking through Celia's garden, and told him to let the others know what she was doing.

Halfway back to Oliver's house, she heard a car driving down the dirt road. She stepped onto the grass verge and looked round to see who it was. Stephen, hurtling towards her, dust billowing behind his Wolseley. He braked when he saw her, and pulled up, switching off the engine.

'Isabella, what on earth are you doing here all by yourself?'

'I'm with Eddie and we're going back to Oliver's house.'

'Why didn't you ask one of us to run you back?'

'A brisk walk helps me. But Stephen, you look exhausted.'

'Yes, I am. I did not sleep at all last night.'

'Oh my. You have been so good. Thank you very much.'

'Hop in, I'll drive you there. And then I will carry on into town.'

Stephen opened the passenger door and Eddie jumped in. Isabella followed, folding her skirt around her legs so it did not catch in the door when he closed it. He walked round to the driver's side and climbed back in behind the steering wheel. He turned towards her, putting his hand on her shoulder.

'Are you alright? I know how much James meant to you.'

The tears started welling up again and she blinked hard, in an attempt to stop them. 'You have been such a help, Stephen. I don't know what we would have done without you.'

'There is a lot that still needs doing. When I get to town, I will register the death.'

'And then what?'

'I will arrange to bring a coffin out here. Oliver is already having the grave dug. It will be near your husband's grave.'

'Of course.'

They drove to the house in silence. Prince came out to meet them and they knew he must have heard the news because he fell onto his knees and started crying as soon as he reached them.

'Prince, please, get up,' Isabella said.

'The Boss, the Big Boss, oh Madam, the Boss,' he wailed.

'Yes, it is very sad for all of us.'

'The *madala* boss,' Prince continued.

'Correct, he was *madala*, and he had a good and long life. But please get up, Prince, and make us a pot of tea. Dr Goldsmith here could do with one before he goes back to Bulawayo. And then, please go and tell your father. Gonda will be mortified,' she murmured.

Stephen looked around. 'So, this is the farmhouse I have heard so much about all these years. I'm sorry I'm seeing it for the first time now, in such sad circumstances.'

'Me too.'

As they talked, Isabella led him into the hallway.

'Very nice,' Stephen said, breathing in the sharp aroma of creosote and thatched roof. 'But there's no time for me to look around now. Let me drink that cup of tea you're promising, and then I'll be on my way.'

*

The funeral was an enormous affair. They held it as quickly as possible after James's death so that there would be no need to take the body back to the mortuary in Bulawayo first. But, despite the rushed arrangements, many people still made the drive out from Bulawayo to pay their last respects to Sir James Brooke. He had been a stalwart of the Bulawayo community for many years, despite the hiccups that occurred around the time his friend and partner, Anthony Craig, died. James Brooke's determination to prove the guilt or innocence of the prime suspects in Anthony Craig's unsolved death triggered a great deal of ill feeling amongst the white settlers at the time. The suspects, Percy and Mabel Brown and Frederick Payne, disappeared when James implicated them in the death. Despite the best efforts of the British South Africa Police to trace their whereabouts, none of them had ever been located. There were reports of them in Australia, in Canada, and having gone back to England, but every investigation led to a dead end.

As time passed, it became accepted that Anthony Craig's premature death would remain unexplained, like many others who had died in the early days of European settlement in Africa.

Some older people who attended Sir James Brooke's funeral may have recalled those difficult times so long ago when they saw Anthony Craig's grave, close to where James Brooke was now being buried. The family had built a low stone wall to enclose the graveyard, with stone pillars and a chain fence looped from one pillar to the next. It could be regarded as a simple enclosure of no real significance, except for the tall gravestone, dated 1905, marking Anthony Craig's grave, a smaller gravestone, dated 1943, marking Emily Craig's grave, and now, a pile of earth, recently dug, for James Brooke's grave.

After the service, the crowd moved back to Brooke House for luncheon. The farm workers, and their families, congregated behind the kitchen wing, which was separate from the house. There, they helped themselves to *sadza* and stew, washed down with opaque beer. The family had slaughtered two cows. Large cauldrons sat on burning embers, keeping the food warm, and there was a strong smell of wood smoke in the air. Meanwhile, family and guests from Bulawayo mingled in the garden and on the front veranda. The garden was neat with the dry lawn mowed and the flower beds weeded and clipped. A large camel thorn tree and other acacia trees predominated. The garden overlooked the river and an oxbow lake, in the middle of which grew a magnificent acacia galpini. The guests sipped gin and tonics, whisky or wine, and helped themselves to a buffet of roasted fillet of beef, served cold, freshly baked rolls and butter, and a selection of salads, laid out on silver platters, set upon the dining room table.

The headmaster of the farm school, Toby Tate, stood with his wife at the edge of the garden. They appeared out of place at this gathering, despite Oliver and Tim being with them.

'You know anyone here?' Oliver asked.

'No, I don't recognize anyone, other than family,' Toby said.

'Lots of strange faces, even for me. The influx of people coming from Europe is astounding.'

'I go nowhere nor see anyone, so most are strangers to me also,' Tim said.

'Let me get us all a drink,' Oliver said. 'What would you like Tim?'

'I rarely drink at midday, but as I'm celebrating my father's life, I'll have a whisky, and make it a stiff one.'

Oliver turned to the Tates. 'We'll have something soft please. Water is fine.' Toby said.

'I'm sure I can find something more interesting than that,' Oliver said.

'What plans have you made for the school holidays?' Tim asked the Tates as Oliver left them. He was in his wheelchair, making it hard for the Tates to hear what he was saying.

'I beg your pardon?' said Toby, bending down, so he was closer to Tim.

'I asked what plans you have for the school holidays.'

'I'm making the most of my spare time, doing carpentry in my woodwork shop, and Pamela is gardening and making jams and marmalade from her fruit trees.'

'Oh good, I hope you will send some this way.'

'I will,' Pamela smiled.

There was an uneasy pause. Oliver had always been friendlier with the Tates than Tim.

'And your children? What are they doing during the holidays?' Pamela asked.

'Heaven only knows, but they always seem to find things to do. You know how it is for children, living on a farm.'

'Yes, they are lucky to have all this space and each other.'

There was an awkward silence, as the talk of children brought to mind the Tate's elder son, Arthur, who had died in France in 1944.

Toby cleared his throat. 'Jermaine is going to help me in the woodwork shop these holidays too,' he said. 'I'm pleased that he appears to have taken after me with his interest in carpentry.'

'Excellent. A very useful skill,' Tim said.

'True.'

'I have a carpentry project he may be interested in. My wife keeps telling me there are many broken chairs and tables at the school. Is this correct?'

'Yes.'

'Would he be interested in fixing them? The farm will pay him for his work.'

Toby glanced at Pamela. 'I will ask him and let you know. He's still feeling out of place here in Rhodesia after his time in Europe, made all the more difficult after losing his brother. He also wants to own a farm, and it frustrates him that he does not. A project like this may do him good.'

'Has he considered using his pay-out from the war to buy a farm in one of the Purchase Areas?'

'We have talked about this with him. But farms in these Purchase Areas are not always arable. And of course, he hates being confined to places that he would not choose to live in.'

'Yes, I grant you, it's a tricky business. But I would advise he looks into it nevertheless. He may be lucky and find somewhere suitable.'

Oliver returned, followed by a waiter with a drinks tray. 'I couldn't carry all the glasses myself, but Jesus here is proving to be an efficient waiter. Serena has done well in teaching your staff different skills, Tim, and being waiters is one of them.'

*

Serena commandeered Barbara Fletcher to help her with the buffet. The Brooke's cook, Tuppence, and two kitchen hands kept the food-filled platters coming to the dining room, but Serena and Barbara stood by to make sure there were no mishaps.

'Dear me, there are a lot of strange faces here,' Barbara said. 'That bunch in the corner must be friends of Graham's from the airbase, judging from their uniforms. Do you know any of them?'

'No.'

'And that striking looking girl with them. I wonder if she's Graham's latest girlfriend. He has a way with women. They just love him. It's his romantic-sounding past. Dashing Spitfire pilot, shot down over Germany, surviving the rigors of a German prisoner of war camp, returning to his home town as a hero.'

Serena rearranged the serving fork and spoon on the silver tray filled with sliced fillet. She twiddled with the parsley around the sides. 'I suppose so,' she murmured. 'Not that he's any more heroic than anyone else who has come back from the war.'

'True. But shush. Here comes the pretty girlfriend,' Barbara whispered.

They tried not to stare as the girl in question took a plate and helped herself to food.

'I'm sorry for your loss,' she said to Barbara when she was alongside them, on the opposite side of the dining room table.

'Oh no, it's not me,' said Barbara. 'This is Mrs Brooke. Sir James's daughter-in-law.' She laid her hand on Serena's shoulder.

'Blimey. I apologise. I thought Graham was talking about you when he mentioned his sister-in-law. Well, I'm sorry for your loss,' she said, staring at Serena. 'Does this mean we should call you Lady Brooke now?'

'No. It was not a hereditary title.'

'Still, you are all so fancy here. You fill this amazing house with antique furniture. You speak with posh accents. Not like us, coming from within the sound of the Bow Bells; but the Germans bombed London's East End to smithereens during the war, and that's why we're here now.'

'Yes. We saw the newsreels.'

'I can't tell you how much we love being here in Southern Rhodesia, with all the sunshine and fresh air and no ghastly air raid sirens. I thought that sound would haunt me for the rest of my life. But since arriving, I've almost forgotten what it was like.'

'And how long have you been here?' Barbara asked.

'Almost two months. Made sure I settled here in time for the royal visit. Even saw the Royal Family at close range, at one function they had, which was exciting for me. Back in old Blighty, I would have been like the blacks here, round the back and out of sight, unless they are serving, that is.' Serena laughed, but a pink glow moved from her throat and spread across her flawless cheeks.

'The reason they are there is because that's where they feel more at ease', Serena said. 'They would hate standing around like we are, making polite conversation, and nibbling on tiny fillet rolls. Instead they prefer to sit down, roll their *sadza* into balls with their hands and dunk them into the meaty stew.'

'Oh, is that what it is. I thought it was a class thing. They're the working class and we're the upper class, and never the twain shall meet.' Serena blushed again. 'Don't worry,' the girl said, noticing. 'We understand all about class systems, coming from England. It's been like that since William the Conqueror there. That's why it's so exciting here, where we're immediately elevated to the upper class.'

'So what do you do?' Barbara asked, changing the subject.

'Secretarial work. Which is what I did during the war.'

'How interesting. And are you planning on being here for a long time?'

'Hopefully forever,' she said, smiling, as she glanced through the window onto the veranda where Graham was standing. 'We'll see how things go.' She nodded and left them, going off to re-join the air force group.

'What a forward madam that is,' Serena said, when she was out of earshot.

'Well, I suppose she is more worldly than us, having been through the war in London.'

'Certainly more opinionated. Thinks she knows how things operate in this country, after being here for just two months.'

'Yes, but working as a secretary in the war office, or whatever, instead of knitting socks like we did here, gives her a certain edge, Serena dear.'

'We couldn't help being stuck here with families and homes to look after. Just like now. If it weren't for me, there would be no food or drink for anyone here. No, they would just be standing around drinking water from the taps, if they were lucky. From almost the moment James breathed his last breath, I have been busy making sure all this happened.' She waved her arm in the air, indicating everything and everyone in the vicinity. 'Food, drinks, ice, flowers arrangements everywhere, fresh towels and soap in the lavatory. Goodness gracious, where do I stop? Yes, I may have Tuppence and his attendants in the kitchen, I may have Jesus and his helpers in the garden, but the truth is, nothing would be done properly in either the kitchen or the garden if it wasn't for me.'

'Yes, you have always had great flair for homemaking and entertaining. This may be a funeral, but it's also an impressive and memorable function, thanks to you. Fitting for James, and what he would have wanted.'

Serena felt bad now about her outburst. 'Well, of course the last thing we needed was for poor Celia or Isabella to have to do any of this. Poor old ducks, I can't work out which one of them is taking James's death the hardest.'

'The husband of one, the friend and benefactor of the other.'

'True. But anyway, that's why I don't need some flibbertigibbet, fresh from England, with her fancy clothes and hairstyle, thinking she can judge us, and how we run things in our homes and our country. And on that note, I'd better go to the kitchens and check that more fillet is being thinly sliced. I can see this platter won't feed everyone, and if I leave the kitchen staff to their own devices, we would end up with great big chunks of meat. And before you know it, there wouldn't be enough to go round.'

Having checked on Tuppence in the Kitchen, Serena made a detour to the lavatory to make sure it was still acceptable. This was a long drop, enclosed by four walls, separate from the main house, and known as the *picanini khaya* or PK because of its minuteness. Serena walked into the garden through a door at the end of the passage to get to it. Too many people had been using it with no one throwing ash down. 'Yuck,' she muttered to herself as she went around the back and found the bucket with ash. It was half full and easy to pick up, but as she was carrying it to the lavatory door, Graham emerged from the passage.

'Here, let me do that for you.' He grabbed the bucket and shuffled into the smelly PK. 'Good God, not a moment too soon.'

Serena could hear the heavy thud of ash hitting the bottom of the hole.

Graham reappeared and took the bucket around the back again and, as he did this, he nodded for Serena to follow.

'You've been working hard. Thank you.'

'Someone has to do it. I'm surprised you noticed. I thought you were too busy entertaining your air force friends.'

'Just being polite. I saw you talking to Irisa.'

'Oh, is that her name? Barbara was wondering if she was your latest girlfriend.'

Graham gave her a long look, and Serena's legs weakened under his gaze. 'She's a decoy because I meant every word I said to you when we were at Sunrising the other night. It's difficult, I know, but it's the way I feel.'

Serena said nothing. She felt a surge of joy, followed by confusion, her heart hammering so hard she feared Graham may notice her chest heaving. She put her hand over it to regain control.

'I'm even giving up my job in the air force to come back to the farm. Ma will need me here more than ever now.'

Serena gasped. 'Graham, you can't. What about Tim and Oliver?'

'We will find a way. We have to. Now let me get back to my guests. Thank you again for the hard work you have put in today. I bet my brother has not uttered a word of thanks or even noticed.'

'No, 'she murmured.

Chapter 9

LILY Sanderson sat on the train, staring at the empty seat in front of her. She was relieved there was no one else in her compartment. She did not feel like making small talk, which was often the case when she travelled by train to the Matopos and someone shared her compartment. Her dad had offered to drive into Bulawayo to pick her up, but she made an excuse. She did not want to be by herself with him. Her holiday in Beira had given her the time she needed to deal with the shock of finding out about his affair, but she was afraid, if she was alone with him, she would confront him, and this worried her that it might open an even bigger can of worms.

She sighed. If only her holiday could have gone on forever. What fun she and Priscilla had had. The train journey there and back; staying with Priscilla's godmother, who, being single, welcomed their company; walking on the beach every morning, exploring the shipwreck; tea dances at the Grand Hotel every afternoon. They had enjoyed everything. On their last night, Priscilla's godmother took them to the Espidral Hotel for dinner where they ate peri peri prawns and drank cheap Portuguese wine, giving them sore heads the next morning, but this did not diminish their pleasure.

The train stopped at the Matopos siding. Lily sighed again as she collected her things. As she walked down the passage towards the door, she noticed her mother waiting for her. She looked as agitated as ever, and Lily felt a surge of sympathy for her.

'Hi Mum,' she said as she alighted from the carriage.

'Lillian dearest, how I have missed you,' her mother said, leaning forward to give her a peck on the cheek. Lily put down her bags and gave her a big bear hug instead. 'What is this all about?' her mother laughed.

'Just lovely to see you again Mum, and I'm relieved you are here to help me with my stuff,' she joked. 'No, I haven't got much, as I brought most of it back last time, but another pair of hands will still be helpful.'

'Look at you; so beautiful and brown. You could be mistaken for a coloured person, except that the sun has highlighted your curls.'

'The beaches in Beira were wonderful, Mum. Priscilla and I took long walks on the beach near her godmother's flat, every morning. We wore our bathing suits, and the sun reflected off the sea and the sand, so of course we both got lovely suntans. When we were hot, we either took a dip in the sea, or otherwise we sat at one of the many beachside cafes and ate ice-cream. It was just perfect.'

'Well, I'm glad you had such a pleasant holiday. You were looking a little peaky and behaving in an odd way before you left, I thought. This break seems to have made all the difference. I think being a teacher is harder for you than your dad and I realise.'

Lily wished this was the reason for her offish behaviour. She was determined to make the most of the few days she would have with her parents, but, try as she might, she found it difficult being at home. From a young age, her father had always asked her to join him on his visits to the communities he oversaw as Assistant Native Commissioner, but this time he did not ask her. This made her wonder why not. One evening, he nonchalantly mentioned that he had dropped in to discuss something with Mr Manning at the Matopos Hotel and Lily was so dismayed to hear this, she fled from him. She ran to the bottom of the garden to compose herself, but her anger refused to abate, so she continued down the dusty road towards the nearest *dwala*. She found a path branching off the road, heading towards this hill made out of a massive rock, but it soon fizzled out and she pushed through long grass to get to the base of the rock. It was easy to climb, but she was breathless when she reached the top. However, her troubled mind began to ease as she sat there and watched the sun sink over the western horizon. The sky became an artist's canvas, with strokes of yellow and orange and blue across it. She found the sight of this, combined with the silence of the sunset, soothing. She wanted to sit and savour it for as long as possible, but, with winter approaching, darkness drew in and the thought of snakes in the grass and baboons on the road soon motivated her to clamber down and go home.

When she opened the front door, she found her father sitting in his usual armchair reading his newspaper. He turned down a corner and studied her as she walked into the room.

'Go far?' he asked. 'You look windswept.'

'I climbed that *dwala* to the right of the road, just after the corner.'

'Oh yes? I often go up that *dwala* too. You get a superb view of the sunset from there.'

Lily bit her lip. This was the sort of thing they used to do together. 'Yes, I watched it set.'

'I wish you had asked me to join you. We could have enjoyed it together.'

Lily did not respond.

'Are you alright, Lily? You don't seem your usual self these days.'

'I'm okay.'

'There is something wrong. You are different.'

'I've just got a lot on my mind.'

'Your job? Your move to the hostel at Milton Junior? I thought you wouldn't mind, after being a border at Eveline for all those years, and then staying in the hostel at Teacher Training College in Grahamstown.'

'I'm sure I will be fine when I get there.'

'That's the spirit. Your mother is having a soak in the tub. I suggested she run a bath, as she said she was cold. You should ask her to leave her water in and then you can hop in afterwards. We don't have enough hot water for two big baths, but the Rhodesian Boiler is pretty efficient and you can get the bathwater piping again if you just top it up.'

'Okay, let me do that. A hot bath sounds inviting.'

Her dad was a convivial person. She hated feeling awkward in his company, but she did not find an opportunity to address any of her concerns in the remaining days of her stay.

*

When it was time for her to go, both parents insisted on driving back to Bulawayo with her. It was cold and damp when they left their home in the Matopos after lunch, and there was no let-up by the time they got to Bulawayo.

'The first cold front of winter,' her mother said, pulling her scarf over her ears.

'Could even be snow on the Berg,' her father responded, glancing at the grey sky.

Lily planned to arrive at the hostel a day early so she had time to settle in before the others came. The headmaster had scheduled a staff meeting for the following morning, and afterwards she wanted to spend time in her classroom, putting up pictures and posters and arranging the furniture the way she liked it.

The matron was standing on the veranda when they drove through the Milton Junior hostel gate. It was not a welcoming sight; a large, burly woman with grey, tightly curled hair and thick glasses, her bright white matron's uniform contrasting with the red brick walls and red polished floors. 'Come in, come in. It's too cold to stand out here,' she snapped, beckoning them through the front door. They found themselves in a narrow passage with wooden sprung floors and bare walls, newly painted in cream gloss paint, judging from the smell. Two passages branched off to the left and right of them, with one in the middle. As they stood next to the front door, the whiff of another smell became apparent too; floor polish. The clashing odours, combined with the bare walls and floors, did nothing to exude an atmosphere of homeliness.

Lily shuddered.

Matron led them along the middle passage and up a wooden staircase at the end. After one flight, the stairs divided, and Matron took them up the right-hand side.

'Your room is situated in the southern wing of the hostel, Miss Sanderson, overlooking 12th Avenue. The north side is warmer at this time of the year, but I'm afraid we allocate the newbies the less favoured rooms. But at least it will be cool in summer.'

They found themselves in front of a double door with round glass windows. Spy holes, Lily thought. Matron shoved the doors open, and they walked into a dormitory, the doors bouncing back with a loud thump as soon as the last person passed through them. There were rows of low metal beds along either side of the room and the mattresses looked thin. At the base of each bed was a wooden locker. Thin blue cotton material was used for the bedspreads and the flimsy curtains were cream.

'This is the standard one dormitory, Miss Sanderson. The standard one boarders will be your responsibility.'

'Yes, Mr Weir told me.'

They walked to the end of the dormitory, their shoes thwacking on the cold concrete floor. There was another white double door, again with spy windows, at the other end of the dormitory. They pushed through these and found themselves in a dark, narrow passage with doors on either side. Matron opened one door.

'This is your bedroom, Miss Sanderson. Miss Child will have the bedroom opposite you, but she will only get here tomorrow. She's in charge of the standard two dormitory.' Matron stepped back into the passage and ushered the Sandersons into the bedroom. They could see why she did not stay in the bedroom with them. It was so tiny, there was little space for even the Sandersons. The three of them looked around, trying not to show their dismay.

'Yes, it looks dreary today,' Matron said from the passage, 'but that's because it's cold and overcast. When the sun is shining, it's much cheerier, and in summer it's lovely and cool. We're lucky to have electricity in these rooms. Newly installed.' She switched on a light and the bare bulb, hanging from a wire in the middle of the ceiling, illuminated. She switched it off straight afterwards. 'We don't need it on now, of course.'

The room had a single bed on one side, a narrow wardrobe on the other, and a wooden desk between these, underneath a small window which looked out onto the street. The bed had a brown candlewick bedspread and cream curtains, similar to those in the form one dormitory hung in the window.

'That's Coghlan School on the other side of the road,' Matron said from the door, pointing out of the window. 'I do so admire the architecture of their school hall, don't you?'

'Yes, it's impressive,' said Peter.

'Not that we don't have a lovely school hall here too,' said Matron. 'Do you not agree, Miss Sanderson?'

'Oh yes, most certainly.'

Ella sat down on the bed, bouncing on it twice, without even realising, to see how soft it was. She squeezed the thin mattress with her hands.

'I hope you brought yourself an extra pillow, Miss Sanderson, to make the bed more comfortable for yourself.'

'Yes, I did.'

Peter opened the cupboard door, his legs brushing Ella's as he tried to make space.

'We don't encourage our junior teachers to bring too much in the way of personal possessions or clothing,' Matron said. 'A few frocks for teaching, and one smart outfit, will suffice.' She glared at Lily's large, bulging suitcase, which her father had left in the passage. 'Once you've unpacked your suitcase, you can put it in the trunk room. Let me show you where this is, as well as the bathroom for female members of staff. We also had bathrooms installed with running water last year, so count yourself lucky, Miss Sanderson. However, I do limit the use of hot water and only allow shallow baths.'

They passed through the standard two dormitory, which was the same as the standard one dormitory, except for orange bedspreads, and through yet another double swing door into the dark passage beyond. This passage took them to the top of a flight of stairs. They descended these, then tramped through another dormitory, "for standard threes," Matron said, through more double swing doors, leading into the next passage, and found themselves in front of a closed door. Matron opened this, and revealed a cold-looking bathroom with white-tiled walls and a polished cement floor, a bath and a basin, and a cubicle enclosing the water closet.

'That's a long way to trek every time poor Lily needs to go to the loo,' Peter said.

Matron looked disapproving.

'How is she going to remember how to get here?' Ella asked. 'It's like a rabbit warren, passages and dormitories, and more passages and more dormitories.'

'Our teachers soon get their bearings,' Matron said. She opened the door next to the bathroom. 'This is the trunk room, where you will leave your suitcase once you've unpacked.' They peered into a room full of empty shelves. 'Now, all I need to show you is the dining room, the teacher's lounge and the prep room, and then you have seen everything.'

She closed both the bathroom and trunk room doors, plunging the corridor into semi darkness again, and marched down the passage, her footsteps sounding militant on the wooden floor.

After a moment of hesitation, the Sandersons followed. The dining room led off this passage, with an open door going to the kitchen on the opposite side of the room. This looked out of place, because every other door in the hostel had been closed.

'The kitchen staff will return tomorrow,' Matron said. 'I warned you to bring yourself something to eat.'

'We ate a big lunch before we left home, and I made Lily some sandwiches,' Ella said.

They continued down the passage, turned another corner, and found themselves heading back towards the entrance hall, passing the prep room and a tiny lounge, "for teachers to sit and relax in" Matron explained. They glanced inside the prep room, with its small wooden tables and chairs, and the sitting room, which was only a smidgen more inviting.

'And here we are, back where we started,' said Matron, looking relieved. She pointed in front of her. 'My quarters are this way, but

I dislike being disturbed. You can see the telephone hanging on the wall, next to the door to my quarters. We use it only in cases of extreme emergencies. Do you want me to show you back to your room, Miss Sanderson?'

'No, thank you. I think I can find my way back.'

'Well, I will say adieu then, Mr and Mrs Sanderson. And I will see you tomorrow, Miss Sanderson.' With this she trudged down the passage and through the double doors to her rooms.

'We'll come back with you and help unpack, in case you've left anything behind,' said Ella.

'No, don't worry, Mum. I will be fine. You need to be setting off back to the Matopos now, otherwise, you will be driving in the dark.'

'Correct,' said her father. 'We don't want that.'

Ella looked worried.

'Don't worry, Mum. All will be well. I've got my nice warm blanket and pillow, my book to read, and the sandwiches you made for supper. I'm just glad I got here today, so I can work out the lie of the land before the boys arrive tomorrow.'

'That's the spirit,' said her father. He hugged her the way he always did, and for a moment she felt a surge of the deep love she had for him, despite what she now knew he was up to behind their backs. She had to blink back the tears. 'Don't worry, girl. We will see you soon. I believe I will be in town again on Friday, so I will take you out to lunch then.'

She was about to say don't when her mother said she would join them. 'I'm worried, Lillian. This place does not seem as homely as Mrs Jenkins's guest house.'

'I know, but at least I will have more money by living here. I'll be earning more and not having to pay rent It seemed like a good idea when the headmaster offered me the hostel job. And don't forget, I'm used to Langdon House at Eveline School. I'll be fine here. At least I have my own bedroom, which I will make as snug as I can.'

Chapter 10

ALTHOUGH Amanda's schooling took place at home with her younger cousins, Harry was strict about following the school calendar. Up until now, Oliver found this difficult, secretly wishing they could have lessons all the time, to keep his daughter busy and out of his way. But when the school term began this time, he did not feel this way. The atmosphere in their home had become more relaxed with his mother around, along with the addition of Frank. Amanda loved her puppy and spent hours rolling around with him on the grass, or "training him". Her earnest desire to teach Frank to sit, to stay, and only to eat his meals when he was instructed touched Oliver. Frank was a dear little dog, so welcoming every time he saw anyone, even if that person had only been out of his sight for a few minutes. Oliver found he warmed to the dog almost as much as his daughter. He wished he had considered getting a dog as soon as he came back from the war, as his mother suggested. This might have saved them many months of discomfit.

Not that their discomfort with each other had completely dissipated. It would take more than a cute little Staffordshire bull terrier puppy to bridge the gulf between them. No one could blame them either. Their strained relationship resulted from the upheavals caused by the world war in the initial five years of Amanda's life, exacerbated by the death of her mother. But little Frank helped, and Oliver vowed to buy another dog when Frank was older. His mother always said that every dog needed their own time as a puppy, and that it was wrong to get another too soon, because it would spoil the special time for the first.

He knocked at the door of the room they called "the schoolroom". On hearing a muffled murmur, he opened it and walked in. Harry was sitting at her desk, her glasses perched on the end of her long narrow nose, her grey hair pulled back in a tight bun at the base of her neck, as it always was.

'Ah, there you are, Harry. Did I buy everything you asked for?'

'I believe so. Thank you.' She glanced at the books, crayons, paper, and pencils laid out on her desk. 'This should last quite a few months.'

'You're not finding it too stressful, teaching all three children?'

'They can be a bit of a handful, especially John, but I cope. You know me, I like to treat my children with a firm hand.'

Oliver smiled. 'You do. Firm but fair.'

'Yes.'

'But you will tell me if you're not managing.'

'Of course. Next year will be better with just the two little girls, once John has gone to school.'

'He should have gone this year; I sometimes feel bad that he did not. But everyone insisted that it would be best for Amanda to have both John and Bea join her for lessons. Well, it was mainly Serena who insisted.'

'Serena is a thoughtful and caring person, and one more year in our schoolroom will do John no harm. He's still a little too precocious and boisterous for my liking.'

'True. I'm sure you will knock this out of him.'

Harry grunted.

'I'm going to ride to Brooke House now, and Amanda will stay here if that is alright. Do you need me to bring anything back for you?'

'No, nothing I can think of right now, thank you. And don't worry about Amanda. She will be quite happy here, I know, going through her Saturday morning training drills with Frank.'

They each smiled at the idea of this.

His horse was ready and tacked up when he got to the stables, less than a hundred yards from his house. He had kept to his resolution of riding his horse whenever possible, first to visit Tim, and then to go checking on everything on the farm.

'Good boy, Como,' he said, patting the horse's neck and tightening the girth as he prepared to mount. 'Everything okay, Bhutu?' he asked the stable hand.

'Yebo, Baas.'

He had bought the horse after returning from the war and named him Como, after Lake Como, the last place he stayed in Northern Italy, before preparing to climb the Alps into Switzerland. The beautiful resort town of Como, in the foothills of the Italian Alps, offered him a quite unexpected respite, despite still being a fugitive and having to stay hidden. The Italian Resistance in the area secreted him in a small hotel on the shores of the lake, the Belavista Hotel. It was owned by an elderly Englishwoman who had lived in Italy so long, she was considered Italian. She went by the name of Mrs Ricci, although she confided in Oliver that her real name was King-Turner. She took great delight in deceiving the Germans whenever she could, and, because of this, she took Oliver in and did everything she could to make him relax. It was the one place he remembered fondly, out of the two years he spent hiding from the Germans and fascists in Italy after escaping from the prisoner of war camp. Mrs Ricci allocated him one of the best rooms in the Belavista and, for the first time since being captured, he slept in a comfortable bed with sheets and blankets. For the rest of his life he would remember how luxurious it felt, when he slid his thin and battered body into those soft, silk sheets after a hot bath. Of course, the room was locked and food sneaked up to him when no one else was around, and there was the constant threat he would be discovered, but he enjoyed his time there nevertheless. Sitting on his balcony, despite the cold weather, enjoying the view of the lake with the Alps beyond gave him the strength to make that last climb into Switzerland in the spring.

I will call my next female pet Bela, after the Belavista Hotel, he thought, as he rode Como towards Brooke House. He kicked Como in the ribs, encouraging him to break into a canter. Nothing like a bit of wind in my face, he thought, blowing the cobwebs away, making me grateful to be alive and free, after all those years of captivity. He chose the long route to the Brooke's, taking the dirt track along the river and around the field.

He rode into the Brooke's stable yard fifteen minutes later and dismounted. Champion was cleaning the stables, and after loosening the girth, Oliver handed the reins to him.

'I will be half an hour,' he told him, as Champion led Como into a small enclosure.

He found Tim as he always was, in his study, sitting in his wheelchair at his desk. Poor bugger, Oliver thought, for the umpteenth time. What a dreadful life sentence, struck down by polio at such a young age.

'You alright?' Oliver asked, thinking he looked a little peaky.

'No,' Tim answered. 'Had a bloody awful night, couldn't sleep, felt liverish after eating too much dinner. And now my limbs are aching.'

'And Daphne? Where is she? Maybe she needs to give you a massage?'

'Serena says she will send her my way once she's finished bathing.'

Tuppence arrived with a tray of tea and toast.

'Thank you,' Oliver said, as he laid it on the table near the door. 'Can I pour you a cup of tea while you wait for Daphne?'

'Yes, please. It may help my indigestion.'

Oliver poured them each a cup and sat down in the leather chair opposite Tim's desk.

'The notion of my bloody brother coming back to the farm is not helping,' Tim said.

'I can imagine. I keep hoping he'll reconsider.'

'Me too, but not likely.'

'Odd. I have always thought the lifestyle in town suits him far better than here, stuck on the farm with just us for company.'

'But he seems to think he's needed now, with Father gone and Ma on her own. He says he shares her love for birds, and the two of them can go on birding jaunts around the farm together.'

'Mm, he has to do more on this farm than just look at birds with his mother. He'll have to find something he can get stuck into. Heaven only knows what. Hopefully, he won't pop in on you too often.'

'You reckon? I bet he will be in and out of here as if he owns the place. You mark my words. The only plus in all this is that Serena does not seem too overjoyed at the prospect of having him as her neighbour either.'

'That's odd when she is so welcoming.'

'Yes, I find it strange too.'

Oliver sipped his tea. 'I'm going to look at the dam site later this morning. You haven't seen it since we started, have you?'

'No.'

'How about I come back at eleven in the car, and you can join me?'

'Yes, I would like that.'

Work was now well underway on both the dam wall and the spillway. The spillway was being built out of rock and cement, on a rocky outcrop three hundred feet west of the river. The wall was being formed out of soil, across a gorge in the now dry river; cumbersome, dirty, and noisy work for the bulldozer hired from CONEX. First digging the soil upstream, the scoop bashing into the hard bank. Then pulling the scoop upwards with wires fastened to one edge, to stop the soil falling out, the arms groaning from the weight. Next, driving down the dry riverbed to the gorge, the tracks crashing and clanging with the bulldozer bumping and heaving over rocks and sand, the engine roaring. Once there, dumping the soil in the gorge, the scoop creaking when lifted and tipped, a great cloud of dust billowing out from the soil hitting the earth. Finally, the arms screeching, as the wires are loosened, and the scoop returned to its normal position. Then the bulldozer compacting the dumped soil by driving over it, before turning round to repeat the process. Again, and again, and again; the wall rising one slow scoop at a time.

Oliver and Tim sat on the front seat of Oliver's Chevy, parked in the road on higher ground, overlooking the construction site. They watched the dust clouds rising from the bulldozer, blowing through the air, before settling on the surrounding vegetation.

'You are right. The wall has come a long way,' Tim said.

'I notice changes every day when I come here,' Oliver replied. 'The hole where they are digging the dirt from is noticeably deeper and bigger as the wall gets higher and longer. The bulldozer goes round and round like this, from sunrise to sunset.'

'I guess they have to if they want to get the job done before the rainy season.' Tim took his pack of cigarettes from his shirt pocket, flicked it onto the dashboard to loosen a few, and offered one to Oliver.

'Thank you, but I've just given up,' Oliver said.

Tim raised an eyebrow in surprise. 'Oh, are you finding it hard?'

'I am, but I'm determined.'

'Well, good for you. Do you mind if I smoke?'

'Go ahead.'

Tim reached in his shirt pocket for his lighter and lit a cigarette. It did not take long for the car to fill with smoke so he wound his window down. 'Hard to imagine the area below us being full of water, this time next year, with luck. I'm still struggling to get my head around it.'

'Me too,' Oliver said.

'Have they seen any crocs in the vicinity?'

'No. Any self-respecting crocodile would have walked as far away as possible once they heard that bulldozer.'

'It makes a bloody awful noise with its tracks banging and the scoop crashing up and down like that. Have you driven on it yet?'

'Yes, I had a go when it was first brought here. It's not an easy machine to drive, I can assure you.'

'I bet.' Tim took a long drag from his cigarette and exhaled. 'God, I can't tell you how depressing it is, being like this and not being able to do all the things I always loved doing before I became a cripple. Like riding a bulldozer, for instance.'

Oliver winced. Tim had always been the most active and athletic out of all of them when they were growing up. He was a year younger than Oliver but kept up with him from an early age. They both went to Sherborne School in Dorset from age twelve, and Tim excelled at athletics and rugby, while Oliver made a mediocre cricket and tennis player. Tim even made Games Captain in his senior year, in recognition of his athletic prowess. Oliver was therefore acutely aware of Tim's frustrations now.

'I'm sorry, old boy. Are you still in pain?'

'No. Daphne's massages are a great help.'

'All those years as a nurse in East Africa would have helped.'

'Exactly.'

'Strange woman, though. Does she not get bored, living out here?'

'I'm sure she must. But she doesn't seem to have a lot else going right now, what with her husband being killed and having no other family, from what I can make out. I think she's just pleased to have a roof over her head and a salary coming in.'

'Shall we try getting her to do some office work? Once we have finished building this dam, there will be a lot of development. We could find a role for her, helping with the paperwork. It would be a way for her to make more money.'

'Yes, I will think about it. She could start by doing some filing.' Tim finished his cigarette and stubbed his butt in the ashtray in the centre of the dashboard.

'Would you like to see how the bush clearing for the new field is coming along,' Oliver asked, starting the engine of his car. 'I can show you what the bulldozer did there, before beginning this dam wall. It was one hell of a job clearing all that thick bush, I can tell you.'

'Bloody hell, Olly. You're certainly developing this fast. It's great seeing our plans coming to fruition so quickly.'

'Now is the time, while other countries in the world are licking their wounds and rebuilding.'

They drove up the rough dirt road from the dam site to the field, through rocky terrain, thick with stunted acacia trees, until they reached the cleared area after a few hundred yards.

'Jeez. The difference is amazing since I was last here.' Tim said.

'Yes, that bulldozer made quick work of the trees and bush. As you can see, we pushed the vegetation to the sides of the clearing and now gangs of men are picking up all the rocks and scraps of twigs and roots, and carting them off the field in wheelbarrows.'

'What a laborious task.'

'Yes, but the only way we can do it, as far as I know. And when they finish, we will need to contour the bottom end of the field so there is no runoff once we start flood irrigation.'

'You'll use wheelbarrows again to contour?'

'Wheelbarrows and shovels. At least the earth is soft now after the bulldozer drove all over the place.'

'Soft and dusty.'

'There's no wind today, but when there is, the dust swirling everywhere is incredible.'

'So how long will the canal from the dam to this field be?'

'Only about 500 yards until we get to this peak, where we are now. You may not notice it, as it looks flat from here, but in fact, the land slopes down. I plan on building a mound along the top edge of the field so the water can run along the outer edge and flood onto the field through gaps we make in the mound.'

'Brilliant. You've got it all worked out.'

'Well, it was the CONEX guys who came up with this design.'

'I wish I could get out of this car and have a pleasant walk around the field.'

Oliver gave him a sympathetic look. 'You should come here more often so you can see how it's going. Maybe Serena can drive you.'

'No.' He stared at the field, his hand twiddling with the button on his jacket. 'Serena and I don't get on too well anymore. Of course, you will have noticed.'

'I guess. It's a great pity.'

'It is. But I'm so inadequate now, well, you know, now that I can't perform. I prefer to keep away from her.'

'Does she make you feel like this?'

'Her mere presence does.'

Oliver had no idea how to respond.

'I cope better when I'm not in her company,' Tim said.

'But that can't be pleasant for her. Knowing you are avoiding her.'

'Mm. Well, we will see how things go. In the meantime, I will ask Daphne to cart me around the place.'

'And maybe you and I can go away later this year.' Oliver said. 'Up to the Gwayi. Do you know the De Wets who live there?'

'No.'

'I have been told they want to sell a property up there. It's excellent cattle ranching terrain, and I think we should look at it, put in an offer. Now that we're turning so much ground over for cropping, we need more land for our beef herd.'

'True. I'd like to go and see.'

'While we're there, we could make a trip of it, and spend a few days at Wankie Game Park, and Victoria Falls too. We've only been to those places once in our lives, and I think they both deserve another visit now. How does that sound?'

'I think it's just what I need, a stint away to recharge my batteries.'

'Right. We'll find a time once the dam is finished.'

Chapter 11

THE waitress showed Lily to a table in the Doulton Tearoom. She straightened the crochet table cloth and centred the small vase of flowers before pulling out a chair for Lily to sit on.

'I will wait for my friend to arrive before we order, thank you,' Lily said.

'Would you like to look at the menu in the meantime?' the waitress asked, handing her one before she could answer.

Lily put the menu down in front of her and took off her hat. She set it on the table, but then decided it was taking up too much room so slid it onto the chair next to her. She glanced towards the door, hidden from where she was sitting by the Aspidistra that grew in a brass pot near the entrance. The table cloth was still rumpled, so she straightened it again and picked up the menu. It was always a treat meeting Priscilla here for tea. They made sure they ordered themselves something delicious. This was the first time they were meeting since the new term started, as they were both busy with sporting fixtures at their schools. The winter term was always busy sports-wise, with boys playing soccer, rugby, and hockey, and girls playing netball and hockey. Both Priscilla and Lily coached hockey, and the matches were on a Saturday.

'Hi,' Priscilla called, as she reached the table.

'Goodness, Priscilla, you gave me a fright. I was so immersed in thought, I didn't hear you.'

Priscilla laughed, sitting down and taking off her hat. It was much smaller than Lily's and she rested it on the edge of the table next to her. She then removed her gloves and arranged them on top of her hat. 'How are you? It's been ages since we last met here.'

'All this dratted sport every Saturday. What with hockey matches in the mornings, and having to support the rugby matches in the afternoons, I find I have little time for myself.'

'Me too. My school sent me to Salisbury, and then Gwelo, with my hockey team last weekend,' Priscilla said.

'Lucky you.'

'Yes, the train journey is always fun. Reminds me of our lovely holiday to Beira. Gosh, that seems like a lifetime ago.'

'It does.' Lily sighed, twiddling with her hat. 'I'm afraid I'm struggling this term, Priscilla.'

'Oh no, things not going well at Milton Junior?'

Lily raised her eyes to meet Priscilla's concerned look. 'The teaching is fine; I love my class. They are such sweet little boys. But the boarding house is another story. It has made me realize I had enough of hostel life after all those years as a boarder at Eveline School. I'm hating it more than I expected because the Milton Junior hostel reminds me so much of Langdon House. Red brick walls, red polished floors, and red painted roofs.'

'Those government school buildings have a similar style.'

'Yes, they do, and my room is like an ice bucket, which doesn't help.' She handed Priscilla the menu. 'Let's order. I can't wait to eat something delicious after the ghastly, ghastly hostel food I'm served every day. They need to sack Cook Matron.'

Priscilla raised an eyebrow. Lily was not usually morose.

'I will order a piece of chocolate chiffon cake. That sounds good.' Lily said. 'And you?'

'I'll have the scones and cream.'

'And how is everything going for you?' Lily asked after they had given their order to the waitress.

'Not bad. Mrs Jenkins has still not put anyone else in our room, and I'm loving having it all to myself. It was somewhat overcrowded with both of us and our bicycles.'

'True. At least I have a room to myself in the hostel, but it's so tiny, there is no way I could fit a bicycle into it. I keep my bike in the trunk room.'

'I still can't believe the trek you have to make every time you need the loo, through dormitories, and up and down stairs. Maybe you should resign from hostel duties next term and come back to Mrs Jenkins's place.'

'I often wish I could. It's pointless being so unhappy there, although Matron keeps telling me next term will be better, as my room will be cool in summer.' They both laughed. 'You're right though,' Lily continued, 'the toilet issue is a problem for me. I make sure I drink nothing from six pm onwards so that I don't have to go to the loo once I'm in bed.'

Priscilla reached over and squeezed Lily's hand. 'I'm sorry you are having a hard time.'

Lily glanced up at her. 'Goodness, this is not like me to feel so sorry for myself. Another of my problems is I miss the bush. I used to go home most weekends, or every second weekend, as you know, to get my "bush fix".'

'Yes. It would help if you felt more relaxed going home for weekends. You don't think you should try again?' Lily had sworn Priscilla to secrecy when she told her about her father's affair, and the embarrassing way she found out about it.

'I must go at some stage, otherwise, my mother will wonder. But I hated being home when we got back from Beira. I'm uneasy around my father, now that I know what he gets up to behind our backs.'

'Maybe you should just confront him Get everything out in the open. Tell him how unacceptable his behaviour is.'

Lily fiddled with the petal of a flower. 'I've considered it, but I worry it'll make everything even more complicated and my mother will find out. I think it would be the end for her if she knew what my father was up to. You know how frail she is at the best of times.'

Their waitress brought their order.

'Well, this looks delicious.' Priscilla buttered a scone and layered it with strawberry jam and cream. 'Oh my gosh, this is straight out of the oven. I'm going to have to eat it with my teaspoon, it's so soft.' She scooped up a large mouthful and Lily had to smile at the look of pure pleasure on her face.

'You make me wish I ordered scones too,' she said.

'Order one for yourself. You can have it after your cake.'

'I can't. I'm not doing enough exercise these days to justify having a slice of chocolate cake and a scone. At least when I was at Mrs Jenkins's guest house I was riding my bicycle to work and back. Now I just walk across the field to get to my classroom.'

'Mm. I feel pretty knackered when I've ridden back to Mrs Jenkins' place after work.' Priscilla was about to take another mouthful of her scone when she stopped. 'Oh gosh, look who's just come in.' She nodded towards the door. 'Do you know her, Serena Brooke?'

'Not personally, but I know who she is, of course.'

'Her parents were friendly with mine when they lived in Salisbury.' Priscilla explained, 'before we moved to the Victoria Falls.'

Serena noticed Priscilla as she was walking to her table.

'Priscilla, hello, how are you? It seems a long time since I last saw you.' She glanced at Lily.

'Hello, Serena. Yes, it's been a while. This is my friend Lily Sanderson.'

'Nice to meet you. I see you girls are treating yourselves to a delicious tea,' Serena said.

'Lily and I do this as often as we can, after which we usually go to the matinee at the Palace theatre.'

'Sounds like fun. What's on there at the moment?'

'We're going to watch "The Two Mrs Carrols" with Humphrey Bogart and Daphne Stanwyck this afternoon.'

'Ah, I've heard about this picture. It sounds good.'

'We're looking forward to it. How are your parents? Are they still in Salisbury?'

'Yes, they love it there, which is a shame because I don't see nearly enough of them.' She paused. 'Do you mind if I sit for a few minutes while I wait for my friend to arrive?'

'Not at all, please do,' Priscilla said.

Serena sat down on the spare chair at their table, knocking Lily's hat off. She bent to pick it up, her hand shaking as she put it on her knee. 'Sorry,' she said. 'It's just that you mentioned the cinema, and I'm afraid I avoid going there these days. Those newsreels they show on post war Europe before the picture starts puts me off. I know we need to know what happened, but seeing what the poor, poor Jewish people went through in those frightful concentration camps is just too awful. And to think this happened while we lived and breathed. Humans can be so cruel.'

'Yes,' Lily agreed.

Priscilla sighed deeply and scooped the last bite of scone into her mouth.

'I'm meeting Barbara Fletcher,' Serena said, changing the subject in an attempt to pull herself back together. 'Do you know her?'

'Oh yes,' Priscilla said, 'but I don't think Lily does. Do you?'

'No. I spent most of my childhood in far-flung places like Nkayi and Nyamandhlovu, so I don't know many people in Bulawayo. My father is in the Native Department, you see.'

'Oh. How interesting,' Serena said.

'Yes, I always loved living in the bush, even though we didn't have a big circle of friends.'

'And what did you do about school?'

'My mother taught me for my junior years, and then I was a boarder at Eveline High.'

'It didn't seem to do her any harm,' Priscilla butted in. 'She's a brilliant teacher herself now, at Milton Junior.'

'Hardly,' Lily said. 'I'm only starting. You're a better teacher than I.'

'No. Your pupils adore you. James Henderson's mum was telling my aunt,' Priscilla said.

Lily blushed.

'Well, I'm glad to hear home-schooling did you no harm. My younger children are being schooled at home too, and sometimes I wonder if we're doing the right thing. It's just that I don't want them to be boarders yet. I'd prefer to wait until they are a little older.'

'I don't blame you.'

The door opened, distracting Serena. 'Oh, good, Barbara has just arrived. I'd better go to my table.' She waved at Barbara as she stood up. 'It has been lovely talking to you girls. Enjoy your film.'

'She's an exquisite looking woman,' Lily said once Serena was out of earshot.

'Oh yes. But I feel very sorry for her. Her husband had polio a few years ago, leaving him crippled.'

'How awful. I wonder if that's why she appears so nervy. Don't you think she seemed on edge? Did you notice that her hand was shaking when she picked up my hat?'

'Yes. And it also surprised me the way she reacted when she started talking about concentration camps. I mean, it's not as if we haven't all known about this for a few years now. But she acted as if she had only heard about it last week.'

'Quite odd, you're right. But anyway, let's finish our tea, and then we can take a slow meander through town on our way to the pictures. I may dislike being a boarder mistress, but I enjoy having more money to spend. I want to buy a pair of kid gloves like yours. Can we look for some on our way to the cinema?'

'Actually,' Priscilla said, 'do you mind if we do something else?'

'Oh, what?'

'Well I haven't told you, as I haven't seen you for a while, but I've been seeing the most gorgeous man, and, when I told him you and I would have a few hours to kill before the pictures, he suggested we visit him in his flat.'

'Priscilla, you devious thing, why didn't you mention him before? And there we've been talking about inane things like boarding hostels and school sport when you could have been giving me all the juicy details about this man.'

It was Priscilla's turn to blush now.

'He's the man we were admiring on the diving board at Borrow Street Pool, all those months ago. And funnily enough, he's Serena Brooke's brother-in-law.'

'Well, I never. The man in the yellow swimming trunks?'

'The very one.'

'Mr Sky Diver.'

'He's a Flight Lieutenant in the RAF. The Germans shot his Spitfire down over Germany in 1940, so he spent most of his war in a prisoner of war camp there.'

'So he is a hero then.'

'Oh yes.'

*

Serena had to work hard to hide her nerves while she and Barbara had tea together. She attempted to relax and enjoy herself, but it was difficult. Barbara asked her a few times if she was feeling alright, to which she answered everything was fine. Thankfully Barbara did not press her further. Bless her. The thoughts racing through Serena's mind would have shocked Barbara.

They separated on the pavement outside the tearoom afterwards, and Serena walked slowly and hesitantly towards Graham's flat. A knot in her stomach tightened, the closer she got. Why, oh why had she agreed to go there, she kept asking herself. His invitation had been innocuous enough; asking her to help him decide what furniture he needed for his cottage on the farm. But they both knew this was not the real reason he wanted her to come to his flat. Since the night they had unintentionally spent alone at Sunrising, after the royal function at Government House, the atmosphere between them was electric. Nothing physical had happened then, but he had made his feelings clear. Talk about chemistry. Her knees weakened, just thinking about him now.

Oh golly, she thought, what am I going to do? Of course, before the war, she had had none of these feelings for him. She was three years older and regarded him as a gangly teenager when she and Tim married back in 1935. Not that she had been that mature herself at twenty one, but she only had eyes for Tim then. Marrying him had seemed the right thing to do. Their marriage delighted both their families, and their splendid wedding at St. John's Cathedral in Rhodes Street was a joyous occasion. Graham was an usher, and she did not give him a second glance, other than to make sure he was smart enough for the occasion.

But now. What a difference a war makes, she thought. Of course, Tim's disability made things much worse. She often wondered if their relationship would be better if Tim accepted his affliction more; if the war had not happened; if all his cousins and friends had not gone off to fight. Those were too many 'ifs', she decided, and that was the problem with their marriage. Whenever someone died in the war or was captured, or had done anything heroic, Tim took it as a personal affront. The more useless he felt, the more he distanced himself from her. She tried to be understanding, she tried to ignore his coldness, but now that a hot-blooded male was showing such interest in her, her resolve to be the faithful wife was becoming ever more tenuous.

She arrived at the block of flats on the intersection of Main Street and Tenth Avenue. It was a new building and a fascinating, art deco design; a square three-story block with rounded turrets on either side of the front facade. Graham told her his flat incorporated one of these turrets, and as she stared up at it, she imagined the lovely north view he must have from its large windows. She was nervous about going inside, so stood on the pavement for a long time, appreciating the architecture. She loved the fact that there were so many new buildings being erected in Bulawayo, and several were just as interesting looking as this one. New buildings to accommodate everyone escaping from Europe. People who had gone through incredibly rough times. People who were looking to build new lives for themselves.

What do I think I am doing, she asked herself? I've had it easy my whole life, and now I am allowing myself to have my head turned by my brother-in-law, just because I'm going through tough times with my husband, the father of my four children. There has been so much suffering, death and deprivation over the last few years, and none of this has ever touched me, yet I stand here feeling sorry for myself. Stop being such a selfish, self-centred bitch, she told herself. And with this she turned around to march back the three blocks she had just walked to collect her car, which was still parked outside the Doulton Tearoom.

But after a few steps, she stopped and looked back at the building. She stared at the windows which she knew were Graham's, and as she did, two figures appeared in the window, two females figures. She squinted, trying to work out who they were and when she saw that one of the girls had long blond hair, while the other had short dark hair, she gasped. Priscilla and Lily, the two girls she had been talking to just an hour ago in the tearoom. Goodness gracious, what were they doing there? Graham appeared at the window too and stood next to Priscilla. She saw him point at something. She ducked behind a tree in case their gaze fell on her.

Now she felt foolish. She thought she was on her way to a clandestine rendezvous with a man besotted with her, when in fact she was just one of what could be many women he planned to meet that morning.

Stupid, stupid her.

She turned around again and strode back the way she had come. Graham could ask those two girls to help him with his furniture choices.

Chapter 12

OLIVER could hear a commotion coming from the schoolroom. It was not like Harry to allow this, he thought, as he walked down the veranda to see what was happening. The three children always behaved from the moment they stepped into the schoolroom until they left, hours later.

When he opened the door, what he saw astounded him. Bea standing on her desk, her legs astride, her skirt pulled up to her thighs, her hands on her hips, mid sway. Amanda sitting at her desk, beating the surface with two wooden rulers. John sitting in a chair next to the window, a cake tin between his knees, his hands at the ready to give it another bang.

'What on earth are you doing?' Oliver yelled. The children froze for a moment. Then Bea's hands fell to her side, and she put her feet together, Amanda blushed and dropped her rulers, but John could not resist giving the cake tin one last bang. 'Stop that,' Oliver shouted, 'and get off the table, Bea. Good God, what's going on? This is where you should be learning.'

'We were practising our um, our music and dance, Uncle Oliver.' John said. 'I was using this tin as my drum and Amanda was using the desk as hers. Bea was dancing to our rhythms.'

Just like him to have a smart answer, Oliver thought as he looked at his watch. 'At eight o'clock in the morning? Surely you should have more serious studies right now?'

'Miss Harry is not here, and we don't know how to do serious studying on our own,' John quipped.

Oliver agreed this much was true. 'Where is Miss Harry?'

'We don't know, Uncle Oliver.'

'Maybe she's having a lie-in,' Bea piped up.

Oliver knew this was not true. Harry took her teaching far too seriously to be having a lie-in on a school day. 'Did any of you consider going to see where she is?'

No one replied.

'Well, next time someone does not come when you expect them, don't fool around, because that is what you were doing. Check on them.'

'Yes, Uncle Oliver,' John and Bea said as one. Amanda stared at her desk.

'Go now and see where she is Amanda,' Oliver said, 'While you two scallywags take out your reading books.' Amanda scurried from the room.

'Which one?' John asked, 'because we have more than one.'

'The one you enjoy reading the most.'

'We can't read properly yet so we don't enjoy any of them.'

Oliver sighed. John's precociousness could be tiring. 'Do the books have pictures in them?'

'Oh yes.'

'Then you can sit quietly and enjoy the pictures, and I do not want to hear another squeak out of either of you while I am gone. Do you understand?'

'Yes, Uncle Oliver.'

The schoolroom had a stable door leading onto the back lawn and Harry's cottage was the other side of this. A path of stepping stones crossed the now brown and crisp grass to a small gate. Amanda had left it open, and Oliver walked through it. Despite the lack of water, Harry was a keen gardener and spent hours tending to her patch. At this time of the year, bright red poppies were the dominant feature.

There was a small lean-to veranda off the front rondavel, with jasmine, about to burst into flower, growing up the pillars that supported the roof. There were also hanging baskets, filled with pink, red, and violet petunias, hooked to either end of a wooden beam. Harry loved to spend her leisure hours on this veranda, enjoying her garden, but right now it was Amanda who was sitting on one of the metal chairs there.

'What on earth are you doing, Amanda? Where's Harry?'

'She's still sleeping, Papa. I knocked on the door, and when she didn't answer, I went in. She was still fast asleep.'

Oliver's face drained. He opened the stable door which led into her little sitting room, the musty smell of old cigarette smoke mixed with the delicate scent of the nasturtiums she had cut, immediately apparent as he stepped in. He strode across the room to the short passage leading to the bedroom. The door was open but the room was dark, with the curtains still drawn. He approached the bed cautiously and looked down at the peaceful-looking Harry. He knew that she was dead, but he still took her hand and put his fingers against her wrist. There was no pulse.

He let out a small sob. He had known Harry his entire life. She had been more like his second mother than his governess.

'What's the matter, Papa?' He turned around. Amanda was standing at the bottom of the bed. 'Have the Angels taken her too?'

'Ah, yes. It appears they have.'

Amanda's lip wobbled. 'I hate it when the Angels take people because then we have to bury them and they are no longer around and then we miss not having them with us.' She started to cry.

Oliver walked around the bed and put his hands on her shoulders, but she pulled away and ran from the room. Of course, Harry would mean a great deal to her also, he thought Harry had been a constant her whole life, too.

He looked down at Harry again and stroked her face. It was cold and waxy. She must've died a few hours before. What on earth had happened? She seemed fine yesterday, not that she would have told them if she was feeling otherwise. A heart attack, he thought. Hopefully, she felt little pain. He touched her long, grey hair; he had never seen it down like this before. She always wore it pinned in a neat, tight knot at the back of her neck. His mother had teased Harry, telling her she looked like a grey heron. Harry responded that, yes, she did, and it delighted her to take after such an elegant-looking bird. She always likened Isabella to a golden oriele, and again, this was apt, even now, when Isabella was almost seventy. The two women had shared a special bond for forty-two years. Harry's death would be shattering for his mother.

He pulled the sheet over Harry's face and left the room. He needed to get to his study to make some phone calls. As he crossed the lawn again, he heard wails and cries coming from the schoolroom. Amanda had broken the news to her cousins. He'd better make his first phone call to Serena, to come and collect the children. He made a quick detour to the kitchen where he found Agnes and asked her to go to the schoolroom and look after the children until Mrs Serena could come and fetch them.

*

Isabella was devastated that she had lost her beloved Harry, but, in the course of her long life, she had learned that, when faced with adversity, it was important to keep busy and focus on everyday needs or interests. After losing her baby in 1904, followed by her husband in 1905, she had mourned and moped for months. It was only after she forced herself to paint again that she healed. She decided afterwards that she would never deal with misfortune like that again, and it was apparent now, that there was something important they needed to sort out as soon as possible. Finding a replacement teacher for Harry.

It was only the last week in June and Isabella felt that the children should not go for weeks without lessons, and, as much as she hated interfering, she knew she was best situated to deal with this problem. At first, she thought of suggesting Serena teach them, but changed her mind. Serena had many skills, but teaching young children was not one of them. Then she considered the headmaster of their farm school, her old friend Toby Tate, but no, running the school as he saw fit kept him busy. Her attention turned to Barnaby Weir, the headmaster of Milton Junior School, who was the son of her best friend, Muriel Weir. He would be the right person to find another teacher for them.

So within a day of dear Harry dying, Isabella was on the phone to Milton Junior. She spoke to the secretary, asking if she could arrange an appointment with Mr Weir as soon as possible. The secretary suggested three-thirty that afternoon.

She had her lunch early as usual, and when Gonda came into the dining room to clear the table, she asked him to tell Admire to have the car ready at three to take her into town. This request surprised him; Madam never went to town on a Tuesday, and even less so during the afternoon.

'I am going to see the headmaster of Milton Junior School,' she explained as he poured her coffee. 'I want to ask him if he knows of anyone we can employ to take over from Miss Harrison.'

'Shame,' he muttered. He put the silver tray on the table and left her to her thoughts. He knew how sad she was that Miss Harry was dead.

Isabella had her usual afternoon rest, while Admire spent his time waxing her already shining car. It was ready and parked at the bottom of the steps at two fifty-five pm sharp. Life was measured and orderly at Sunrising.

They drove through the gates of Milton Junior at three-twenty, swooping around the circle in front of the school hall. Admire stopped the car outside the big front door. He got out and ran round to open Isabella's door, placing a small stool next to it to make it easy for her to alight.

She glanced at the school buildings as she straightened her hat, put on her gloves and slid her handbag strap up her forearm. She had always loved the shutters on the windows of this school, not dissimilar to Sunrising, she thought, as she made for the secretary's office.

'Good afternoon, Mrs Craig,' the secretary said, glancing at the clock above the door. 'Let me tell Mr Weir you are here.'

He must have heard her, because he came through moments later, extending his hand to shake hers. 'So lovely to see you, Mrs Craig. Please, come into my office. Can I ask Miss Smith to bring in some tea for us?'

'Oh yes, I would like that, thank you.'

They sat in the easy chairs on either side of his fireplace, a low coffee table between them. There were some old school magazines spread out on the table. The secretary was soon back with a tray and poured them each a cup of tea.

'Thank you, Miss Smith. I will call you if I need anything else.' Barnaby Weir turned his attention back to Isabella. 'I don't believe I've seen you since prize giving last year when you presented us with your painting of the front view of our school. Can I take you to see the painting when we have finished here? It's hanging nearby, in the hall foyer.'

'I would like that very much, thank you.'

'But what can I do for you now?'

'We have had a tragedy, Barnaby.'

'Sir James. Yes. Please accept my deepest sympathy.'

'Thank you. But no, I was not talking about him. We have had another loss since. On Monday, that is, yesterday, Miss Harrison, do you remember her? Our governess of over forty years. She died.'

'Oh heavens, that is sad. Of course I remember her.'

'Oliver found her dead in her bed. Suspected heart attack.'

'I'm so sorry to hear this. How wretched, and especially because you have now had two people close to you die in quick succession. It must be unsettling for all of you.'

'It is indeed, and even more so for the children. They loved both Sir James and Miss Harrison very much.'

'It's too bad.'

'The thing is, Barnaby, Miss Harrison was teaching the three youngest. At my insistence, as they could have been attending schools now. But I did not want this just yet, because I thought Oliver and his daughter, Amanda, needed more time to get to know each other. She has had a tumultuous start to her life, poor girl, losing her mother when she was three, and then only meeting her father for the first time when she was five. The last thing she needs right now is for us to shunt her off to boarding school.'

'I agree with you.'

'Amanda lived with me after Emily died, and was reluctant to leave and go off to live with Oliver when he returned, but I insisted she did, so that the two of them could get used to each other.'

'That was the right thing to do.'

'She and Oliver still have a strained relationship, although she seems to enjoy living on the farm, and she loves her youngest cousins, John and Beatrice Brooke, who live nearby. So, to make things easier for Amanda, Tim and Serena agreed to have Miss

Harrison teach their two children also, for at least this year, and next year too if necessary.'

'I see your dilemma. Three young children without a governess and you consider yourself responsible.'

'Indeed. That is why I have come to you. To ask if you can suggest anyone we can employ to take Miss Harrison's place as soon as possible.'

'I will need to think about this. Let me speak to my deputy. Can you give me a bit of time?'

'Of course.'

'I will telephone you when I have discussed this matter with him.'

'I am planning on travelling to the farm tomorrow for Miss Harrison's funeral. We are burying her in the family graveyard there. Would you be able to telephone Oliver instead?'

'Certainly. I have his number and I will do so as soon as possible.'

'Thank you.'

'Would you like another cup of tea, or shall we look at your painting?'

'One cup of tea is enough for me.' Isabella said, reaching for her handbag on the floor beside her feet. 'Let us look at the painting. I was most honoured when the school board asked me to do it.'

*

'I cannot believe we are all here again so soon, burying another family member,' Isabella whispered to Celia as they walked towards the newly dug grave. Although Harry was the children's governess, she had been with them for so long, they all considered her part of the family.

The coffin lay on the ground next to the grave, ropes passing underneath it and coiled to the sides. These would lower it into the hole after the ceremony.

The teachers gathered the children from the farm school behind the grave, and they sang songs in *SiNdebele*. Toby and his wife stood to the side of them, along with the other teachers from the school. They all knew Madam Harry, as they called her, because she made a point of going to the school once a month, to discuss teaching matters with them. She had done this for years and maintained they all learnt a great deal from each other.

The only other people attending the funeral, besides the Brooke and Craig families, were Isabella and Celia's brother, Edward Braithwaite, and his family, and the Greaves from Nyamandhlovu. Harry had worked for the Greaves when she first came to Rhodesia, leaving them in 1905 to come and work for Isabella, where she had been ever since.

They planned for the ceremony to take place in the morning, followed by a light lunch, to give the Braithwaites and the Greaves time to get home afterwards. The weather was freezing. Wind whipped up dust around the graveyard and clouds skidded across the grey sky. The surrounding vegetation was dry and dusty with barely a leaf on any of the trees or thorny scrub.

'It could not be bleaker today, could it,' Isabella said to Celia.

Celia gave a small sob. Isabella reached for her hand and squeezed it. It was hard for all of them, seeing the fresh pile of dirt so close to where James had been buried a few weeks before.

Toby Tate said a prayer and read from the bible, after which Oliver moved forward to the grave to say a few words.

'We are all going to miss dear Harry,' he said. 'Most of us cousins don't remember a time when she was not around; a stoic, solid, and sensible figure in our lives. I had hoped she would be here for many years still, to have the same positive influence on the next generation's lives, and I'm sad that this will not be so, but we must be thankful for the years we had with her. She was so much more than a governess; she was a much-loved member of our family. We are all going to miss her.'

With this, Bea and John started sobbing. Serena admonished them while Edward Braithewaite said a few words. Isabella's mind started wandering, recalling how poorly she was when Harry first came to work as Oliver's nanny. He was just a few months old, and she was suffering from severe depression, having lost her husband a few days before Oliver was born. She glanced at Anthony's grave now, reading for the millionth time, the words on his gravestone.

Anthony Craig
Born 1875 Died 1905

She and James had pondered long and hard about what else should be written on it. Yes, they could have put 'Beloved husband of Isabella', but then what about Oliver? He never knew his father, so they could hardly write, 'Beloved father.' And then what about little William, who had been dead almost a year when Anthony died? Did you mention him as one of his sons? In the end, they decided this was all too complicated, and it was best to leave it simple. Isabella had instructed Oliver to bury her in the same grave when her time came, and he could add her name on the gravestone then.

'Well, that was lovely,' Celia whispered, dabbing her eyes with her handkerchief when Edward finished talking. He walked back to his place next to his wife, Alice, and Isabella realised she had not heard one word of what he said.

Toby led the congregation in a closing prayer and then the school children broke into song again. The family and friends could hear their singing as they trailed back to Oliver's house. There, they found fires blazing in both the sitting room and dining room, making the rooms cosy and welcoming after the freezing graveyard. The dining room table was laden with crusty bread loaves and dishes of butter, and there was a pile of soup bowls and spoons, ready for everyone to help themselves.

The teachers and schoolchildren also walked back to the house when they finished singing, and congregated around the fire outside the kitchen. The kitchen staff had cooked cauldrons of *sadza* and relish for them. They rolled the *sadza* in their hands and dipped it in the relish, as they warmed themselves next to the blazing fire and sheltered from the icy wind behind the kitchen wall.

Isabella made a point of inviting Toby and his wife to join them in the house for soup and bread, even though she knew they were never entirely at ease mixing with the family like this. It saddened her that, after everything they had been through together, they all still felt this way, despite everyone's best efforts to be more relaxed.

At least this time she had something to talk to Toby about; a project she hoped would ignite his imagination.

During the royal visit in April, she had met the Reverend Paterson from Cyrene Mission, who was also a keen artist. He told her he encouraged his artistic pupils, and even some young men who lived at the mission, to paint murals on the walls of the chapel. He said the result of their work was breath-taking, and painting them had proved most rewarding for everyone involved. This intrigued Isabella and, in the months since, an idea of instigating something similar in their farm chapel took shape in her mind. She had not talked to Toby about it before, but she did so now. His eyes lit up with interest.

'So, what do you think?' she asked when she finished telling him about the Reverend Paterson. 'Do you not consider this a splendid idea?'

'I do. What a legacy it would be, for future generations to enjoy.'

'Indeed. I wondered if you and I should go to Cyrene and look at what they have done. I don't think the mission is over twenty miles from Bulawayo, on the Plumtree road.'

'I'm happy to do that. I will find it most interesting.'

'I am planning on staying here at the farm until next week, so we could go there on Friday morning? Would that suit you?'

'Yes. I will make sure another teacher fills in for me while we're away.'

'Well, good. We will leave from here and Admire can drive us in my car.'

Chapter 13

LILY found a letter in her staffroom pigeonhole when she checked it first thing in the morning.

Dear Miss Sanderson, she read.

May I request a meeting with you in my office at two o'clock this afternoon? If this is not convenient, please let my secretary know, otherwise, I will see you then.

Yours sincerely

Barnaby Weir

Lily bit her lip. The headmaster had never asked for a meeting with her before. What could this be about? Had she done something wrong? Had he found out how unhappy she was in the hostel and he was angry about this?

She tried to get on with her day and concentrate on her pupils, but she found she could not stop worrying about the impending meeting. At least she had a small class, and her pupils were easy to control, enabling her to set them work and watch them as they got on with it.

When lunchtime came, she felt so sick in the stomach about what Mr Weir might say to her, she hardly touched anything on her plate, despite it being one of Cook Matron's better meals. Roast chicken.

I must stop this, I must stop this, she kept telling herself. I worry more and more as I get older, and if I'm not careful, I will end up like my mother.

She arrived at the headmaster's office at two minutes to two.

'Mr Weir told me to bring you straight in,' Miss Smith said, as she knocked on the headmaster's door.

'Miss Sanderson is here to see you, Headmaster.'

'Good afternoon, Lily,' he said, getting up from his desk. 'Please, do take a seat.' There were two chairs in front of his desk, and Lily slid into one of them as he sat down again behind his desk. 'Heavens, it's cold these days, isn't it.'

'Yes, the last few days have been miserable.'

'We have to have at least one icy patch every winter to bring on good rains later in the year. But this cold spell seems more severe than usual, don't you think?'

'I suppose so,' Lily said, thinking that surely he had not asked her to come to his office to discuss the weather.

'I bet the hostel is like the Antarctic at this time of the year. I hear they have allocated you one of the less comfortable rooms, on the south side of the hostel.'

Lily hesitated. She did not wish to complain to him about her room. 'Well, at least it will be cool in summer,' she said.

'True. But this brings me to what I need to discuss with you, and maybe, if it turns out a certain way, you will no longer be in the hostel during the summer.'

Lily paled. Was he going to fire her?

'I had a Mrs Craig come and see me last week. Do you know her?'

'I met her when the Royal Family visited the Matopos. My father is the Assistant Native Commissioner, and we were therefore involved with the royal visit. They commissioned Mrs Craig to do a painting of Rhodes's grave for the Royal Family.'

'Of course. Mrs Craig is a very talented artist, isn't she? You may have seen the painting she did of this school, hanging in the foyer.'

'Yes, I have.'

'Lovely, isn't it?'

'Oh yes.'

'Anyway, the Craig family has a problem. Mrs Craig's granddaughter is being schooled at home, on their farm. This poor young girl's mother died during the war when she was three, and she did not meet her father, Mr Oliver Craig, until she was five. She was born in 1940, and by then he was in North Africa. Because of all these upheavals in her life, the family thought it better for her to spend a few years at home, being schooled there and getting to know her father, rather than sending her off to boarding school.'

'Yes, I understand this.'

'She has two cousins, almost the same age, and they are all having lessons together, so it's not as if she is on her own.'

'That's a good thing.'

'Indeed, but their governess died unexpectedly a few days ago. They think she had a heart attack. Her name was Miss Harrison. She had been working for the family since Oliver Craig was a baby himself, and so, besides losing someone of whom they were all very fond of, the three children are now without a teacher. Their best-laid plans have fallen apart, so to speak.'

'Oh dear.'

'Mrs Craig and I go back a long way, and that is why she called on me. She asked me if I knew anyone who could step in at the last minute. I spoke to my deputy about it, and we both thought of you.'

Lily was too taken aback to say anything.

'Please don't think that we're trying to get rid of you, Miss Sanderson. We think you are a splendid young teacher.'

'Oh, um, thank you.'

'The reason we thought of you is that, first, you are new here, second, you are single, and third, you teach the same age group as the children in question. Mrs Flanagan, the other standard two teacher, has been teaching at Milton Junior for many years and would be reluctant to up sticks and go off to a farm, especially as it would mean leaving Mr Flanagan to fend for himself.'

'Yes.'

'The deputy and I have looked at the size of your class and Mrs Flanagan's. They are both small, and we could therefore combine them, until we find a replacement for you, which would be next term.'

'Oh.'

'Mrs Craig asked if we could find someone to start as soon as possible, to reduce the disruption to the children's lessons. As for your hostel duties, Matron says everyone does one weekend duty every six weeks, and you have done yours, so they would only have to find someone to replace your weekly prep duty, which they say they can manage.'

'I see.'

'So what do you think, Miss Sanderson? Would you consider helping these people and going to the farm to teach their children? The farm is twenty to thirty miles north of Bulawayo. I have been there many times and can vouch that it's beautiful out there. Open spaces, interesting wild animals, and comfortable homes with attractive gardens. Of course, you would not have to be there all the time. You could go away for weekends, and you would have the holidays off. Obviously. And once the three children are old enough to attend proper school, in town as boarders, we will happily take you back onto our teaching staff here. If you still want us, that is.'

'Um.' Lily fiddled with the pendant on the chain she was wearing around her neck. 'This is all very sudden.'

'It is. Maybe you need to see for yourself what it's like out there before you decide. Mrs Craig expected this. She telephoned me yesterday to say she's driving into town on Friday with the headmaster of the farm school, Mr Tate. They are going out to Cyrene Mission to look at murals artists there painted on the chapel walls. Have you heard about these murals?'

'No.'

'Neither had I, before she mentioned them to me. Anyway, they are going to the mission first thing Friday morning, so should pass through town somewhere around lunchtime. She suggested you may like to return to the farm with them and stay Friday and Saturday nights. This will give you enough time to see how the land lies, so to speak. Someone could bring you back to town Sunday morning.'

'Um.'

'Did you have plans for the weekend?'

'Well, sort of. My friend and I usually go to the cinema on Saturday afternoons when there is no sport.'

'Oh dear.'

'I suppose I can cancel our arrangement.'

'Excellent. Shall I telephone Mrs Craig to tell her she can prepare for your visit, or shall I wait to hear that you have successfully cancelled your Saturday afternoon trip to the flicks?'

'No. I don't think my friend will mind. She teaches at Coghlan, so, I will walk there and tell her, before she leaves to go back to where she stays.'

'Thank you very much, Miss Sanderson. I know it will be a great relief for the Craig and Brooke families to get this sorted out as soon as possible.'

*

Mrs Craig's Rover pulled into the Milton Junior hostel gate just after one o'clock on Friday afternoon. Lily was waiting on the front veranda, a small overnight bag at her feet The vehicle came to a halt next to the veranda. Lily could see Mrs Craig and a middle-aged man of mixed race sitting on the back seat. He opened the back door and got out of the car.

'Good afternoon, Miss Sanderson. I'm Mr Toby Tate. Can I take your bag?' He took the bag to the boot, which the chauffeur had already opened. 'You sit in the back with Mrs Craig and I will ride up front with Admire.'

'Miss Sanderson, how lovely it is to meet you again,' Mrs Craig said, sliding a little further towards the opposite door so that Lily had more room on the back seat. Lily climbed in, clutching her handbag on her knee. 'How are you?' Mrs Craig continued.

'Fine, thank you,' Lily said, fiddling with the strap on her handbag.

Admire started the engine, and the car glided out of the hostel gates, turned right and travelled north up Borrow Street, passing the swimming pool which Lily so enjoyed using during the summer months.

'I hope you do not mind, but we are going to stop off at my house for a spot of luncheon, before heading out to the farm. Mr Tate and I are famished after our morning at Cyrene Mission.'

'Mr Weir told me not to have lunch at the hostel.'

'I telephoned him to tell him about our plans for luncheon.'

'Thank you.'

'Not at all. But before we continue. How are your dear parents? The Assistant Native Commissioner, and his excellent wife?'

Lily blushed, remembering how they behaved when they met Mrs Craig in April.

'I have not seen them for a while, but I believe they are well, thank you.'

'I hope so. Do you go back to the Matopos often to see them?'

'No. Not as frequently as they would like.'

For the rest of the journey to Mrs Craig's house they talked about the murals they had seen at Cyrene Mission. Mrs Craig told Lily how the Reverend Paterson inspired delinquent teenagers and young adults, who were being schooled at the mission, to paint murals on the chapel walls. They were told they could paint their interpretation of bible stories, and the resultant artworks were quite breath-taking, according to both Mrs Craig and Mr Tate. Mrs Craig was so inspired by what she had seen, she now wanted to encourage the school children at their farm school to do the same. From the way he was talking, Lily could see that Mr Tate was also interested in art, and he was going to instigate this project.

After leaving the main part of town, they drove through burgeoning new housing developments, "for everyone moving to this country from Europe. Builders cannot keep up, so great are the numbers flooding here," Mrs Craig explained. Finally, they came to a grand looking gate and Lily noticed a sign on the one of the posts with "Sunrising" written in polished brass letters.

Mrs Craig saw Lily reading this as they swept through the gates. 'It's the name of the house' she explained. 'Sir James Brooke, who built it, named it Sunrising before we moved here, back in 1905. Sir James Brooke is the late grandfather of two of the children we hope you will teach. He named it Sunrising when the house was first built back in 1898. When I moved in, I thought it a most appropriate name, especially for people like my husband and me, who had arrived in this part of the world just a few years before, when there was little or no development here, so it was a new dawn for us.' She sighed. 'Those were amazing times when I think back on them. Everything was so wild then.'

The car stopped in front of a flight of steps leading up to the veranda which wrapped around the entire house, as far as Lily could make out. Several French doors led onto this veranda, all with tall shutters on either side. From one of these doors emerged an elderly African man, dressed smartly in a black suit, resplendent with a crimson tie and shiny black shoes. The chauffeur came round to Mrs Craig's door and opened it, placing the little stool she used to climb out of the car on the ground. All this intrigued Lily, and she could not help being reminded of the Queen, just an older version.

'No need to come down the steps Gonda, we have nothing to carry in,' Mrs Craig called to the elderly man who was now hovering at the top of the steps. Lily wondered who he was.

'Good afternoon, Madam, Mr Tate,' he said, with a little bow. 'Your cold luncheon is ready in the dining room, but the drinks tray is on the western veranda if you would prefer to go there first. It is warm enough, now the weather has improved.'

'Thank you, Gonda. We will after we have freshened up. This is Miss Sanderson, the new governess, we hope. Please show her to the Lavender Room.'

Lily realised he was the butler as she followed him into the house, through a large hall, and down a passage. There were two marble pillars at the beginning of the passage. All the ceilings were high and made from slatted wood, painted white, and the house smelt of furniture polish. It was colder in the house than outside, now the cold spell was over and the sun shone brightly again.

'When you have finished, you should go back down the passage to the hall. The door opposite the passage takes you through the drawing room to the veranda where Madam will be,' Gonda said as he opened the door to the Lavender Room. He bowed and left Lily.

The Lavender Room was as beautifully furnished as the rest of the house appeared to be, Lily thought as she looked around. Cream curtains with sprigs of lavender flowers hung in the window, and the bedspreads on the two single beds were lilac. There was a large painting of a bowl of lavender on the wall between the beds. Lily looked at it and saw 'Isabella Craig, 1909' written in the bottom right-hand corner. Goodness, this lady has been painting for a long time, she thought. She sat down on one bed and it squeaked under her weight. She felt quite overwhelmed by her surroundings. She had never been into such a grand private home before. So much grander than all the Native Department houses she had lived in all her life. As she sat there, she noticed a chamber pot near the window and she smiled to herself. For all its grandness, she thought, they do not have a water closet, like Mum and Dad have in their Matopos home. This made her feel a little better.

Chapter 14

MOST people would consider the way Harry passed away a blessing, to die with no warning in your sleep, when you are old but still leading an active and full life. She would have hated becoming decrepit and incapacitated, having to rely on others to look after her, but this did not stop Oliver from struggling to come to terms with her sudden death. It's no wonder I feel depressed, he said to himself, losing two people I have been close to all my life, within weeks of each other. He understood what Amanda meant when she said she hated anyone dying. He missed James and Harry a great deal.

Oliver ate an early lunch and then lay on his bed for an afternoon nap. He did this most days when he was on the farm, a habit he developed after returning from the war. So different from when he was a prisoner for all those years. Then, one boring day stretched into the next, but he could never relax or sleep properly.

When his squadron was first captured in Libya they were too nervous to rest, mainly because they did not know what was going to happen to them. The day after their capture they were taken to a makeshift prison in Benghazi, where they huddled around in groups, stunned and afraid.

It happened in November 1941. They were watching a battle raging at Sidi Rezegh from the top of an escarpment, their tank engines ticking over, ready to go in and help if necessary, when a colonel came onto the radio announcing that a German column had been spotted heading their way. The colonel instructed them to leave, but their brigadier decided to separate from them. He went down the escarpment instead to round up the Gloucester Regiment who had been fighting in the battle. He wanted to bring them back to join their squadron. They agreed they would fire off two flares at dusk, the first white, the second green, so the brigadier would know where they were. Once they found their new location about ten miles from Sidi Rezegh, they arranged their twelve tanks in a laager, with three tanks on each side and the truck that served as their headquarters parked in the middle. After this, they had nothing to do except wait for the brigadier to arrive with the Gloucester Regiment. Oliver and his sergeant, a man by the name of Arnold, stood in front of their tank smoking, like most of the other men. The two flares were fired off from their headquarters truck at sunset and, shortly afterwards, they heard tanks rumbling in from the west. Their staff captain ran around, yelling, 'Don't shoot, it's the brigadier coming back.' The light was fading, but Oliver and Arnold could see tanks from the Gloucester Regiment approaching in two columns. He and Arnold even walked out towards them, waving their arms above their heads, directing them where to go, but as the tanks got closer, they noticed something odd; a motorcycle with a sidecar driving out from between the columns and racing to the back of the line.

'We don't have motorcycles with our tanks, do we, Arnold?' Oliver said.

'No Sir.'

A moment later they spotted German tanks behind the lead tanks. It caught them completely by surprise. Later, they found out that the

Germans often drove captured tanks at the front of their columns, to deceive the enemy when they were approaching. However, right then, all they knew was that the Germans were fast approaching. They dashed back to the safety of their tanks, but the Germans surrounded the laager. Three tanks on the east side managed to start up and drive off, but the rest of them, grasping the severity of the situation, started firing at the Germans. Another battle ensued and there were many fatalities and injuries, including their squadron leader, who had taken cover underneath his tank. A shell hit the petrol tank, blowing it up, and killing both him and his sergeant. Recognising that they were both outmanoeuvred and out manned, Oliver and Arnold ran to the headquarter truck and set it on fire, to destroy all their documents, managing to get back to their tank before the Germans could identify that it was them who had done this. By now, the Germans were swarming all over their tanks.

A smart young German officer in riding breeches and highly polished boots sauntered up to Oliver. He spoke excellent English.

'Are you an officer, Sir?' he asked.

'I am,' Oliver said.

He took out a silver cigarette case and offered Oliver a cigarette, which he accepted, and then took one for himself. He lit both their cigarettes with his lighter.

'But you do not wear an officer's uniform,' the German said.

'We all wear the same clothes,' Oliver responded, which was true. They were all dressed in khaki trousers, a khaki shirt, with a vest underneath, and brown overalls, with no insignias on anything. 'The officers will identify themselves,' Oliver explained.

'Why did you wave to us at first?' the German asked.

'We were expecting Allied tanks, and we sent up the flares to tell them where we were. When we first saw the column, we only saw the tanks you had captured.'

'You fell for our trick,' the German officer laughed. 'Well, the war is now over for you, my friend.'

The Germans separated the officers from the men, something the Allies fighting in Egypt and Libya never did. They took the men off to one side, while the officers crouched between the tanks. They dragged the injured into the relative shelter of the laager. Dr Harvey, their regimental doctor, did what he could to ease their pain, and the German general told his men to take off their overcoats and put them over the injured. For the main part, it was a hopeless situation, sitting there listening to the groans of the wounded which, for many, turned into a death rattle.

It was a long, cold, and frightening night, and the beginning of many years in captivity.

*

Oliver came back to reality with a start, feeling hot and clammy, even though it was cool in his bedroom. He stared at the photograph of himself and Emily on their wedding day, which he kept on his bedside table, trying to regain his composure. But looking at it just made him feel worse. Emily was dead too. Her last breaths had probably been that awful rattle also.

He pushed the photograph face down and kicked the rug off his legs, shoving his feet into his shoes. He tied his shoelaces and walked onto the wide veranda, passing the stable doors of the other bedrooms leading onto the veranda, until he was at the other end, outside the drawing room. He sank into an easy chair there. Prince must have been looking out for him because he soon appeared.

'Would you like your tea now, Sir?'

Oliver glanced at his watch. His mother should be back any minute with Miss Sanderson, or Lily, as he had called her on that strange night in April.

'Yes, please, Prince. Put four cups on the tray.'

He gazed at the view from the veranda and gradually calmed down. They had built the house on a hill, with an impressive view of the surrounding bush. Despite the scrub being brown and grey and dusty, he loved it. He had known bush like this all his life and he didn't mind that the trees were leafless, and the grass more yellow than brown at this time of the year.

Prince arrived with the tea tray and Oliver poured a cup, putting the tea cosy back over the large brown teapot so it would remain hot for the others. He helped himself to a slice of banana bread from the plate on the tray. He was not happy with the idea of Lily filling in for poor Harry, although he accepted that they needed a replacement sooner rather than later. But Lily? He recalled how they were mutual witnesses to her father's escapades with the lady-proprietor of the Matopos Hotel. He remembered with amusement the squeaks and squeals coming from the flower bed. It had mortified the poor girl. She would surely also feel uneasy with the prospect of meeting him now. She must be embarrassed, knowing that he knew something she would prefer to forget. He never thought he would see her again after that night. What a coincidence that Barnaby Weir had picked her, of all people, to fill in for poor old Harry. Barnaby thought he knew everything about everybody, just like his mother, Muriel, but he knew nothing about that fateful night. God, imagine if he did. Pompous git that he was, he would have postulated long and hard about it. Barnaby and Oliver were born just weeks apart and, because their mothers were such grand friends, they had been thrown together from birth. But as they grew older, they grew apart. Barnaby attended Milton Junior School, followed by Milton Senior, while Oliver went to REPS, and then completed his schooling at Sherborne, in England. After school Barnaby attended a teacher training college in Birmingham, while Oliver went to Cirencester Agricultural College. When war broke out, Oliver travelled to North Africa while Barnaby stayed in Rhodesia. As the headmaster of a school, the authorities deemed his position critical, which meant he did not have to fight, even though many others like him did. Oliver could also have applied to stay at home, as farming was an essential service too, but he felt it was his duty to go, knowing his cousin Tim could manage the farms, despite his disability.

The roar of a car engine broke Oliver's chain of thought. He was glad of this. His driveway and garages were on the opposite side of the house from where he was sitting. He remained where he was, listening to car doors shutting, followed by murmurs, and then some movement and talking in the hall. This hallway stretched from one side of the house to the other, with a door leading onto the veranda. He stood up and walked towards this door as Isabella appeared.

'Hello Mama,' he said.

'Here you are, Darling. Lily, come this way and meet my son again.'

'Hello Lily, welcome to Brightside,' Oliver said.

'Thank you.' Lily's eyes darted away from his.

Oliver shook Toby's hand.

'Let's all have a cup of tea and then we will show you around, Lily. You will stay for a cup, won't you Toby, before going home?' Isabella said.

'I can't, thank you. Pamela will expect me home around now.'

'Well, that's a shame, but we will be in touch soon about our project. Thank you for accompanying me to Cyrene.'

'It was very interesting.'

He made his farewells and departed while Isabella settled herself in a veranda chair.

'So where are the children?' Isabella asked as she accepted a cup from Oliver.

'They are at Brooke House. I told Serena I would telephone her when you got here, and she will bring them over. Let me do this now while you have your tea.'

He left them and went into his study, picking up the receiver and twisting the handle, two long turns, followed by one short turn. He had to do this several times before Serena answered.

'Hi Oliver, they're back are they?'

'Yes.'

'Not a moment too soon. These children are driving me crazy. I'll drive them over to meet Miss Sanderson now.'

'Won't you show Lily to Harry's old rooms?' Isabella asked when he returned to the veranda. 'I need to freshen up, and I am sure you would like to too, Lily.'

The last thing Oliver wanted was to be alone with Lily, but he could not refuse his mother's request

'We built a cottage out of two rondavels for our late governess many moons ago,' he explained, as they walked through the hall, and out onto the back lawn. 'She was the one who requested rondavels, oddly enough.' They stopped at the gate into the private garden, so Lily could see what the place looked like. 'It's quaint, isn't it?' he said.

'Um, yes.'

'Harry was happy here. In recent years, when she wasn't teaching, she spent much of her time pottering about in this garden, or sitting on her veranda, enjoying all her efforts. It's north facing, so a sun trap in winter.'

'Yes. I,… I can see.'

'Most often the kitchen staff brought her meals here, and she ate in her sitting room or on the veranda,' Oliver said, opening the door into this sitting room. 'The kitchen is just to the right of the path, so she also used to pop in and help herself to whatever she wanted. She preferred her privacy, even though she was always most welcome to join us.'

'I would do the same as her,' Lily said.

'Of course, but this weekend, while you are here, you must have all your meals with us, if you don't mind.'

'Thank you.'

'My cousin-in-law, Serena, removed all Harry's possessions so the rooms are quite sparse now but they'll soon become homely enough again.'

'After my room in the hostel at Milton Junior, this looks cosy.'

Oliver threw her a sceptical look. 'Really? You don't mind this? Just a sitting room, leading into a little bedroom.'

'It's… it's lovely.'

'Well, I'm glad you approve. I'm afraid the PK is back through the gate, on the right as you go towards the house. Harry always used to have a chamber pot.'

'I'm sure I can manage.'

'I intend installing some proper plumbing soon.'

'My parents had a water closet put in their house before the royal visit.'

'Yes, I remember your father telling me.' Oliver noticed her biting her bottom lip, wishing she had not brought up that time, he thought, but he felt he had to ask after them now that she had mentioned them. 'Your parents are well, I trust?'

'Um. To be honest, I don't see as much of them as I used to.'

'Oh dear, because of, well, you know what?'

'Yes.'

'I'm sorry to hear this. You haven't spoken to your father about your discovery?'

'No. I don't know how to broach the subject.'

'Yes, it's a tricky business.' He paused. 'Well, I'll leave you to unpack. When you're ready, come back to the veranda and I will show you the schoolroom. The children will be here by then.'

Chapter 15

LILY did not mean to talk about her parents during her weekend at the Craig's farm. She could have kicked herself when she mentioned the water closet. However, afterwards, she was glad she had because it broke the ice between her and Oliver. Until then, she felt embarrassed in his presence, knowing what he knew about her father, but when she brought her dad to mind, by mentioning the plumbing, it seemed quite natural to discuss the secret they shared.

Once they were over this hurdle, she relaxed and enjoyed her time at Brightside. She loved everything about it, and, before she went to bed on Friday night, she decided she would leave her job at Milton Junior and come to work here. It was so much more interesting and exciting.

First, there was the little cottage she would live in, incomparably more homely than the Milton Junior hostel. The garden was dry at this time of the year, as were most gardens in Rhodesia, but it was still lovely, with a flower bed full of red poppies and cascading jasmine and petunias on the veranda.

Then there were the families. Lily was fascinated by all the Craigs and Brookes, and the way their lives were entwined. Being a single child, like her mother, her father's brother and his family were her only close blood relatives. But after the war they moved to a farm in Melsetter, hundreds of miles away in the Eastern Highlands, so they saw little of each other. Therefore, the family dynamics she witnessed here intrigued her. The Brookes came over on Friday night, at Mrs Craig's insistence, for a drinks party to meet her. All the Brookes that is, except the two older children, who were away at boarding school, and Mr Brooke, the children's father. She was told that he preferred to stay at home on account of being left crippled from the polio virus he contracted before the war. But old Lady Brooke came with Graham, and of course Serena and the two younger children.

'How surprising that we met recently at the Doulton when you were there with your friend Priscilla,' Serena said. Her eyes danced towards her brother-in-law, who was standing with them. Lily expected him to mention that he knew her and Priscilla too, and that he and Priscilla saw a great deal of each other these days, but when he did not, she decided it was not her place to bring it up. 'What a coincidence that you are here now, to fill the much-needed position of a teacher for our children, if we're lucky,' Serena continued. 'I have been trying to give them lessons this week and discovered I don't have the patience or the know-how.' She gave a small giggle. 'Oh dear me, I never thought teaching would be so difficult.'

'Gin and tonic is the drink of choice for all of us at drinks parties,' Oliver said, as he came over to where they were standing. 'Can I pour you one, Lily? You'll have, won't you, Serena? Graham?'

'Oh yes,' they both said.

Lily rarely drank alcohol, but she liked the idea of a gin and tonic now.

'Yes please,' said John, before she replied.

'I wasn't talking to you, young man, as you well know,' Oliver said.

'But you said, "all of us" Uncle Oliver.' John gave a mischievous giggle.

'All of us over a certain age, Brat. Now stop getting ideas above your station. Go to the kitchen and help Prince with the tray of snacks,'

'But I want to talk to Miss Sanderson.'

'Time for that tomorrow. For now, you can bring the snacks and offer them around. That should keep you busy.'

'Aw, Uncle Oliver.'

Oliver handed out the gins. 'Sorry about my youngest son,' Serena said. 'I'm afraid we need to keep him in his place, which Uncle Oliver is good at doing. I have another boy who is much less precocious. Hopefully, this one will become more like his older brother.'

Oliver lifted his glass. 'Cheers, and good luck, with whatever you decide to do,' he said to Lily.

'We will have just the one gin, and then be on our way,' Serena said. 'We thought it would be useful for you to meet most of us now, Lily. I'm sorry my husband couldn't come.' She gulped her gin nervously.

'Time enough for that,' Oliver said. 'He and I had a long session again this morning, discussing how the new irrigation scheme will work, so he'll be tired now.'

'I suppose so,' Serena said. Lily noticed her eyes darting towards Graham again as she said this.

'Has anyone told you we're building a dam here?' Graham asked.

'We?' Oliver said.

'For God's sake Oliver, don't be so pedantic.' Graham flashed his charming smile at Lily.

'No,' she said. 'No one has mentioned a dam.'

'It's almost done,' Oliver said. 'We're working hard to have the wall and spillway finished before the first rains, and then we can sit back and relax while we enjoy watching it fill up.'

'Hardly,' Graham snorted. 'You relax and enjoy; that'll be the day.'

Oliver ignored him this time. 'Hopefully, it will transform our farming operations, not to mention our lives too.'

'Absolutely,' Graham said, nudging John to offer Lily a snack from the silver tray he had carried from the kitchen. Lily chose a sausage roll, while the others helped themselves to pieces of biltong. 'Homemade,' Graham said, chewing his and grabbing another piece.

'Now offer your grandmother and great aunt, John, before you gannets tuck in,' Serena said. The two old women were sitting together on the sofa next to the fireplace, with Mrs Craig's dog lying between them. Amanda and Bea sat on the carpet in front of the fire, playing with Amanda's puppy. Amanda took a piece of biltong and gave it to him, which caught the attention of Mrs Craig's dog, who jumped off the sofa and sniffed at the tray John was still holding.

'Now look what you've done, Amanda. You can't give one dog and not the other,' John said, throwing a piece of biltong to Frank.

'Oi. Bring that tray back here,' Graham said. 'That biltong is for us, not the dogs.'

'May I suggest the children come over early tomorrow morning for a session in the schoolroom,' Serena interrupted, 'so you can get to know them better before you decide?'

'Thank you, I would like that,' Lily said.

'I'll send them around first thing, with Champion in the mule cart, which is the way they usually travel here. And then, how about you all come back to my house afterwards for a spot of lunch?'

*

"The schoolroom", as they all called it, was large, with one stable door opening onto the front veranda, and a second stable door leading into the back garden. Both these doors were closed during their morning lesson, as it was chilly when they started. However, a fire smouldered in the fireplace next to the teacher's desk, making the room warm. A far cry from my draughty classroom at Milton Junior, Lily thought.

'Do you like it here?' John asked as they were finishing their lessons. 'Are you going to teach us?'

'I like it very much,' Lily answered.

'Oh goody, because we like you, don't we girls?' When he said this Bea giggled and Amanda blushed.

'You need to learn to talk less and work more, John, if you want me to stay.' Lily noticed this shut him up for a moment.

'You see,' Bea whispered.

'Now let us pack everything away and go down to the stables. I'm looking forward to travelling to your house in the mule cart.'

'Do you ride horses?' John asked.

'I've only been on a horse once or twice, so I'm not competent,' Lily said.

'Well that's fine,' Amanda said, 'because Bea and I are just learning too, so you can learn with us.'

They set off in the mule cart, with Champion driving and Lily sitting next to him on the front bench. The children and Frank squashed into the back.

'Mum always says Champion is a champion with mules,' John quipped from where he was sitting on the tailgate. Lily glanced at Champion, but he either did not understand John's joke, or he had heard it many times before, because his expression remained unchanged as he manoeuvred the mule cart out of the stable yard.

They met Oliver cantering up the road as they lumbered towards Brooke House, his hair swept back, his face ruddy.

'He will have been talking to Uncle Tim about the fields again,' Amanda said, as Champion pulled on the reins, bringing the cart to a halt.

'Morning all,' Oliver said, also reining his horse to a standstill. 'How was your lesson?

'Very good, Uncle Oliver,' John piped up. 'Miss Sanderson said she's pleased we've been taught our seven times tables.$1 \times 7 = 7$, $2 \times 7 = 14$, $3 \times 7 = 21$.' He opened his mouth to continue.

'Okay, okay, we get the picture. Enough now,' Oliver said.

'You can be such a pain, John.' Bea poked him in the ribs.

'Enough,' Oliver said again. 'I'll ride back to the stables, and come over a little later in the car. See you then.' He nudged his horse and dashed off.

The children and Lily disembarked from the cart in the stable yard behind Brooke House a short while later. They walked across the dry lawn to the front of the house where the view over the riverbed immediately caught Lily's attention.

'Do you know what we're looking at down there?' she asked the children, pointing at the scene in front of them.

They scrutinized where she was pointing, their eyes flitting across the vlei and dry river bed.

'I don't think I can see anything interesting right now,' Bea said.

'Although there are often impala, kudu, and, and other stuff,' John said. 'But nothing at the moment.'

'You have no idea what we are viewing?' Lily asked. 'The sweeps and bends the river has made in the landscape have a special name. You don't know it?'

The children stared out at the view again. It was as familiar to them as the back of their hands, but no one had ever pointed out anything unique about it.

'The Umguza River,' Amanda tried.

'That's the name of the river, but what we're looking at down there is an oxbow lake.'

The children gazed in silence.

'It takes thousands and thousands of years for an oxbow lake to form. Some rivers shape them when a wide meander is cut off, creating a free-standing body of water. You see that curve in the bank. That was where the river once ran,'

'But there isn't any water in it,' John said.

'Not now, but does it fill in the rainy season?'

'Yes, most often. We like to play in it, although Mum doesn't let us if she thinks there may be a crocodile.'

'I can imagine.'

'But we've never seen one,' John said

'That's an acacia galpini tree in the middle,' Bea said. 'We've got a whole forest of them further down the river.

Isabella and Celia were sitting on the veranda, watching and listening to Lily with the children.

'So interesting that she's pointing out the oxbow lake to them,' Celia said. 'It was one of the principal reasons James built the house here, and none of us have mentioned it in years, have we?'

'No. That's what fresh eyes do. The more I get to know Lily, the more I like her,' Isabella said. 'Let's hope she takes the position.'

*

Before Lily left, she signed a contract with Oliver to fill the teaching post until the end of 1948. She would start the following Monday, as Mr Weir said they would release her as soon as necessary. Now she had seen the place, she could not wait to begin.

Admire drove her and Isabella back to Bulawayo on Sunday morning. The arrangement was that Mrs Craig would stay the week at Sunrising and the two of them would travel back to the farm the following Sunday, with Isabella staying there for a few weeks while Lily settled in.

As Lily walked into the hostel, smelling the usual strong odour of floor polish and hearing the echoing sounds of people moving in sparsely furnished rooms and empty passages, a sense of relief that she would be leaving overwhelmed her. She had lunch in the teachers' dining room, thin beef stew and well-boiled cabbage, and then set off on her bicycle to Mrs Jenkins's boarding house. She wanted to share her news with Priscilla.

'Oh gosh, you are such a lucky fish,' Priscilla exclaimed when Lily finished telling her about Brightside and Sunlands. 'I'm green with envy, and not just because of the interesting teaching position.'

'Yes, I can imagine.'

'Was he there? He did not contact me at all this weekend. And there I was, alone, and not even able to do anything with you.'

'Yes, he was there, and so was his brother, Tim, although I did not meet him. He keeps to himself most of the time because of his polio a few years ago. Isn't that too awful?'

'Yes, Graham has told me. And Oliver, what's he like?'

'He's fine, although he and Graham don't appear to get on'

'Oh, why?'

'I don't know. I just thought that. He and his daughter also have a difficult relationship, but I don't think it's his fault. It's because of what happened. His wife dying and him away until 1945.'

'He's quite old though, isn't he?'

'In his early forties. Older than Graham. Maybe that's why they aren't that friendly.'

'Could be. And Serena. She's so lovely, isn't she?'

'Oh yes. And full of energy too. I was amazed at how much she does. Overseeing the housekeepers, cooks, and gardeners, arranging meals, drinks, snacks, and whatever.'

'Graham told me he's going to live on the farm,' Priscilla said.

'Yes, I heard. I wonder what he intends doing out there.'

'He told me something to do with flying still,' Lily looked surprised, because no one had mentioned this. 'Oh Lily, you are lucky. I so wish I could work there,' Priscilla went on. 'Do you think I can come and visit you sometime?'

'I will try to arrange it. They all seem accommodating enough, I can't see why they would mind. You could stay in the rondavel cottage with me.'

*

'I'm making some big changes in my life, Mum,' Lily said when her mother answered the telephone.

'Oh dear Lillian, now what?'

'It's all rather sudden, I know, but last week the headmaster, Mr Weir, asked me if I would consider leaving my position at Milton Junior for the rest of this year, and next year, to help some people who need a governess for their children.'

'Oh, who?'

'The Craig and Brooke families.'

'What? You're, you're joking,' her mother spluttered.

'No. They need someone to teach the three youngest children on the farm, so they don't have to be boarders yet.' She hesitated, waiting for her mother to respond, but as she said nothing Lily continued. 'Their elderly governess died, and they need someone to fill in as soon as possible.'

'I don't believe it. Peter, come here and listen to this,' her mother yelled to her husband, from the passage, where the telephone was fixed to the wall. Lily imagined him sitting in his usual chair in the sitting room. She heard her mother telling her father the news.

'You can't do this, Lillian,' her mother said when she picked up the receiver again.

'Of course I can, Mum. I'm twenty-four, and old enough to decide. It's not such a big deal. It's not as if I'm being fired from Milton Junior. Mr Weir assures me the reason he asked me is that I'm the right fit for the job; young and adaptable, with no dependants. When I finish at the end of next year, they will give me back my position at Milton.'

Mrs Sanderson started crying. She must've rammed the telephone into her husband's hand because Lily could hear sobs in the background.

'I'm afraid your mother is not happy about this, Lily,' said her father.

'But why? What's wrong with it?' She explained to him how she spent Friday and Saturday nights at the farm and how much she loved it. She told him how much she hated living in the hostel at Milton Junior. 'I understand many people don't mind hostel life, Dad, and there is nothing wrong with the hostel but, when I moved here, I realised I've had enough of institutional life.'

'Should we see if Mrs Jenkins can take you back into her boarding house again?'

'I've signed a contract with the Craigs, Dad. I would hate to backtrack now. And what's more, they are paying me more than I'm being paid at Milton Junior, even with the top up as a boarder mistress. I will have free accommodation, free food, and more money. I cannot see why Mum can't be happy for me.'

'I'll talk to your mother and try to make her see reason.'

'Thank you. Would you be able to come and fetch me on Friday after school, and I will stay Friday and Saturday nights. I need to take all my stuff from here back home, and I don't want to lug my heavy suitcase on the train again.'

'Absolutely my dear. I look forward to seeing you then.'

'I will catch the train back into town on Sunday and afterwards travel back to the farm with Mrs Craig. I'm not planning on taking a lot out to the farm.'

*

The weekend with her parents did not go well. Her father could not talk her mother round and, although she refrained from crying again, she was sulky and sullen and kept making derogatory remarks about the snobbish Craigs and Brookes and how superior they thought they were. For the first time since she found out her father was having an affair with Mrs Manning, Lily almost understood why.

It was a relief to get onto the train from the Matopos siding back to Bulawayo on Sunday morning. Admire was at the station to pick her up, and they drove back to Sunrising. She and Mrs Craig had a light lunch, and then they set off for Brightside. Lily felt nothing but excitement for what lay ahead and was determined her mother would not spoil it for her.

Chapter 16

THE first month of Lily's teaching job on the farm passed by in a flash, and, before anyone knew it, the August school holidays were upon them. Oliver wanted Lily to stay on at Brightside for at least a week or two of the holidays, not to teach, but just to be around. He appreciated how much Amanda enjoyed having her there, and he dreaded four weeks with the two of them alone again.

He went to find Lily in her cottage on the Sunday morning before the term finished. This was the first time he had been there since she moved in. He was always aware of her presence around the place, but they did not see much of each other. She ate most of her meals in her cottage, except for Friday nights, when she ate with them in the dining room. His mother suggested this, and it became a habit from then onwards.

He rang the cowbell hanging from the veranda roof and Lily must've been in her sitting room because she appeared at the door straight away.

'Hi, can I come in?' he asked. He thought she looked embarrassed, seeing him there, and he wished he had asked her to meet him in his study. But it was too late now.

'Of course,' she said, stepping back into the room so he could come in. 'Please, sit down.' He chose the chair he always sat in when he had visited Harry. There was a moment of discomfort.

'I have a bottle of homemade lemonade here. Would you like some?' Lily asked. 'Otherwise, I can go to the kitchen and get some tea?'

'No, lemonade would be great. Is it the stuff Prince makes?'

'Yes, and Agnes always leaves a bottle of it on the tray for me, with a jug of water.' She slid the crocheted doily off the jug, the glass beads clinking on the metal tray as she did, and poured them each a drink. She set the glasses on the coffee table in the middle of the room and sat down in an armchair opposite him.

Oliver felt uneasy being there, alone with her. He had not expected this. He picked up his glass and sipped the juice. 'Delicious,' he said, holding the glass and glancing around the room. 'I don't notice many changes since you've moved in.'

'Well, no. I didn't want to bring much stuff with me when I first came, not that I have a great deal, as I haven't had a home of my own yet.'

'Of course.'

'Nonetheless, I find it cosy and comfortable. I love sleeping under a thatched roof.'

'You're not worried about bugs and spiders dropping out of the rafters.'

'Oh no. When I was small, and my dad worked in the Nyamandhlovu area, we lived in thatched rondavels. The roof beams were much dustier than these. Your staff is meticulous about cleaning.'

'Yes, my mother's influence. She's always made them clean the rafters every few months.'

'It shows.'

'So you've been with us a month now,' Oliver continued. 'Is everything okay?'

'Oh yes. I love being here and the children are a delight to teach. Even John.'

Oliver began to feel more relaxed. He crossed his legs and sipped his lemonade. 'I'm glad to hear this because I can see how Amanda has warmed to you.'

'We get on well. I find her easy-going. She's one of those children who likes to please.'

'She is, although she's still reserved with me.'

'But she's getting better, isn't she?'

'Yes,' Oliver said, although he knew that some of the awkwardness between them still was his fault. He needed to make a greater effort to be less reticent with her. He blamed his sometimes distant manner on having no siblings and going to boys' only boarding schools from the age of ten.

'I'd be lying if I said John was easy,' Lily continued. 'But he means well, and I just need to keep him in check all the time.'

'Excellent. I'm glad to hear this.' Oliver finished his drink and set the glass back down on the coffee table.

'Can I offer you some more?' Lily asked.

'No, that was good, thank you. In fact, I came over to discuss the school holidays with you. If you haven't made plans yet, I would be most grateful if you would consider staying here for part of the time. For extra pay, of course, and no teaching duties.' He noticed her eyes widen with surprise. 'Just for a few weeks.' He cleared his throat. 'As I mentioned before, I can see how much Amanda enjoys having you around and she and I are still uneasy with each other.' Lily still didn't respond. 'Sorry, I shouldn't have asked.' He gave a small laugh. 'You'd be right in thinking I should make more of an effort with my daughter and not expect others to help me.'

'No. Please. Not at all,' she blurted. 'It's just that I have made plans. First, to spend time with my parents. I will have to go back there for a while. It will distress my mother if I don't.'

'Of course.'

'And then I'll be meeting up with my best friend Priscilla. She's a teacher at Coghlan. We always spend some of our school holidays together. Her aunt and uncle live in Suburbs, and we've arranged to stay with them for a week. We have such fun together, swimming at the Borrow Street Pool, if it's warm enough, going to the cinema, having tea at the Doulton Tearoom, shopping at Sanders and Haddon and Sly and Meikles. Um....' As the list of her planned activities grew, he regretted more and more asking her if she would stay. Compared to all of this, life on the farm must seem dull. As if to drive her point home she concluded by saying: 'and of course they have tea dances at the Grand Hotel, which are fun too. I'm sure we will attend at least one of those.'

'Ah, it all sounds most exciting. And a girl your age needs all this. I'm sorry I asked.'

'On no.' She flushed. 'It's different from life on the farm, but as I said before, I enjoy being here as well. Maybe I could go off for the first few weeks of the holiday and then come back here for the last two weeks. That way I can catch up with my parents and Priscilla, and still help with Amanda.'

'Well, mull it over for a few days and we can finalise things before you go. If you need to make any telephone calls, use the telephone in my study.'

'Thank you. Although the postal system seems to work well enough. Bhutu takes Amanda and me to the end of the road in the mule cart every week to send and receive the mailbag. It's become a bit of a ritual for us.'

'I'm sure Amanda loves it. Everything the two of you do together will be enjoyable for her. Collecting the mailbag; walking the dog;

picking vegetables in the garden; fetching the butter and milk from the dairy. I'm afraid she and I would not be relaxed if I suggested doing any of this with her.'

*

Lily decided two-and-a-half weeks was long enough to spend time with both her parents, and Priscilla, and then she would return. While she was away, Oliver made a concerted effort to spend more time with his daughter, and he discovered the activity that worked the best for them was horse riding. Every afternoon Bhutu saddled up Como, and an elderly piebald pony by the name of Poppet, and the two of them rode down to the newly prepared fields together. The first few times they walked with Oliver holding a leading rein attached to Poppet, 'In case he shies, unlikely, but better to be safe than sorry,' he explained. However, Amanda soon gained enough confidence to ask if they could trot.

'Grip with your knees, Amanda, and try to raise yourself up and down, in rhythm with Poppet.' He couldn't help smiling as he watched her bobbing around like a sack of potatoes, gripping the saddle with her small hands to stop herself bouncing over and off, her face a picture of concentration. But it only took a few days of this before she controlled her movements and rose in time with the pony. 'That's it, that's it, well done. I'm most impressed,' Oliver said. 'Easy does it. Up, down, up, down.' The look of concentration turned to relief as she felt more in control. 'Now let's see you bring Poppet to a standstill. Pull your reins, that's it, whoa, whoa.'

Both horses stopped and Amanda looked at her father, her face flushed and red, her eyes bright, delighted with herself.

'Can we try that again, Papa?'

'Of course, let's trot to the far corner where the road opens onto the field? Can you manage that?'

She did not reply, but pulled in her reins, clutched the pommel of the saddle, and kicked Poppet in the ribs. The horse moved off at a sedate trot again.

'Try not to hang onto the saddle,' Oliver called. 'Grip with your knees instead.' However, he noticed she continued to hold on to the saddle, and he did not blame her. Poppet was a placid pony, but he was still much bigger than his daughter, and he could understand her innate fear of falling off. She would learn to let go of the saddle in good time, he thought. In the meantime, the progress she was making delighted him.

The dirt road they trotted down took them through stunted mopane trees, leafless after so many dry months. Dust flew from their horses' hooves, despite their going at a slow pace. The heavy, clay soil in this area was not suitable for growing crops, unlike the sandy soil in the field they rode towards. They soon reached the field and reined in their horses as they surveyed the vast open space in front of them. Oliver glanced at the cloudless sky; creamy grey, from the millions of minuscule particles of dirt in it. How he hoped for an early rainstorm or two, to settle the dust. But they would only plant their maize crop mid-November, once the rains started properly, with luck. Next year should be different, he hoped, with good rains to fill the dam enough for them to irrigate. What a change this would make to their lives.

The sound of a horse galloping behind them interrupted his thoughts. He turned round to see his cousin Graham pelting down the road at high speed. Oliver tightened his reins and grabbed Poppet's, just in time to stop him from bolting as Graham's horse descended on them, still at a pace.

'Whoa, whoa,' Graham called, pulling his horse to a standstill as he reached them.

'For God's sake, Graham, Amanda is a beginner. The last thing she needs is for her horse to take off in fright.'

'Didn't think about that. Sorry, Mands. You ok, honey?'

'Yes, thanks.' Amanda grinned at him.

'Excellent. You see old chap, no harm done. You look splendid on that pony, Amanda. I can see you are going to have what we term "a good seat".'

'Thank you, Uncle Graham.'

Typical, Oliver thought. He can't help turning on the charm.

'I think we need to encourage your cousins to ride more. We can't have you being way ahead of them. Maybe I should start taking them out like your Daddy is taking you.'

'Papa said he'd take all of us. He's just been teaching me to trot though, because John can trot already. But Bea can't.'

'Well, I'll teach her to trot this afternoon, so the two of you can trot together, side by side.' He winked at Amanda and she beamed back. Oliver looked straight ahead, so they could not see his irritated expression.

Although Graham had moved back to the farm a few weeks before, Oliver still found it a struggle having him around full time. He went to town a lot, but not enough, in Oliver's opinion. Instead, he always seemed to get in Oliver's way and steal Oliver's ideas. This was a perfect case in point, trying to take over the children's riding lessons, with no consideration for any plans that were already in place. As far as Oliver was concerned, the only benefit to having Graham back on the farm was that it made his Aunt Celia happy. He had moved into a cottage near her, and being so close was a great comfort to her.

'I'm racing around the farm on Captain, deciding where to put my airfield,' Graham said.

This was another bone of contention for Oliver. He knew Graham had as much right, as any of them, to earmark a piece of land for his use, but the idea of an airfield still irritated him.

'All Tim and I ask is that you don't insist on any of the lands we have designated for cultivation after the dam has filled. We'll need all the arable land for cropping once we've got the irrigation scheme going.'

'I know, I know, the two of you go on about this every time I mention it. I get the picture.'

With this, he lifted his hat to them and bolted off again. Oliver was thankful he was still holding Poppet's reins, because otherwise, he may have followed.

Chapter 17

PRISCILLA and Lily met up as planned, but it turned out Priscilla's mind was far from the fun Lily thought they would have during their time together in town. 'Please, please, ask Mr Craig if I can come out to the farm with you when you go back,' Priscilla said, no sooner were they settled in her aunt and uncle's house. Lily glanced at her, surprised. 'I'm desperate to see Graham Brooke. It's weeks since I last saw him,' Priscilla continued. 'I'm in love Lily. Remember how I was when I first clapped eyes on him at the swimming pool. You were with me. You know I was smitten, and nothing has changed.'

'But you hardly know him.' Lily giggled.

'Don't laugh Lily. It was love at first sight. I never believed in it before, but now I do, and that's why I need to come back with you, so that we can get to know each other better.' Lily stared out of the window, at Priscilla's aunt's lush garden, wondering how it would work, having Priscilla at Brightside. 'I know I'm putting you in difficult position, asking you to ask,' Priscilla said. 'It would just be until school starts again.'

'Oliver is nice. I don't suppose he'll mind,' Lily said, turning around to face her again. 'You could stay with me in my little cottage, so it's not as if he needs to see much of us or anything like that.'

'Lovely.'

'It's just the meals that will be awkward because they provide all my food. I'm sent a tray from the kitchen for most of my meals. Except for Friday nights, when I eat with Cliver and Amanda, and Mrs Craig if she's there.'

'Maybe I could offer to pay for my meals.'

'They are not the sort of people who would accept that.'

'Oh dear. So what do you think?'

'I will ask Oliver. I'm sure he will say yes, and you can bring a few eats as gifts.'

'Shall we make a delicious fruit cake? I know Aunt Estelle bought some dried fruit. The good thing about fruit cake is that it lasts. They can keep eating it for weeks after I've left, even though it looks as if Mr Craig eats very little.'

'Yes, I've decided he's so thin because he had a tough time during the war.'

'Does he talk about it?'

'Not to me.'

'You're probably right. Going back to what to do, though, I could also ask Enock to make some shortbread. His shortbread is delicious, and I'm sure Mr Craig would enjoy it too.'

Lily smiled. 'Well, let me ask him first, before you plan on anything else to bake, although it will surprise me if he doesn't agree.'

*

The following week Oliver fetched Lily and Priscilla from her aunt and uncle's home in the Suburbs of Bulawayo. Priscilla was bursting with excitement at the prospect of seeing Graham, although she would never tell anyone but Lily about this.

'Thank you so much for allowing me to come and stay, Mr Craig,' Priscilla purred, as soon as they were on their way.

'Not at all. I'm glad Lily will have company. I'm sure it's boring for her, with just my daughter and me there.' He glanced at Lily in his rear view mirror, but she was looking out of the window.

The journey passed quickly, with Oliver doing most of the talking. When they were almost there, he pulled the car to the side of the road, just after a low-level bridge and told them that this was the place his parents always stopped at on their treks to the farm in the early days. He explained how they left before dawn, so they could arrive at the farm and set up camp before nightfall.

'Before we continue, let's stretch our legs for five minutes,' he suggested, switching off the car's engine. 'I always enjoy this place, not that I stop here often.'

'Ooh, rather,' Priscilla trilled.

They climbed down into the dry river bed and walked in the sand. There was a stagnant pool of water in a rocky outcrop, and Oliver halted next to this pool.

'They called this place "The Breakfast Spot" because they used to eat their breakfast here. It would be late morning by the time they arrived, and they would take out their packed breakfasts and eat them, before proceeding with the rest of the journey. It will only take us twenty minutes to get home, but for them, it would have been another couple of hours. Of course, the mules or oxen, whichever were pulling their carts, needed a break and a drink of water too by then, and they would let them drink in this pool. The first time they stopped here, a crocodile took my father's beloved Labrador.'

They all stared at the pool as if they were looking for the wretched crocodile that had done this deed all those years ago. But the surface remained still.

'How awful. They must have got such a fright,' Priscilla eventually said.

'I'm sure they did,' Oliver agreed. 'My mother is a great dog lover. She's been quite paranoid for the safety of her dogs ever since.'

'Life was different in those days,' Lily murmured.

'It was. Nowadays we can travel around in comfortable automobiles on well-maintained roads, not to mention the bridges, making the journey out to the farm an easy drive. My mother used to tell me how precarious it always was crossing the rivers in their carts. It got to the stage where she preferred to ride a horse rather than hang on to the seat of the cart, as it lurched over rocks. Now, the only time we encounter a problem with crossing rivers is in the rainy season, when there has been a heavy downpour causing the water level to rise and flood over the bridges. But even this isn't a big problem, because we just wait a few hours for the water to go down again.'

*

'Gosh,' Priscilla said when she and Lily walked into her cottage, 'this is quaint. I adore it. You are so fortunate to have landed a job here. I'm green with envy.'

'Yes. I count myself lucky.' Lily pointed at the sofa. 'You are going to sleep there if that's okay with you?'

'Of course.'

'Oliver said I could take some sheets, blankets, and a pillow from the linen cupboard in the house, and we'll fold everything away and store it on top of my wardrobe during the day, so it won't get in the way.'

Priscilla walked through the door into Lily's little bedroom. 'Too, too gorgeous. Oh, if only I had something like this.'

Lily laughed. 'Shall we go for a walk? I could do with a bit of exercise after that slice of chocolate cake we had with our tea.'

'Do you always join your boss for afternoon tea like that?'

'Oh no. He suggested it because we'd just got back and he wanted you to meet Amanda. In actual fact, I don't see a great deal of him, and he's often reserved. It amazed me how much he opened up when we were driving back today.'

'He's lovely. So interesting, and full of fascinating stories. From the way you've spoken about him, I thought he'd be dour, but he isn't in the least.'

'I guess not.'

'And so good of him to invite us for dinner tonight. You said you only ate with him on Friday nights.'

'It's usually that way. We started doing it when I first got here. Mrs Craig was staying, and she suggested it, and we carried on from then onwards. I enjoyed it when she was with us, but felt uneasy when she left. As I said before, he's reserved, and his relationship with his daughter isn't the easiest, which doesn't help.'

'I'm surprised to hear that. But still, I'm looking forward to dinner with him tonight. It'll give me a chance to wear the smart frock I brought with me.'

Lily laughed again. Priscilla was always considering the way she looked.

It soon became clear to Lily that Priscilla brought out a side to Oliver's character that she had not seen before. In the month she spent at Brightside before the school holidays, he was always polite, but distant, keeping to himself. Now, he was charming, outgoing, and exceedingly agreeable company. It first became apparent in the car journey back to the farm, and it did not change once they were home.

At dinner on that first night, he could not have been a more attentive host. When Priscilla mentioned how "stunning" his house looked, he insisted on pouring them each a gin and tonic and taking them on a guided tour. They moved from one beautiful room to the next, with Priscilla gushing over everything. Before then, Lily had been into few rooms, so it was fascinating for her too, but she refused to compete with Priscilla's eagerness. However, she was interested to see that he was converting one of the smaller bedrooms into a bathroom with running water. This was a recent development since her departure.

During dinner, he told them about his riding lessons with his daughter. Also something new.

'She has come on well,' he said. 'We go for an evening ride, and sometimes in the mornings too, and it has amazed me how she's picking it up.'

Amanda was as quiet as ever, but she looked pleased with this compliment.

'That's tremendous,' Lily said, reflecting how satisfactory it was that they were enjoying an activity together. 'I'm going to have to work hard to catch up to you, I can see.'

'I'm sure you will find it easy, Miss Sanderson. All you need to do is hold on with your knees,' Amanda responded.

'It's so much easier if you learn to ride when you are a child,' Priscilla said. 'I was lucky enough to have riding lessons when I was about your age, Amanda.'

'So can you ride well, Miss Clark?' Amanda asked

'I guess I'm pretty competent. I used to ride in gymkhanas and shows when I was young. It was always great fun, although I'm afraid I have little time for it these days.'

'Well, that's a shame because I was going to suggest you come with us tomorrow morning,' Oliver said.

'Oh, I would love that,' Priscilla said, flashing him a bright smile. 'It will be a tremendous way to see the farm.' Then her face fell. 'Oh dear. I'm afraid I didn't bring any proper riding gear with me, just a pair of trousers and some tennis shoes. Will you mind if I wear these?'

'Of course not. Wear what you like, as long as you are comfortable.'

'I'm so excited at the prospect of this,' Priscilla said, sipping her wine. 'Would you mind if I call you Oliver?'

It was then that Lily felt a stirring of discomfort. Was Priscilla flirting with Oliver? She glanced at Oliver but his face was blank.

Priscilla and Lily left shortly afterwards, with Lily feigning fatigue when Oliver asked if they wanted to join him for a nightcap in the drawing room.

'Gosh, what a lovely, friendly man Oliver is,' Priscilla said again when they got back to the cottage. 'You never told me how fascinating he is. The way you spoke, he sounded like a fuddy-duddy. Okay, he might be older than us, but he's attractive, with his chiselled features and brown hair with only a few streaks of grey around his temples. There I was, assuming Graham was the only dish in the family, but Oliver has an air of vulnerability which I find appealing.'

'Honestly, Priscilla. You are the end. It's only because he's so thin, after his wartime experiences.'

'I must ask him about this,' Priscilla said. 'All these heroes amongst us, since the war.'

'The question is,' Lily chuckled as she threw the blankets onto the sofa for Priscilla, 'who is the most heroic? Graham or Oliver?'

'Mm, well as you know, I have only had eyes for Graham Brooke, but maybe I could change my mind.'

Lily went to bed feeling discomfited about what had transpired; Priscilla drooling over Oliver like that, and him enjoying it. What man wouldn't? Priscilla was an attractive-looking woman, with her long blond hair and flashing blue eyes, and always so enthusiastic.

Unlike me, Lily thought. It's no wonder Oliver keeps his distance when I'm here alone. Oh dear, what would she do if Priscilla usurped her? As much as she treasured their friendship, she was happy with the way her life was going, but she could hardly ask them to stop flirting with each other.

*

The next morning Lily rose early to walk down to the stables with Priscilla where she was meeting Oliver and Amanda for their ride. Summer was on its way and the early morning was balmy.

'This is my favourite time of the year, with the trees sprouting new leaves and the smell of flowers in the air,' Lily said, as they strolled down the dusty driveway and turned through the gate to the stable yard.

'Mm, it's not bad, but I think I prefer April, when the skies are bright blue, and everything looks crisp and clean. Now, the bush is brown, or grey, with dust. Even the sky is grey,' Priscilla said.

Bhutu had saddled three horses and was waiting for them next to the trough, holding their reins. Oliver and Amanda arrived a few minutes later, Oliver carrying a spare riding hat for Priscilla.

'Morning girls. Morning Bhutu. I see you chose Granger for the madam,' he said.

'Yes, Baas. He needs a ride today as I did not ride him yesterday.'

'That's fine. He's a pretty steady mount, Priscilla. You shouldn't have any problems with him.'

'I'm sure I won't.' Priscilla took the reins and patted Granger's nose.

'Do you need a leg up?' Oliver asked, causing Lily to flinch.

'No, no. I can manage.' Priscilla checked her girth and stirrup lengths, then slipped her left foot into the stirrup and pulled herself up, swinging her right leg over the horse's rump and feeling with her foot until she found the other stirrup.

Lily watched Priscilla with envy, wishing she could join them. Once they left, first walking and then easing into a steady trot, with both Oliver and Priscilla calling out instructions to Amanda, Lily decided she would take her mind off them and go for a walk to the family graveyard. She and Amanda went there first when she was new to Brightside and, since then, she visited it often. The view of the farm was magnificent from there, and the four graves always moved her. One over forty years old, the others more recent. She often climbed the large rock next to Oliver's father's grave and pondered on the lives of the people buried there; and especially Oliver's father, dying so young. And then there was Oliver's wife's grave. She wondered too what had caused her to die so young.

The gate squeaked as she opened it, and a flash of movement in the graveyard caught her by surprise. It was Graham Brooke, standing up from where he must've been sitting next to his father's grave. His brow was furrowed and his eyes blurry, and for a moment Lily thought he might have been crying.

'Oh dear, I'm so sorry to disturb you,' she said.

His face cleared, as he reverted to his usual jaunty self. 'No problem,' he said. 'I was just saying hello to the Old Man. I do this most mornings, now that I'm living here again. But it's nice to bump into you. When did you get back?'

'Yesterday. I come here often too, but not usually this early.'

'Well, how about we coordinate our visits so they coincide?' lily's eyes widened in surprise. 'It's amazing how little I see of you,' he continued. 'It's not as if Oliver's house and mine are that far apart. Only a couple of miles. But then, Oliver rarely invites me there, or anyone else.'

'Well, I'm tied up with the children during term time.'

'Serena tells me you're doing wonders with them.' Lily shook her head. 'No seriously, as much as we all loved dear old Harry, I'm told that having you here is doing them the world of good.'

'Thank you. I do my best.'

'But you've returned earlier than I expected. I'm sure the school holidays only finish in another week or more.'

'Oliver asked me to come back earlier if I could.'

'Did he? The sly devil.'

'He thinks Amanda is more reassured with me around. Although, saying that, the two of them have started riding together, and this seems to have drawn them closer.'

'Yes, I often see them on their rides.'

'In fact, that's why I'm out and about now. They're on an early morning ride now. My friend Priscilla has come back to the farm with me, and she has joined them.'

Graham raised an eyebrow. 'Priscilla is at Brightside?'

'Um, yes.' What else could she say? It wasn't as if she could tell him the reason for Priscilla being here was her desperation to see him, especially as she didn't seem that desperate anymore. Instead Lily said: 'Yes, she wanted to come and see what the farm was like. She and I stayed at her uncle and aunt's house in Suburbs, and now she has joined me for the last week of the holidays here.'

'Oliver has all the luck. Two beautiful young ladies staying a stone's throw from him. And not a mention to any of us at Sunlands about this.' Graham laughed to himself. Lily couldn't decide if he was joking or not. 'He's a dark horse, that one,' he muttered.

'We made the plans at the last minute,' Lily explained.

'But as you girls are here, how would you like to meet for a picnic later, so that I can show you about too?'

'That's kind.'

'There is a lovely spot along the river where we often picnic. If you brought your bathing suits, we could swim in the river when we get hot.'

'Aren't there any crocodiles?'

'I don't believe there are. I will ask Serena and the children if they want to join us, and my mother too. We will make a real family outing of it.'

'That sounds lovely. I know it will please Priscilla when I tell her.

Chapter 18

SERENA telephoned Oliver later that morning to invite him to the picnic. He had washed and changed after his ride and was sitting in his study, catching up with his paperwork.

'Graham tells me Priscilla is staying with Lily,' Serena said. 'He thinks they will enjoy a day down at the river, and we should all join them.' Oliver was not sure he wanted to be part of a family day down at the river, arranged by Graham. Serena may have sensed his reluctance because she said; 'It's not as if I feel like it either, you know. But it will be rude if I stay away, especially as my family and Priscilla's have been friends for many years. So you old stick in the mud come and join us. Amanda will love it, and it'll do her good to see you enjoying yourself with all of us too. You don't have to worry about food. I've got Tuppence onto it already. We're going to have a braai. Boerewors and rolls. Very simple, but you know how the kids love a fire. Just bring a couple of cold beers for yourself. I'll have homemade lemon juice and gin.'

'Alright then,' he groaned. 'The girls can go in the cart and I'll ride Como down later. That way, I can escape when I've had enough. Will we meet at the usual place on the river?'

'Yes.'

'Priscilla tells me she's experienced at handling a mule cart, so she can drive them down there. This means Bhutu won't have to take them and hang around when it's his afternoon off.'

'Great. And Amanda can show Priscilla the way. Don't be too long after them though Oliver.' Serena said.

'I'll try not to be.'

He replaced the receiver and went looking for Amanda. She was on the front lawn, rolling around with Frank. The dog leapt up and ran towards him wagging his tail, a smile on his face, the way Staffies always do when they first see someone.

'Down,' he said, as Frank was about to leap up at him. 'It's only been a few hours since I last saw you. Down.'

Amanda giggled. 'He's always like that, Papa. He loves everyone.'

'True.'

He told her the plans for the rest of the day, and her face lit up.

'So you're happy to go down there in the cart with Miss Sanderson and Miss Clark?'

'Oh yes, Papa. Can we go now? I love it there.'

'They may not want to go right away, but you can ask them. I will join you later. I need to finish off some paperwork in my office first.'

He did not see them again before they left, but, as he was considering getting ready to go, the telephone rang, three shorts and one long; his ring.

'Oliver, Oliver. Thank God I've got you,' his mother said when he answered it. 'Oh Oliver, the most terrible thing has happened.'

'What Ma, what's the problem?'

'We've had a bush fire here and my studio has burnt down.' He made no response as the significance of her words sunk in. 'Did you hear me, Oliver?'

'Yes, yes Mama, I....I did,' he spluttered. 'I don't know what to say. How bad is it?'

'Bad. My studio is burnt to a cinder.' He realised she was crying.

'Oh, Mama, I'm so sorry.' He could not remember the last time he had seen or heard his mother cry, but now great wracking sobs could be heard down the telephone.

'Is anyone hurt?' he asked when the sobs ceased.

'No, thankfully not.'

'And your car?'

'It's fine,' she murmured. 'Admire and I were out in it when the fire started.'

'But you have a fire break, Mama.'

'The fire jumped clean over it.' Isabella started weeping again. 'It's windy here, and the bush is dry,' she said.

He glanced out of the window. 'Yes, the wind has risen here too. I'll come now. It sounds like you need help.'

'Well, I've got the staff doing what they can, but oh dear, it is terrible.' The tears started again.

'I'll leave as soon as I can,' he said.

He ran to the kitchen where he found Prince finishing his morning chores, looking forward to a relaxing afternoon off.

'There's been a fire at Sunrising,' Oliver said.

Prince's face fell.

'No one was hurt, but my mother's studio sounds bad. I'm going to drive into town now. Please make me a sandwich to eat on the way, and a bottle of water. Then go to the stables and tell Bhutu I will not need my horse after all, but he needs to go to the river to tell the others that I will not be joining them.'

'Yebo, Baas. Baas, that is terrible.' Prince said.

'Yes, but at least it hurt no one,' he repeated.

Oliver prepared himself for a shock as he drove into town, but it was still far worse than he expected. The devastation was apparent as soon as he turned through the gate and his heart sank. He parked his car next to the fishpond, out of harm's way, and, as he opened the car door, the smoky smell of the bush fire hit him like a slap. Instead of climbing the steps into the house, he walked along the veranda to the corner, where he could see the studio roof beams, stretching from the smouldering walls like thin arms held up in surrender. Oliver shuddered, taken back for a moment to his days of hiding in Italy.

He shook his head. Seeing his childhood home burnt like this was heart-breaking, and, on a practical level, it was appalling. He dreaded to think how many of his mother's beautiful and valuable paintings had been in the studio. Years and years of work, gone up in smoke.

He found Isabella in her favourite spot, sitting on the veranda, looking westward onto the vlei. The stream at the bottom of the garden was dry at this time of the year, as was the garden, but it was still a beautiful view. Except, as he looked northwards, the remnants of the bush fire were still noticeable. Smoking earth, scrub with flames licking from them, blackened trees, and smouldering grass. Isabella was sitting on the large sofa she had had out there for years, stroking Eddie's head, rubbing his ears, staring out at the vlei.

She looked broken.

'Mama,' he said. Tears welled up in her eyes again when she saw him. She took a soggy cotton handkerchief from her pocket and dabbed her eyes and nose.

'Oh Darling, it's too awful.'

'I'm sorry.' He walked up to her and stroked her shoulder. She grasped his hand in hers. 'You know what we both need?' he said after a while, 'a good strong whisky.' He moved back into the drawing room and took two glasses from the drinks cupboard. There was always whisky in a decanter on the silver tray, and he poured a large tot into each glass and then, after scrutinizing them, poured a little more. He carried the glasses through to the veranda. 'Do you want ice, Mama? I can go to the kitchen to get some.'

'No thank you.'

He placed the drinks on the coffee table in front of the sofa and sat down next to his mother. 'It's a terrible, terrible shame. Have some of your drink, Mama. You are in shock.'

She gulped her whisky, shuddering as she swallowed it.

'Where were you when the fire broke out?' he asked.

'Town. Admire and I travelled to town this morning. I needed to buy some groceries as the Weirs and the Fletchers are coming for luncheon tomorrow. If I had known there was going to be a fire, I would have stayed. There is a chance I could have stopped it.'

'Probably not. You know how these bush fires are when they get going on a windy day. I'm afraid once they take hold there's not a lot one can do, except back burn from the fire break.'

'Indeed, but if I had been here, I would have made sure they did this. I don't believe anyone even considered it. The staff all looked pretty sheepish when I asked them.'

'It would have swept in before they knew what was happening.'

'They were all in the compound having their tea. Except Gonda, who has gone off on his leave.'

'Yes, I have seen him at Brightside. But what is done is done. It's pointless blaming yourself, or any of them, or thinking you could have stopped it.'

Isabella bit her lip, trying to stop the tears from welling up again. 'Fortunately it did not hurt Edward, or anyone else.'

'Exactly.'

'But all my work.' She could not help herself. The sobs started again.

'Between you, me, Celia, and the other Brookes, we have many of your paintings.'

She looked at him as if she did not believe a word he said. He waited for her to stop crying, knowing there was nothing he could say that would make her feel better. He knew how much her paintings meant to her.

'All those paintings for "Archie in Africa",' she murmured.

Isabella did a whole series of paintings of her first Staffordshire bull terrier back in 1906. She submitted them to the publishers, MacMillan of London, in the hopes they would illustrate Percy Fitzpatrick's book, 'Jock of the Bushveld'. MacMillan's turned them down, but the ever pragmatic Isabella did not let this stop her. She sat down and wrote her own children's story about the dog in the paintings, Archie, and she called it 'Archie in Africa'. As a child, Oliver loved that book, as did many other children in Southern Rhodesia.

'What about those paintings Mama?'

'They were in a cupboard in my studio. They will have burnt.'

'Oh no. That is a shame. I thought the paintings were in your bedroom.'

'I always meant to take them out and have them framed. The biggest irony is that seeing how much Amanda loves her dog, and knowing how much she loves the book, I was going to give them to her this Christmas. I decided she was old enough now to appreciate them.'

'That is too awful. What a treasure that would have been.'

'Oh yes. And there were many other paintings too.'

'I'm sure.'

Silence fell as they contemplated their loss.

Isabella eventually broke it. 'Oh Darling, I feel utterly wretched. I am so depressed. I do not want to stay here and look at that burnt shell and consider everything I have lost.'

'No, that would be depressing for you. I think the best thing is for you to come back to the farm with me.'

'I suppose.'

'Why don't you pack a bag while I sort things out? For starters, we need to cancel your luncheon tomorrow.'

'Oh yes.'

'I'll phone the Weirs and the Fletchers while you pack.'

Before he did this, he walked down the veranda to have a better look at the damage, but found he could not get close to the building. It shocked him that so much heat still emanated from it. The roof was gone, save for some blackened and burnt beams, and just a few stumps sticking out of the wall remained of the studio floor. The tractor, always parked in the garage underneath the studio, was burnt to a frazzle, the red paint now grizzled and blotchy.

'Bloody hell,' he muttered, sitting down on a bench on the veranda facing it.

His mind drifted back to the last time a house of significance to him burnt down. It was in Italy in 1943, and the house belonged to a family by the name of Albertini. They were part of the Italian Resistance and agreed to hide him for a while, allowing him to stay in a tiny room off their kitchen. The Albertini family comprised Bino and his wife Hilda, Bino's brother, Silverto, and their mother. They treated him as well as they could, although his room was hardly more than a cupboard and only had one small window looking onto the wall of the house next door. It was claustrophobic, but he could not move around unless he had to, for fear of being heard by a fascist couple the Albertinis were forced to accommodate in their rooms downstairs. This couple was pro-Nazi, and the whole neighbourhood was intimidated by them. Oliver and the Albertinis constantly worried that someone would become suspicious and inform on them.

Hilda worked out an elaborate plan for the times when the bedpan was not sufficient for his needs. She spent most of her time sewing in a small sitting room next door to the kitchen, and he would tap on the wall behind his bed when he needed to use the privy. On hearing this, she would put on a pair of wooden clogs and stomp down the passage to where the privy was situated. Once there, she slid the clogs off and crept back to the sitting room, patting the wall to tell him to proceed. He would then sneak down the passage in his socks, do what was necessary, and flush to let her know he was finished. After this he would climb out of the window, step across a gap, and in through the kitchen window, which Hilda made sure was open. While he was doing this, Hilda tiptoed down the passage again, slipped the clogs back on, and clomped back to the sitting room. Such a ridiculous rigmarole, but Hilda decided this was the best way to deal with his calls of nature.

Now and then, the Albertinis let Oliver join them in the kitchen if they thought no one was around. They always listened out for the sound of anyone climbing the stairs, but one fateful morning Oliver was sitting in the kitchen with Hilda and her mother-in-law when two children appeared at the doorway without anyone hearing them. Maybe they had also learnt to be sneaky; everyone did those days. Oliver acted as if he was a friend paying a visit, even answering them in Italian when they addressed him. But after this, he could no longer stay there, in case the children mentioned him to their parents. That night Bino and Silvertini had three bicycles left in the churchyard nearby and they sneaked out around midnight and rode seventeen miles to Parma, where the Resistance had arranged another safe house for him.

Oliver got away, but the damage was done. When Bino and Silvertini returned to their home in the morning, the fascist officer was waiting with German soldiers, and they were marched away to be shot. That night, when the fascist couple was asleep in their beds, old Mrs Albertini lit the curtains in the downstairs hallway and the house went up in flames, killing everyone in it. The news of their fate devastated Oliver when he heard about it a few days later.

He thought now that he would tell his mother this story one day. It would put her loss into perspective.

Chapter 19

ISABELLA knew she would get over her loss quicker if she kept busy, and therefore she threw herself into what she termed, her "mural project"; to paint murals on the walls of their farm chapel, similar to what had been done at Cyrene Mission. Their chapel was near the farm school, beyond the compound where all the farm workers lived. Three days after the fire, she asked Lily and Priscilla if they would like to join her on a visit there.

'We would love to,' Lily said. 'You have told me so much about what you want to do with this chapel.'

'Good. And you'll come too, won't you, Amanda. We can take both dogs.'

'Yes please, Granny.'

'We'll ask Bhutu to take us in the mule cart,' Isabella suggested.

'I can drive it, Mrs Craig,' Priscilla offered. 'We had a pony and trap when I was young, and my mother often let me take the reins, so I'm pretty experienced.'

'Mm,' Isabella murmured. 'Mules can be a great deal more troublesome than ponies.'

'I drove us to the river the other day with no problems,' Priscilla said.

182

'She did, Granny,' Amanda agreed.

They set off with Lily and Priscilla on the front bench, while Isabella and Amanda sat on a box in the back, the dogs at their feet. Once they were out of the stable yard and heading down the dust road, Priscilla pushed the reins into Lily's hands

'You give it a go,' she said.

Lily bit her lip. 'Are you sure? You've just been telling us how experienced you are.'

Priscilla laughed. 'Try it.'

So Lily took over the reins and the whip, relieved that the mule continued trotting down the dusty road without noticing. Fifteen minutes later they were passing the farm compound.

'Let's stop for a moment. I need to get my bearings as it's been a while since I was last here,' Isabella said.

They had built the compound over a large area and it consisted of individual homesteads, demarcated by rough stick fences. The homesteads varied in size, with the smallest having just one or two thatched pole and *dagga* huts, and the largest, five or six. Whatever their size, each included an elevated wooden structure where the inhabitants stored dry maize cobs. Each also had a kitchen hut, identified by the smoke that rose from the blackened grass roof. Householders swept bare the yards surrounding their homesteads, with loose sand making soft ridges against the fences and leaving compact earth around the huts. Chickens pecked around the edges, hoping to find insects and grain. Well used dusty paths threaded between the homesteads. There was little vegetation around any of the huts, other than a few large trees, underneath which people sat.

'We like to keep things traditional here,' Isabella said, noticing both Priscilla and Lily staring at everything with interest. 'I believe they prefer it that way. Except for Gonda, of course. My late brother-in-law, Sir James, took him to England when he was a young man so that he could learn the ways of the professional servants in the grand old houses there. After that, he became quite anglicised and preferred a brick house, or "four corners", as he refers to it. We, therefore, built him one here many years ago, although, until now, he has spent most of his time with me at Sunrising.' She paused. 'What an asset that man has been all these years. Every time I hear my friends complaining about their staff, I know, yet again, how lucky I am to employ Gonda. I often say I will die when Gonda dies.' She laughed.

'Don't say that, Granny,' Amanda squeaked.

Isabella squeezed her hand. 'I was only joking, Darling. Don't worry, I've got many more years left in me yet. Of course, full-time domestic work fell by the wayside in England after the Great War,' she continued, 'so we are lucky to still have people working in our homes and gardens here, aren't we?'

'You think so?' Priscilla said. 'We have Judah and Zachariah working in our house and garden, and my mother is always complaining about them. "Miracles they do not perform", is her favourite mantra.'

'But I am sure they do,' Isabella said 'Your mother would not like it if she had to do everything herself.'

'True.'

'We had better get going,' Isabella went on. 'Those people sitting under the tree over there will wonder what we are doing.' She looked around. 'Now, let me see. All these haphazard tracks are a little confusing.' She pointed. 'Ah ha. That is the one we take. It should go around the perimeter of the compound. The school, the chapel, and Toby's house are the other side of that hill.' She pointed to a low, flat-topped hill nearby.

'Do you want me to take over the reins, Lily?' Priscilla asked. 'Although you have controlled the mule well so far.'

'Thank you. I thought so too,' Lily laughed. 'Don't worry, I can carry on driving.'

She flicked her whip across the mule's rump and he started walking again. Another flick and he broke into a slow trot as they headed towards the hill.

The school nestled at the base of the hill and included two buildings made of stone, with thatched roofs, and running parallel to each other. The staff and pupils kept the surrounding area well swept, just like the compound.

'We built these classrooms back in the late twenties' Isabella said. 'There was so much rock lying around, we decided to use it, with clay for mortar. It has held up well, although we may need to do a bit of patching at some stage. That's the chapel over there.' She pointed to a building, situated beneath an impressive-looking camel thorn tree and built from bricks with a corrugated iron roof.

'What a lovely picture that makes,' Lily said.

'I think so too,' Isabella agreed. I did a painting of it. One of the many I lost in the fire, I'm afraid.' She sighed.

The girls glanced at her. 'I'm sorry,' Lily said.

'Mm. One day I may do it again. But for now, I am more interested in painting murals on the chapel walls. If you had seen the chapel at Cyrene Mission, you would understand my enthusiasm. How beautiful they are. The artists painted murals on both the inside and outside walls there, but we will only paint on the inside walls here.'

'Oh, why?' Priscilla asked.

'The chapel at Cyrene has a veranda right around it, offering the murals some protection from the elements. As you can see, there is no veranda here. Save for taking the roof off and rebuilding it with a veranda, which I know Oliver will not agree to, as he is pouring every spare penny into that dam of his, we have to satisfy ourselves with painting the interior walls only at this stage. Let us find Mr Tate. His house is the other side of the school, up the hill over there. Tie the mule to a tree, Lily dear, and we will walk.'

It did not take long to climb up the incline to the Tate's cottage, although Isabella became a little puffed towards the end. Their cottage was also built of stone with a corrugated iron roof. It had no garden, except for some fruit trees; banana, mango, pawpaw, mulberry and what looked like a lemon tree.

Mrs Tate was sitting on the little front veranda.

'Mrs Craig, what a pleasure' she said when she saw them, lifting herself onto her feet. 'Oh dear, we were so sorry to hear about your studio.'

'Thank you. I was devastated when it happened. But you know me, I always try to look forward, and the first thing I have set my sights on is to paint murals on the chapel walls here. Toby told you about Cyrene Mission, I am sure.'

'Oh yes.'

'These two young ladies are staying with us and I have brought them over to show them what we want to do. Have you met Miss Sanderson, Miss Harry's replacement?'

'No, although my husband has told me about you.'

'How do you do, Mrs Tate,' Lily said.

'And this is her friend, Miss Clark, who is also a teacher, but will go back to Bulawayo in a few days for the start of the school term.'

'Hello,' Priscilla said.

Toby appeared at that moment.

'Hello Mrs Craig. I overheard you telling my wife why you are here. Please, come and sit on the veranda and have a drink, while we discuss our project?'

'Thank you, yes,' Isabella said.

'Would you like some home-made lemon juice?' Mrs Tate asked.

'That sounds delicious,' Isabella said, flopping into one of the four slatted chairs on the veranda and leaning her walking stick against the wall next to her. She removed a handkerchief from her pocket and patted her brow.

The veranda was cramped, so Lily and Priscilla sat on the low wall enclosing it while Amanda perched on the steps to keep the dogs out.

'Would you like to take those dogs off their leads so they can sniff around the place? I'm sure they would love that,' Toby suggested.

Amanda agreed, and the dogs bounded towards the chicken coop at the side of the cottage. 'I'm going to keep my eye on them, so they don't get up to mischief,' she said, getting up and following them.

'About the murals,' Toby continued. 'We have painted nothing yet because we had to get the chapel walls plastered again. The original plasterwork was rough, and it would have been almost impossible to paint any sort of picture on them. I asked Oliver to come and look, and he agreed and sent the builder to redo them. All this took a bit of time, as he has been so tied up with the dam.'

'I can well imagine,' Isabella said.

Mrs Tate came back with a tray of lemon juice. She handed them each a glass, leaving Amanda's on the wall for her to drink when she returned.

'What a lovely view you have,' Lily said, taking a sip of her lemon juice. It was strong and warm and she had to stop herself from grimacing as she swallowed it.

'Isn't it just?' Mrs Tate said, not noticing her discomfort. 'When we first married, we lived in pole and *dagga* huts near the school, but when Mr Craig had the chapel built, he insisted on building us a house too, and allowed us to choose the site. We decided a house with a view would be best, as it's breezy up here, which is lovely in the hot weather. As it will be in a few weeks.'

'Oh my, I am not looking forward to the heat one bit,' Isabella said. 'I struggle more and more with hot weather the older I get.' She paused for a moment while she sipped her drink. 'So, when did they finish the plastering, Toby? Is it dry enough for us to paint?'

'I think it will be.'

'I've been thinking about it, and believe we should do what the Reverend Patterson did; start the ball rolling by painting murals ourselves, you and I.' She turned to the girls. 'Mr Tate is a talented artist, too.'

'Not in your league,' he said.

'That is only because I have more time on my hands to practise. But I know you will do a beautiful job, Toby.'

They finished their drinks and made their way down to the chapel, with Amanda hitching the dogs back onto their leads to stop them running off to the compound. They got to the chapel and, when they found the plaster was dry, they took some time choosing where each of them would paint their mural. They eventually decided that Isabella's should be over the altar, as she was the "famous artist", and Toby's would be next to the front door.

'Why don't you get Lily to paint one on the other side of the door,' Priscilla piped up. 'She isn't half bad with a paintbrush either.'

'Oh, I'm not,' Lily gasped.

'You're very capable,' Priscilla insisted. 'I've seen some stuff you've done for your classroom walls.'

'The murals won't need a great deal of detail, or be perfect,' Isabella said. 'Most of the paintings at Cyrene are basic, but that's what makes them so intriguing. The artists used bright colours, and, although their style is simple, they are still glorious. Their size makes them impressive, as they cover most of the walls. If you decide to do one, you will need to spend many hours here, Lily.'

'I can help you, Miss Sanderson,' Amanda said. 'I'm quite good at mixing paint and colouring in.'

'You are indeed, Darling,' Isabella said. 'You can help all of us with mixing paint and colouring in.'

'Well, that settles it then,' Lily said. 'I will do my best.'

*

'I find Mrs Craig's friendship with Mr and Mrs Tate strange,' Priscilla said later when she and Lily were back at Lily's cottage and having tea on her little veranda. 'They seem to know each other well, which is odd, considering Mr Tate is a coloured, and all that. I don't know of any other European in Bulawayo who goes off visiting coloured people. Do you?'

'Well, my father has to pay visits to black people in his districts. It's part of his job as Assistant Native Commissioner. Some of the people he visits look like coloureds.'

'I'm sure, but I bet he doesn't treat them like they're great friends. I mean, there is nothing wrong with it, as Mr Tate seems pleasant, it's just not usual in this part of the world.'

'Yes, I suppose you're right.' Lily sipped her tea. 'I will be interested to see how his mural turns out. He seems as keen on the project as Mrs Craig. I couldn't believe you suggested I do one too, Priscilla. For goodness sake. I'm not skilful enough.'

Priscilla laughed at the idea of Lily sweating over her painting, trying to keep up with the talented Mrs Craig and the artistic Mr Tate. 'I'm sorry, I don't know why I came up with the idea, but you know what, I bet you'll do a brilliant job. There is nothing wrong with a bit of simplicity in a mural. At least it'll give you a goal to work towards in your spare time.'

Lily had to laugh too. 'You're right.'

'Oliver asked me if I want to join him on an early morning ride tomorrow. I shall try to glean some more information about Mr Tate, and how he and Mrs Craig became such good friends.'

'You and Oliver have become pretty good friends yourselves,' Lily said, forcing herself to sound normal.

'Well, this will be the third time we have gone off on a ride together, and with each one, I like him more But Graham is younger and comes with less baggage, so maybe I should keep my sights set on him still.'

Lily was relieved when she heard Priscilla say this. 'Yes, Graham is closer in age to you, and always charming, a bit like yourself.'

'True. I think he and I are two peas in a pod, character-wise. Of course, I could never keep up with his flying. But I love the idea that he's going to be a commercial pilot. What fun, to own a private airstrip here, and an aeroplane. Have you ever heard of a, um, now let me think what did he say the plane he wants is called? A De Havilland Dragon Rapide, or something like that.'

Lily laughed. 'No, of course I don't know of such a plane. I know nothing about aeroplanes.'

'He was telling me the other day that there are lots for sale at reasonable prices, now that the war is over. He's planning on buying one to use for air charters. Take people to Nuanetsi Ranch in the south, or Chiredzi in the east, and all over the countryside. Maybe he will need an air hostess, and I can apply for the job.'

They both laughed at the idea of this.

'I bet you've never even been in an aeroplane in your life,' Lily said.

'Nope, but I hope that will change. I just wish I didn't need to go back to Bulawayo so soon. It's such fun out here.

Chapter 20

PRISCILLA'S original intention to use her stay at the farm to get to know Graham better failed. She discovered, instead, that Graham was an elusive man and she saw little of him, despite her best efforts. However, on her last morning she received a note inviting her and Lily to join him on a jaunt to his airstrip that afternoon. Not the most interesting place on the farm to visit, they both agreed, but Priscilla was happy for any excuse to spend time with him. He collected them from Lily's cottage mid-afternoon in his sporty MG TA, and drove them to the airstrip.

'What a lovely car this is,' Priscilla warbled, as she slid into the middle of the seat so that she sat between Graham and Lily.

Graham patted the dashboard. 'Yes, I love her. I left her here in my parents' garage when I went away to the war. Every week, Isaiah, their gardener, turned the engine with a shaft, so that she would be in adequate running condition when I returned.'

'And was she?'

'Oh yes, she started almost straight away.'

Graham parked at the bottom of the airstrip and they looked about them. As expected, neither Lily nor Priscilla found anything fascinating about a two hundred yard wide and mile long gash in the virgin bush. However, Priscilla gushed about it in her usual way, saying how exciting it would be when he was using it to take off and land in his new aeroplane. Lily sat in silence, staring at all the dead trees, chopped down and dragged to the edges to make the clearing.

'Let's walk to the top,' Graham suggested.

This was more interesting because a small herd of impala were grazing there, although they skipped into the bush as they approached.

'You must see a lot of game here, with it being so open,' Priscilla said.

'Oh yes' Graham replied. 'Kudu, warthog, impala. I've even seen eland and zebra grazing here.'

'How wonderful,' Priscilla enthused, but Lily turned around and started walking back down the strip. She wanted to leave them alone, so they could make plans to meet again once Priscilla was back in town. She wracked her brain, trying to think of a way to do this, without seeming too obvious, but other than taking off at a sprint, she did not know how else to get away from them.

'Hey, wait for us,' Graham called, leaving her with no alternative but to walk back to the car with them.

'Would you like to come to my place for some refreshment?' he asked as they were sliding back into the car.

'Oh, rather,' Priscilla said, but when they got there Lily drank her tea in silence, again trying to find an excuse to leave them alone. Then an idea took shape.

'Listen,' she said, interrupting Graham's conversation about his plans for air charter. 'I don't want to appear rude, but it's occurred to me I should see your mother while I'm here, as she lives close by.' They both stared at her, wide-eyed. 'Um, I don't come to this part of the farm often, and Mrs Craig said I should look at a series of paintings she did many years ago, which your mother has.' This astonished them more. 'Mrs Craig says they are good examples of what she calls a "Simplistic style".' Lily raised her arms, quoting this with her fingers. 'For the mural, Priscilla.' She stared at Priscilla as she said this.

'Oh that, right, I'll tell you about it,' Priscilla said to Graham.

'So I'll pop over there now,' Lily went on. 'I won't be long. Half an hour at the most.'

Graham still looked surprised. 'Well, okay, I'm sure it will please my mother to see you. You can take a shortcut through the bush. The path is just off the driveway. You'll find it, I'm sure.'

Lily could hear Priscilla's chatter about the murals at Cyrene Mission fading as she walked through Graham's dry garden towards the path. A happy change from all the talk about aeroplanes, she thought. She hoped they would use this time to arrange to meet up again soon. However, when she returned, they were still sitting as she had left them, with Graham deliberating about whether he should buy more than one plane, and if he should take on a partner.

He broke off when he saw her. 'You're back,' he said. 'Was that useful?'

'Oh yes. Mrs Craig's style has certainly evolved since she painted those paintings your mother showed me. She sends her love and asked if you would go round for a drink with her this evening.'

Graham looked at his watch. 'Mm, I suppose I need to get you girls back then.'

He dropped them at the cottage gate, with only a 'See you sometime,' as he sped away. Priscilla looked disheartened as they walked inside.

'Oh dear,' she said. 'I'm afraid I'm losing hope with that man. He tends to blow hot and cold, I've discovered.'

Unlike Oliver, they soon found out.

He invited them for dinner again that night and was as interesting and attentive as he had been on Priscilla's first night. Mrs Craig and Amanda were with them this time and somewhere during their meal, they got on to the topic of the war and he told them about some of his experiences during that time.

They learnt he joined the 6th South African Armoured Division in Egypt at the beginning of the war, but in 1941 Germans captured his squadron when they were fighting in Libya. They mistook the Germans for British because the Germans drove captured British tanks at the front of their column.

'We were waiting for our brigadier to return with tanks belonging to the Gloucester Armoured Division,' he said. 'They were involved in combat close by and we were told to look out for them. We sent up a flare to tell them where we were, and when tanks came rolling towards us a little later we first saw the four tanks from the Gloucester Division at the head of the column. By the time we realised they were using the Allied tanks as a ruse, it was too late. We were surrounded.'

'Oh gosh, how awful,' Priscilla said.

'What's a flare, Papa?' Amanda asked.

'It's something you shoot into the sky to produce a brief burst of light. You choose the colours you want for each shot and discuss with your comrades what colours you are using, so they know where you are when they see the flashes in the sky.'

'What happened next?' Priscilla asked.

'Well, we tried to fight them off but they outnumbered us fourfold, leaving us no alternative but to surrender.'

Amanda looked at her father wide eyed. 'Were you scared, Papa?'

'I suppose so, because we had no idea what was going to happen, and we were told nothing. The day after they captured us we were trucked to a town called Benghazi, where we spent a few days in a large war prison. At first they gave us no food and very little water to drink.'

'How inhumane,' Isabella said.

'After a week or two at the camp in Benghazi they shipped us to Italy,' he continued. 'That journey was not pleasant either, with hundreds of us squashed below deck, forced to spend most of the time there. Thank God it was winter, otherwise, we would have suffocated. The stench from the buckets we were given for toilets was appalling.'

'Oh Darling,' Isabella said, reaching out and squeezing his hand. 'Emily and I were so worried about you when we received the telegram saying you had been captured.' He glanced at her, a pained expression crossing his face and Lily realised this was the first time she had heard anyone mention his late wife.

'We sailed via Crete,' Oliver went on, 'where they allowed us up onto the deck. Some locals heard who we were and rowed out to our ship with their small boats filled with oranges. They threw these up to us. It was some time before the German guards saw what they were doing, and as soon as they did, they herded us below deck again. However, I managed to catch one orange, which I shared with Charlie Duff and Guy Parks, who were not so lucky.'

'So did you spend the rest of the war in a POW camp in Italy?' Priscilla asked.

'No. I spent two-and-a-half years in different camps. First in a transit camp in the south, when we landed. From there they made us march thirty miles to a more permanent one. It was near a place called Brindisi, in the heel of Italy. It had an ablution block, where we showered and shaved for the first time since being captured.'

'How appalling,' Isabella said. 'Not being able to wash for so long.'

'You get used to it. But we weren't at this camp for long. A few days later they marched us to a railway station and put us on a train. We weren't told where we were going. It was a long journey, sitting upright on hard wooden benches all night, not even allowed to open the windows to let fresh air in. We arrived at a place called Piacenza, and from there they marched us to our next camp. It was called Montalabo and was a fifteenth-century castle built on the top of a hill.'

'Fascinating,' Priscilla murmured.

'I'm afraid, it was not. It was dreary and deathly cold in winter, especially after we had been there a while and our clothes were threadbare. Also, there was never enough food. Thank God for the Red Cross hampers otherwise we may have starved to death.'

'How long were you there?' Lily asked.

'Fourteen months, until March 1943, when the Germans took over the camp for their own use, and we were marched off again. This time to a place near Parma, a camp in Fontanellato. It was an old orphanage, and much better than Montalabo, because the camp commandant was pro-Allies. But we were only there until September.'

'Why Papa?' Amanda asked, engrossed in his story.

'The fascist dictator, Mussolini, ruled Italy. By 1943 things were not going well for the Italian war effort, and the king wanted Mussolini out. You will have heard about some of this.'

'Oh yes,' Priscilla said. 'We watched a newsreel about him when we went to the cinema a while back. About Mussolini when they executed him and his mistress and…....' She stopped and looked at Lily who had kicked her under the table, motioning her head towards Amanda.

Amanda looked at both of them. 'What? We didn't see any newsreels when you took me to the cinema, did we, Granny? I don't even know what a fascist dictator is.'

'No, we saw nothing about Mussolini, and we would not have wanted to anyway,' Isabella said.

'But I still don't know what a fascist dictator is,' Amanda said.

'It's a leader who always thinks he's right, and won't let anyone else tell him he's not. He will hold on to power and keep doing things the way he wants, no matter what.' Oliver said. 'With everything going so wrong for Italy in the war, they forced Mussolini to resign and, without making it known, some Italians entered secret negotiations to surrender to the Allies. They signed an armistice in secret at the beginning of September, but only announced it a week later. As soon as our camp commandant heard about this armistice, he opened the camp gates and ordered the guards to ignore us so we could all escape.'

'Oh my goodness, that is unbelievable,' Lily said.

'Yes, we were pretty shocked, as you can imagine. Of course, we knew nothing about the armistice then. We had an idea that things were going well for the Allies in North Africa, but knew nothing about any Italians wanting to change sides. However, Germany would have none of it, and as soon as they found out about the armistice, they cracked down wherever they could in Italy. They arrived at our camp hours after our escape. The commandant had warned us they might come our way, so we got as far from the place as possible. We couldn't stay together so broke off on our own, or in twos. I was on my own, and for the first few days I just hid.'

'Where?' Lily asked.

'At first in the woods, and then in the thickets along river banks, disused barns; walking and running when I was not too tired; getting as much distance between myself and Fontanella. After a few weeks, I managed to make contact with the Italian Resistance. They had what we called "safe houses" and they sneaked me from one safe house to another, a few weeks here, a month there, depending on how easy it was to move around. I planned to climb the Alps and get into neutral Switzerland, but I was held up and got to the base of the Alps too late, at the beginning of winter, when snow covered the mountains. So I waited until it warmed up again. By then I was able to speak Italian well enough to pass myself off as an Italian, so I helped the Resistance over the winter until the snow melted enough for me to climb over the Alps late spring.'

'Gosh, all of this is just amazing,' Priscilla said. 'Tell us about your climb.'

Oliver looked at Amanda. 'Mm. I think we all need to call it a night. I've kept our young lady up late enough, and she needs to go to bed.'

'No, I'm not tired, Papa.'

'I think you may find you are when your head hits the pillow.'

'Indeed,' said Isabella. 'Say good night to everyone and go and clean your teeth. I will come and tuck you in.'

Amanda stood up. 'Good night, Papa,' she said to Oliver, putting her thin arms around his neck, much to everyone's amazement. She had never done this before. She then hugged Lily and Priscilla. 'Let's go, Frank,' she called to her dog, who was lying underneath the table.

'I'm afraid, I need to do some work in my study, so I will say good night too,' Oliver said, giving his mother a brief kiss on her cheek as he walked past her.

*

Oliver took Priscilla back to Bulawayo the following morning, and Lily felt as unhappy as ever with the thought. She tried to find a reason to go too, but failed. Her parents were visiting her uncle in Melsetter, so she couldn't use them as a reason to go to town. Oliver intended on staying the night at Sunrising so she couldn't even suggest she came for the ride. No, she would have to accept that Priscilla would spend a few hours in the car alone with him. Lily wondered if he would continue telling her about his wartime experiences on their drive. Knowing Priscilla, and her easy-going manner, she would coax him into telling her the rest of his story.

Lily felt a wave of possessive jealousy sweep through her. How amazing, she thought, I have become infatuated with Oliver Craig.

Chapter 21

OLIVER and Tim sat in Tim's office, strategising, as they did most mornings when they were both on the farm. Tim rarely left, but Oliver came and went a fair deal. He found himself busy these days. First, buying everything needed for the farm, and second, sorting out his mother's affairs. After much deliberation, Isabella had decided to sell Sunrising. She said she could not bear living there and looking at her burnt-out studio every day, and the idea of rebuilding it was beyond her at this stage of her life. For her, it was better to sell Sunrising and remember the amazing life she had there for over forty years

Besides the fire destroying her studio, she also disliked the way the area behind Sunrising had changed in recent years. Many of her beloved landmarks had disappeared, or were unrecognizable now; destroyed to make way for a residential suburb for the new immigrants. A beautiful tree here, an interesting rock formation there, a grass covered vlei, a river crossing - she used to so appreciate these when she was driving to and from Sunrising, but the area had now changed into small plots, each containing a bungalow, a garage and a *khaya* at the back. The Europeans moving into these homes would hopefully love them, compared to the war-torn places they were leaving, but for Isabella, they were just a reminder of how her world had changed.

'Stroke of luck finding a buyer so quickly,' Tim said to Oliver.

'True. They want to convert the place into a residential hotel. The developers are unable to keep up with the influx of people coming into this country. Sunrising is in a prime spot. The buyers think, as a hotel, it will be full for years, with people staying there while they wait for their houses to be built.'

'I'm sure. And it will become a vibrant, busy place again. It has been a bit like a museum since you left to go to boarding school, if you ask me,' Tim said.

'Mama still has her luncheons and the odd dinner party. But you're right, the place has been sedate for a long time. Nevertheless, I'm sad to see it go.'

'Me too. It always reminds me of my father.'

'Of course.'

'But, that's life for you. Nothing lasts forever, as the saying goes. And it's a great relief for me, knowing Ma and Aunt Isabella will be together here on the farm. She has struggled since Father died. Amazing how those two old ducks are still so close after all these years. Unlike myself and my siblings. Patricia is far too bossy for my liking, and Graham will always be a spoilt brat in my eyes. I mean, look at him now. Buying that De Havilland Dragon Rapide and cavorting all over the countryside in it.'

Oliver wondered if there was some jealousy in this statement. He wouldn't blame Tim if there was. Stuck in a wheelchair all day, every day. As he thought this, he said to himself that he must make more of an effort to take Tim around the farm with him. He also needed to make plans for their trip to Wankie National Park and the Victoria Falls.

'On to business matters,' Oliver said. 'This heat wave we're having should bode well for an excellent rainy season this year.'

'I bloody well hope so as I can't stand being so hot. It makes me feel like I'm suffocating. If no one knew it before, they'll understand now why October is "Suicide Month" in these parts. I bet all those Brits who moved here recently are struggling with it too.

'I've no doubt. Getting anyone to do a decent day's work on the farm right now is difficult.'

'Always is, at the best of times, if you ask me,' Tim answered.

'True. Did I mention that I changed the starting time forward to five-thirty, to make the most of the cool hours in the early morning?'

'No. But I knew this because I hear the siren at the workshop go off.'

'Oh yes, of course. Anyway, we've finished preparing the field for maize, and we're on track to plant mid-November. And I am looking forward to trying out tobacco next year. It's doing well in the north of the country, we need to see if it does just as well here.'

'I agree. How are the tobacco barns going?'

'Slowly, like everything else. We've finished making all the bricks and digging the foundations. I wouldn't mind if you looked at them before we pour the concrete. You may see something that I've overlooked. Two heads are always better than one.'

'Do you want me to come today?' Tim asked, glancing around the room, looking irritated for a moment. It was awkward for him to go anywhere, and he liked to have advance warning.

'No, not today, old boy. Later this week is fine. I'm going to town with Mama. We're spending a few days at Sunrising while she makes a last sweep through the place, deciding what she wants and what she does not want.'

*

'Are you sure about this, Mama?' Oliver asked as they drove into town later. 'It's not too late to change your mind.'

'Oh no. I have quite decided it is for the best. If nothing else, I cannot let Celia down now. She is so relieved that we are going to set up house together. I wish I did not need to sell so much of my furniture, but unfortunately, there will not be space for everything. Celia has given Graham most of her precious pieces, in preparedness for me bringing some of my own, but as you know, she has a lot anyway.'

'You mentioned the Fletchers are coming round to see what they may like.'

'Yes. That beautiful house of theirs is in keeping with all my furniture. I invited them for drinks tomorrow evening, and we can look around then. It will have given me time to decide what I am going to keep, although I am pretty much decided already. I have been thinking about it a lot while I've been staying with you.'

'Oh, and there I thought you were busy planning the mural you are painting on the chapel walls,' Oliver joked.

Isabella smiled. 'Well, of course I am, but that doesn't mean I can't think about furniture too.'

'How are the murals going?'

'Lily is quite capable, you know, after going on about how she is not. Hers is going to be lovely, bright and simple. She is such a sweet girl. We are so lucky Barnaby headed her in our direction. And Amanda adores her too.'

'Yes, I can see that. It has made life easier for all of us.'

He met her eye for a moment, and they smiled at each other. 'I intend picking out some furniture and nick-knacks for her too,' Isabella said. 'I get the impression things are awkward at her home.'

Oliver did not respond.

'I am also going to give a few bits and pieces to Toby and Pam. I know they have enough in their cottage as it is, but they may want to make a few changes, and they can always sell some of their stuff, or give it to their children.'

'You are kind, Mama.'

'Not in the least. Toby and I go back such a long way.'

'You do.'

'I always found it most unfortunate that he has not had the opportunities we had, because he is a coloured man. He has always had so much potential.'

'But you have given him great opportunities, Mama.'

'Hardly, Darling. Given the freedom to choose, I am not sure he would have been the headmaster of the small school we built on the farm. I believe he could have done so much more with his life, without the segregation that exists here. Humankind is so prejudiced, and where does it get any of us? Just consider my experience, for instance? Stephen and I were very fond of each other when we first met, but it would have broken his mother's heart if we had married, not to mention what my father would have said. Why? Because I am a gentile and he is a Jew. Ironically, his family changed their surname from Goldstein to Goldsmith when they moved to England. But marrying a non-Jewish girl was not acceptable. So we put aside any thoughts of being together, and he married Deborah instead. I do not know the ins and outs of their marriage, but they did have three lovely children, who they could raise as Jews. And then, look at what happened during the war. It's unbearable to think what that ghastly man Hitler did to the Jews, and all those other people too. Unbelievable. All because of prejudice, intolerance, and bigotry. The world is full of it.'

'You never told me about yourself and Stephen Goldsmith before Mama. I often wondered about your relationship.'

'Friends Darling. Pure and simple. We became close again after poor Deborah died, but, well, it has never been quite the same. But I would never discuss this sort of thing with you when you were a young boy. I'm afraid it just was not what we did back then.'

'I understand. But he is still a good friend. I hope you will keep up with him when you are living on the farm.'

'Oh yes. We will meet for lunches when I go to town, as I will with my other dear friends.' Isabella sighed. 'I hope you find someone else, Darling. We did all love dear Emily, but it would be sad for you to go through the rest of your life alone. I am sure she would not have wanted this either.'

'You never married again, Mama. Do you regret it?'

'No. But I have my art. This has always been my passion. And of course, my beloved dogs are such wonderful company. You are passionate about farming, I know, but it differs slightly from the passion I have for my art.'

'I need to meet someone first, Mama.'

He glanced sideways at his mother. She was staring rigidly at the road ahead. 'Just start looking around,' she said.

Chapter 22

AMANDA is becoming a proficient little horsewoman, Oliver thought as he watched her slip her foot in the stirrup and pull herself into the saddle, flinging her right leg over Poppet's back as she did this. When they first started riding together, she always asked either Bhutu or him to help her up, but now, a few months on, she was happy to do it on her own.

'Well done,' he said. Amanda patted Poppet's neck, a look of pleasure crossing her face. 'Let's go then,' he continued. 'It looks like it could rain in a while. Now wouldn't that be lovely, after these last few weeks of scorching weather?' It was late afternoon, and, although the sun was low, it was still hot, while the sky in the north was dark with brooding clouds.

'We will have to canter back if it rains. Papa. I can canter quite fast now, but I can't gallop.'

They walked out of the stable yard and headed down the dusty road towards the fields. Oliver had been there earlier in the day when the maize was being planted. All the farm workers had knocked off now, and he wanted to check that they had finished planting. He and Amanda trotted down the road, mopane trees either side of them, and then, when they turned the last corner, an open field replaced the scrubby vegetation. A vast, fifty-acre clearing in the bush. The red earth was loose-looking, after being recently ploughed and planted with seed. Scrubby, dry-looking, grey, brown vegetation edged the field, with the odd taller tree protruding a little higher.

'Now, is that not a magnificent sight,' Oliver said, breathing deeply. 'I never tire of this scene. It's especially pleasing this minute, seeing those dark clouds in the distance. Oh, for them to drop their load right here. That would be brilliant, to get our maize going.'

Amanda glanced at the menacing sky. The wind blew into their faces, driving the clouds their way. The sun disappeared.

'Let's go for a quick canter around the perimeter of the field and then we'll head for home. Is that okay?' Oliver asked. Amanda only nodded, preparing herself and Poppet.

They tightened their reins, nudged their horses in the ribs, and took off at a gentle pace. Oliver felt exhilarated, with the wind blowing in his face, and he urged his horse to go faster.

'No, Papa,' Amanda squeaked from behind him. 'I'll fall off.'

He immediately reined his horse in again and continued at a slow canter. When they returned to the road, having gone all the way around the edge of the field, they stopped. They were both panting after the exertion of their ride, as were their horses.

'Hopefully, in a few days, the maize will sprout and the surrounding bush will be greener. It never ceases to amaze me how quickly everything springs to life once there has been a bit of rain. Water is life, and we don't have nearly enough of it in this part of Africa. That's why I'm excited about our dam. It's going to make such a difference to the way we farm here.'

Amanda squinted at the sky.

'Alright, alright. I can see you want to get back before the rain.' Oliver said. 'Do you want to trot or canter back up the road?'

'Canter Papa, but not too fast.'

Oliver scrutinised the mopane scrub, looking for something in particular, which he quickly found. 'See that felled tree trunk over there? Why don't we jump over it? Have you ever tried jumping Poppet before?'

'No, Papa.'

'Well, it's easy, and I'm sure you'll enjoy it once you've tried a few times. Just trot or canter up to the log and, as you get there, give Poppet a bit more rein, lift your bum out of the saddle, and let yourself glide with him as he jumps. I'll go first, so you can see how it's done.'

He jumped over the log, and she followed, beaming as she pulled Poppet to a walk afterwards.

'I told you you'd enjoy it. Next time we ride, we will find other things to jump over. Ditches, ridges, etc. When I was your age, I jumped over everything I could find.'

They got back to the stables as the rain started. First, a few drops, but it soon began to pelt down. They walked their horses into their stalls, Amanda unsaddling her horse and doing as much as she could, despite Bhutu hovering like a mother hen. She loosened the girth and threw it over Poppet's back, then unbuckled the throat latch and slipped the bit from his mouth. Finally, as she was lifting the saddle from Poppet's back Bhutu could watch no more, and he took it from her, carrying it to the tack room next door and returning with a bucket of food. The stables were constructed from homemade bricks, with a roof of gum poles and thatch, muffling the sound of the rain. After watching Poppet tuck into his supper, Amanda stepped onto the little veranda running along the side of the stables. Oliver was already there, observing the rain falling heavily in the stable yard. It felt chilly after the cosiness of the stalls, with their windowless walls and hay-filled floors. Water poured off the roof, splashing along the edge of the veranda, gushing down the side. They could see lightning flashing and then, a few seconds later, they heard a crash of thunder.

'Magnificent. Don't you just love the smell of the first rains, falling onto the dry earth,' Oliver said, inhaling deeply, but Amanda couldn't hear him because she had her fingers in her ears. She sat down on a hay bale, while Oliver prodded the roof, checking what looked like a leak. It took a while for the storm to abate, the heavy rain stopping as quickly as it started, with just drizzle and a lot of water and mud to show for itself.

'I believe we can walk back to the house now,' Oliver said.

The storm had breathed new life into an array of creatures and they awakened in the surrounding bush. Frogs croaked, crickets chirped, guinea fowl grated, and francolin screeched.

'Look at all these flying ants emerging from the ground,' Oliver said, pointing at them with the toe of his riding boot. 'They'll make a delicious supper for lots of different animals.'

Amanda bent to pick up a chongololo in her path. She lifted it in her fingers and observed it as it wriggled and curled while it's hundreds of legs kept moving, before putting it back on the path.

'Next time we ride, please can we ask Miss Sanderson if she wants to come too,' she said. 'She's nearly as good as me because Uncle Graham's groom has been teaching her. She said she can also canter slowly now, although she hasn't tried jumping over anything yet.'

'Why didn't she just get Bhutu to teach her?' Oliver asked.

'Uncle Graham told his groom to come here with a horse for her every few days, and it's just carried on from then.'

Typical, Oliver thought. Graham taking over like that, although a part of him wished he'd considered it before Graham.

'Of course, we can ask her,' he said. 'But she will go back to Bulawayo soon when the school holidays start.'

'Oh no, does she have to go?'

Oliver laughed. He had been thinking the same thing. Since her arrival in July, he found himself enjoying her presence more and more, as she quietly became involved in different activities on the farm besides teaching. Driving his mother and daughter to the chapel in the mule cart three or four afternoons every week; going to the dairy early every morning with Amanda and her dog to fetch the milk in a pail; pottering in her garden in the evenings; and now he discovered, having riding lessons too. Yes, he enjoyed having her around.

To Amanda, he said: 'I'm sure she will want to spend time with her friends in town, and of course her parents will want to see her.'

'I suppose so. But she will come back next term, won't she?'

'Oh yes. In the meantime, we will see if she can come for rides with us. It will be fun for me to watch the two of you riding together, so I can judge who is making the most progress.' He gave Amanda a playful shove.

'Aw, Papa,' she said before Frank distracted her as he bounded across the grass to meet them.

*

The three of them rode most evenings after this, and with each ride, the two beginners improved in both ability and confidence. They developed their favourite routes; to the field to assess the progress of the newly planted maize; to the dam wall to measure the rising water level; to a lookout point further up the river to gauge the rate the water was flowing after a soaking rainstorm; to the chapel to admire how the murals were coming along.

A few days before the start of the school holidays, Lily arrived at the stables without Amanda. Oliver was already in the yard, checking his girth. He looked up when she greeted him.

'Amanda isn't well,' Lily said upon seeing his raised eyebrow. 'She was lying on her bed.'

'That's not like her.' Oliver replied. 'She never wants to miss out on her rides with us.'

'I know. Maybe I should go back and sit with her. She said she's nauseous.'

'Agnes is there, isn't she?'

'Yes, I told her to stay with Amanda until we get back.'

'As we're all dressed and ready for a ride, let's go anyway, just down to the lands. As you know, I love watching my maize sprouting.'

Lily smiled. 'Oh yes, I have noticed.'

'I live in fear that the rains will suddenly dry up and the maize crop won't give an adequate yield. That's the problem with dry-land cropping in this part of the world. The rains are not reliable, hence the need to build dams.' By now they were on their horses and walking out of the stable yard. 'Do you want to try a slow canter again?' he asked as they turned onto the road.

'Yes, that's fine,' Lily said, taking up her reins in preparation.

They cantered down the dirt road through the mopane trees towards the field.

But they never got there.

A hundred yards before the road opened onto the lands, a ground hornbill frantically flapped into flight, next to where Lily was riding, its huge black wings flailing with white undersides and red neck flashing. Lily's horse shied violently, veering away from the bird, his ears back, his head down. He shot into the mopane thicket at pace, darting and diving to avoid trees. Lily pulled at the rein and hung onto the saddle, but first her knee hit a low branch and then her head hit a high branch and the next thing she knew she was on the ground, winded and shocked. She lay there, dazed, becoming ever more aware of the pain in her hip.

When she opened her eyes, Oliver was kneeling over her, his face a picture of concern.

'Oh my God, are you alright?'

She looked at him and bit her lip, trying to stop the tears she could feel welling up. 'I, um, I...' She could not stop them. Her eyes blurred. He wiped her cheek with his gloved hand, but this did little more than smear dirt across her face.

'I'm sorry,' he said, stroking her arm, not knowing how to comfort her. She closed her eyes tight and willed herself to stop the tears. She opened her eyes again.

Oliver was staring at her. 'Where does it hurt?' he asked.

'Mainly my hip, it's sore.' she rubbed her left hip.

'Can you move your leg?' She slowly straightened her leg, wincing as she did. 'Well done, and your ankle, can you rotate it?' She did this. 'Well done again. And what about your toes? Can you wiggle them in your boot?'

After a moment she said, 'Yes.'

'That's a relief. Anywhere else sore?'

'Not really. I guess my left wrist is a little tender, but not too bad.'

'Your head and neck are alright? You've got a gash on your cheek.' She immediately put her hand to her face. 'It's here,' he said, touching her left cheek, below her eye. 'I don't think it's deep.'

'I remember bumping my head, but it feels okay. Thank goodness I have my riding helmet on,' she said.

'Yes. Bloody hell, that happened fast. One minute you were riding next to me and, the next thing I knew you were taking off into the bush. That ground hornbill jumped up right next to you as we were riding past it.'

'Is that what it was? As you say, it all happened so fast, I didn't see it. Where's Whisky?'

'Home by now, I'd say.'

'Oh no. That means I will have to walk.'

'I'll help you. Are you ready to get up?'

'I guess. I can't lie here all night.'

'Exactly. Now how shall we do this so that you experience the least amount of discomfort?' He got onto his haunches, and she lifted herself off the ground, wincing again. He put his hands behind her shoulders to help her up and, as he did this, their eyes locked and in that moment they both knew something changed. Lily pulled herself up to a sitting position and Oliver, still with his hands on her shoulders, leant forward and kissed her, first on her cheek and then on her mouth.

'Wow,' he murmured into her ear. Lily blushed, and her lids dropped. He stroked her cheek, then pushed his hand under her chin to unclip the chinstrap of her riding helmet. He pulled it off, and Lily's hand flew to her hair, sensing it plastered against her head. She ran her fingers through it, combing it back from her forehead. He smiled at her vanity, taking off his helmet, his hair also matted against his skull. 'There we're both the same,' he said, 'although you are a good deal more beautiful than I, even with your dishevelled appearance.'

'No, I'm not.' She glanced up, her eyes on a level with his sun browned throat, and she saw his pulse beating with frantic speed. 'I have thought you handsome from the day I first met you,' she whispered. She lifted her eyes to his face and noticed the colour deepen beneath the tan of his cheeks.

'Really, even though I'm so much older than you?'

'You don't look your age,' she said.

'Do you know how old I am?'

'You told me when we first met, forty-one.'

'I was forty-two at the beginning of October. And you?'

'I was twenty-four in June, a few weeks before I first came here.'

'That's a big age gap.'

'I suppose. My mother will be forty-two next year.'

Oliver smiled. 'Oh my God, so I'm older than your mother. Now that is a scary notion.'

Lily smiled too. 'It is a bit. But my mother was young when she had me. Seventeen.'

'Come, let me help you up. My old legs are cramping.' She threw him a concerned glance. 'Don't worry. I am joking,' he said.

He helped her onto her feet and pulled her towards him, and then, holding her head between his hands, he kissed her again. She was so overwhelmed, she thought for a moment her legs were going to buckle from underneath her. But he put his arms around her, clasping her tightly, her head tucking into his shoulder. She could feel his collar bone against her cheek as she breathed in his musky smell and, as thoughts of everything he went through over the last few years rushed through her head, she knew all she would ever want from then onwards was to be with him and help him heal.

'Lily, Lily, Lily,' he said. 'What are we going to do? You are so lovely, and I'm an old man, with way more baggage than anyone your age needs to deal with.'

'No, you're not.' She pulled away. 'I, well, I, I think you're just wonderful, so, um, so kind and thoughtful.'

'Thank you. And I think you're wonderful too. How many days until you leave for the holidays?'

'Ten, I think.'

'That's not long, but let's make the most of these ten days, and use the time to mull things over. I'm certainly going to miss you when you're away.'

'Me too.'

He hugged her to him again. 'Now, do you want to get onto Como, and I'll walk next to you, or shall we walk together, and I'll lead Como. As much as I would like to suggest that we ride together, with you wedged in front of me, so I can put my arms around you and breathe deeply over your shoulder, just like actors do in films, I fear you would be uncomfortable.'

Lily laughed. 'Yes. Let's both walk,' she said.

'If your hip becomes too sore, you'd better get onto Como though.'

'Okay.'

He untied Como from a nearby tree, and putting the reins in one hand and taking her hand in his other, they set off back up the road. Despite her sore hip, Lily did not believe she could be happier.

'You know what today is?' Lily said.

'What?'

'It's the day Princess Elizabeth is marrying her Philip Mountbatten, now the Duke of Edinburgh, I heard on my radio last night.'

'Is it really? I had forgotten that.'

'I think it's a good omen for us, because we met for the first time when she and her family were here.'

'That's true.'

'And it was then that I found out what a lovely man you are. You were so kind to me when I discovered what my dad was up to.'

Oliver squeezed her hand, and pulled her to him again.

*

Before Oliver took Lily back to town ten days later, he asked her to marry him. There was nothing Lily wanted more. The only person they spoke to about their plans was Isabella, who was more than delighted with this turn of events. The three of them sat each evening in the drawing room after dinner and discussed how everything would unfold.

They decided they would not announce their engagement until Oliver had asked Lily's parents for her hand in marriage. Lily dreaded the idea of this, because of her mother's irrational dislike for the Craigs. Lily knew it was illogical, but felt she needed to tell Oliver and Isabella about it.

'But that is so strange,' Isabella said. 'Why on earth would she not like us? The only time we have ever seen each other is when we were all staying at the Matopos Hotel during the Royal Family's visit.'

Oliver and Lily glanced at each other. 'Maybe she's jealous of you, Mama,' Oliver suggested. 'Seeing you being singled out, commissioned to do the painting for the Royal Family.'

'I can't believe something like that would make her so jealous,' Lily said. 'It's not as if she ever had any aspirations to be an artist or anything like that.'

It would have to remain a mystery to them.

Oliver drove Lily back to town when the school term ended, both sad to say goodbye, but confident that their separation would be short-lived. They planned that after one week Oliver would come and visit her parents. That would give Lily enough time to spend with them before her life changed forever.

Chapter 23

LILY found her stay with her parents more relaxed this time, mainly because her father did not keep disappearing. On previous visits, he kept coming home late and, when he returned, he would give them long, convoluted stories about being held up by a chief needing his help, or an incident that only he could settle. His excuses may have been real, but every time she listened to them, Lily wondered if Mrs Manning was the actual reason for his delay. The thought irritated her. However, he did not behave like this now; leading Lily to hope that the affair was over. He came straight home from work and was back to his attentive and friendly self.

Things were so pleasant between them that Lily even joined him on two of his trips.

*

The first was to the small village of Kezi, south of the Matopos Hills, to visit a chief. They drove in the departmental Bedford, along the strip road through the hills, weaving their way through huge, lichen splattered, *dwalas* and *kopjies*. Formed of granite.

'I need to paint some *kopjies* like these in my mural with rocks full of lichen,' Lily said as she gazed out of the car window, admiring the scenery.

'But you told me you were depicting the story of Moses in the bulrushes. Surely you just need a painting of a river, river banks and lots of reeds,' Peter said.

She laughed at how simple he made it sound. 'Yes, I've got all that, but I've been struggling with the background. At the moment it's just a grass covered *vlei* and a big, blue sky. I think I should add some *kopjies*. It will make it more interesting.'

They crested a rise and rounded yet another granite hill, where an even more spectacular vista spread out in front of them.

'Hey, let's pull over and enjoy this view for a few minutes,' Peter said. He slowed down and eased the car off the two thin strips of tar, watching out for the drop off onto the gravel. 'After it has rained, water sometimes gouges the gravel out next to the tar, leaving a nasty step which can puncture a tyre in a heartbeat,' he explained. 'But I see this road is well maintained, with lots of mitre drains, enabling the water to run off. Thankfully the roads department are efficient at their job, because it makes my job that much easier, what with all the driving I have to do.'

He switched the engine off, and they sat in silence for a moment, staring out of the windows, hearing only the twittering of the birds in the bush nearby. He felt for his cigarettes and lit one, and the car soon filled with smoke.

Lily opened her door but remained seated. 'The grass is long after the rain we've been having,' she said.

'Yes, but excellent for thatching. In a few months there'll be lots of women out here cutting this grass to thatch their roofs.' He sighed. 'Although there are going to be some upheavals soon.'

Lily glanced at her dad. 'What do you mean?'

'Well, I don't like to discuss my work in too much detail, but one reason I'm going to see this chief is to talk about moving some people from areas in the Matopos which have become overpopulated. When Rhodes had his *Indaba* with the chiefs back in 1896, when he negotiated a peace deal with them, he told them we would not disturb the people living in the Matopos. However, fifty years later, we can no longer fulfil this promise. Mr Rhodes did not know the population would swell the way it has, with the introduction of clinics and medicine resulting in a higher life expectancy. Unfortunately, the area can no longer sustain so many people, without becoming irreversibly damaged and so, some are going to be moved. As Assistant Native Commissioner, I will be involved with this. I'm afraid many people will not be happy about it.'

'What else can you do?'

'It's a tricky business, and I can't answer that question. It's one conundrum of colonialism. The population has swelled fourfold since the turn of the century, when white people first started settling here. But most indigenous people still live the way they did when there were just a few hundred thousand of them. It did not matter then if they destroyed the natural resources because everything was abundant and it soon revived. But that's changing now.' He stubbed his cigarette out in the ashtray and started the engine. 'Close your door. We had better get going. I'm just putting off the inevitable.'

They arrived at the chief's homestead and parked under a large, shady tree. Lily remained in the car. It was a muggy day, and she wound all the windows down, allowing a breeze to blow through the vehicle. Traditional villages were nothing new to her, but she still enjoyed sitting there, observing the activities of the inhabitants, living a life that was so different from her own. The chief's homestead comprised pole and *dagga* huts of varying sizes, all with thatched roofs. She identified the hut where they cooked, by the smoke coming through the blackened thatch. A skinny looking dog slept under the eaves of the biggest and neatest looking hut, flicking its ears every time a fly landed on him. Scantily dressed children came to stare at her and the car. She counted twenty-four of them, of varying ages, and she wondered if the chief was the father to them all. This made her speculate how many wives he might have. She understood what her father meant about the population exploding. If it carried on like this, it would cause enormous problems one day. Women were sweeping around the huts, and another two popped out from the bush near where she was sitting, carrying buckets on their heads, having collected water from a river. She imagined these people were living much the same way previous generations had. No electricity, no running water. The only changes were that there was a clinic to go to when they were sick, they were wearing clothes made from cloth, and they had the use of wheels, in the form of a donkey cart and maybe a wheelbarrow.

*

A few days later Lily's father suggested they visit Cyrene Mission. 'I need to see the Reverend Paterson and it will give you a chance to look at those murals you have been telling me so much about.'

'Oh, I would love that Dad. Thank you for thinking of this,' Lily responded.

This time they drove down the strip road towards REPS School, turning onto a dirt road after the school.

Her father stopped the car.

'Hop out,' he said, 'it's time you had more driving experience, and what better place is there than on this road that has little or no traffic.'

After stalling a number of times, Lily managed to drive at a slow but safe speed to the Plumtree Road, after which her father took over.

They arrived at the mission with no mishaps and left the car in the shade of a large tree near the chapel. This was a sight to behold and Lily decided Mrs Craig's descriptions had not done it justice. Stunning, simply painted murals covered both the interior and exterior walls from roof to floor with the artists using orange, yellow, turquoise, blue, brown, and green in vibrant, but flat hues.

Reverend Paterson pointed out the mural he did, to show the artists the way, just as Lily, Mrs Craig, and Mr Tate were doing now. Lily drove back from Cyrene Mission feeling inspired. She could not wait to get back to the farm and use what she had learnt to finish her mural before starting the schoolchildren on theirs.

*

As the time approached for Oliver to come and see the Sandersons, Lily became ever more nervous. She worried about their age difference and what her parents would have to say about this, fearing that her desire to marry someone older than her mother would be difficult for them. All she hoped for was that they would change their minds when they saw how much she and Oliver meant to each other. She believed her father would be tolerant, but she was not so sure about her mother, knowing how opinionated she often was about the Craig family. Lily could not understand this, but hoped Oliver's charm would change her mother's mind.

The telephone rang in the passage on the night she knew Oliver would call, and Lily felt her heartbeat quicken and her hands break into a sweat.

'Now, who can that be?' her father murmured, getting up to answer it.

She heard him say, 'Oliver Craig. Well, hello. This is a surprise.'

The conversation continued for some minutes, with Lily not picking up much of it, but as soon as her father finished, he came through to the sitting room to tell his wife and daughter.

'Well, well, well, I have just had a telephone call from your employer, Lily, asking if he can come for a visit tomorrow.'

'What,' said her mother? 'Who?'

'Mr Oliver Craig.'

'Oh no. He's the last person we need here,' she said.

'I did not want to say no to the man, Ella.'

'You should have. I do not want him here.'

'For God's sake Ella, he's Lily's boss. We have to be polite.'

'No, we don't. I would much prefer it if Lily got a proper teaching post again, at one of the lovely junior schools in Bulawayo, instead of being stuck on that farm. We hardly ever see her when she's there.'

'But I love it, Mum.'

Her mother gave her a side-long look. 'I can't understand why. You were having such a lovely time in town, going to the pictures every weekend with Priscilla, tea here, shopping there, bathing at the swimming pool just down the road from Milton School. Now you're stuck in the middle of nowhere with those dreadful people.'

Lily had no idea how to respond. It mortified her to hear her mother speak like this.

'Well, I said yes,' her father said. 'And I expect you to be polite, and give him a cup of tea and a slice of cake, at the very least Ella. We're going to meet in my office at two o'clock, as he said there is something he wants to discuss with me, and then we will come back here for tea.'

Lily was so anxious about what was going to happen the next day, she did not sleep well that night. Things were no better when she sat down to breakfast with her mother the next morning. Ella carried on and on about what snobs the Craigs were, and how she had always detested people like them. After listening for a while, Lily could bear it no longer. She excused herself, picked up her plate, and walked to the kitchen to make a vanilla sponge cake for their tea. This helped calm her nerves and she knew her mother would not bake anything.

The hours ticked by and Lily stayed in her room, reading her book as best she could; "The Diary of a Young Girl," by Anne Frank. Her interest in what people had gone through during the war had increased a great deal since Oliver told them about his wartime experiences. Priscilla's aunt had sent this book out, and Priscilla gave it to Lily when she finished reading it. Goodness, Lily thought as she read it now, I must never, ever complain about anything in my life again.

However, this resolution was soon to be sorely tested.

From her bed, she could see the road through the window, and just before two o'clock Oliver's Chevy drove up the road and parked outside her father's office. Her heart raced when he got out. He looked tense too, she thought, as she watched him straighten his tie and look around, before going through the gate. She could not concentrate on her book after that, so she got off her bed and sat at her dressing table, staring out of the window, and waiting. She sighed. How in love with him she was and how fortunate that he returned her feelings.

After what seemed like a long time, she heard her father and Oliver talking as they walked up the path to the front door. They sounded amicable enough, Lily thought, as she stood up, her legs feeling shaky. Their house was small, so she heard them come through the front door. Her father called out to her, and she wasted no time going through to them. Oliver was standing next to the sideboard, his hands in his pockets. Their eyes met, and he smiled. Her heart was hammering but she managed to smile back.

They were both relieved that her father broke the tension.

'Well, well, well, Lily. You have been a secretive little thing, haven't you?' Lily could feel her cheeks burning.

'I couldn't say anything to you, Dad, until Oliver spoke to you.'

'No, of course not. Where's your mother?'

'I'm not sure.'

'Let me find her.'

As soon as he left, Oliver strode across the room to Lily, grabbing her in his arms and giving her a quick kiss and a hard hug.

'I've missed you so much,' Lily whispered. 'Was my father okay?'

'He was a bit surprised at first, but I have talked him round.'

'I knew he wouldn't mind. It's my mother, I'm afraid of.'

'We need to be on our best behaviour then.' He gave her one last squeeze and broke off from her. 'You sit there, I'll sit here.'

The Sandersons soon joined them.

'Lily and Mr Craig here have something to tell us, Ella,' her father said. Ella stood inside the door, turning her stare from Oliver to Lily but saying nothing. 'They have decided they want to marry,' her father continued.

Ella gasped, then her face went rigid.

'Aren't you going to give them your blessing? Mr Craig assures me they care for each other, and he will do everything he can to make her happy.' Peter smiled at Lily. 'As she will him, I know.'

'They can't marry,' her mother stated. 'I will not allow it.'

'Ella dear, Lily is twenty-four years old. You can't tell her what she can and cannot do.'

'You can't marry him, Lily,' her mother repeated.

'Mum, why are you saying this? Oliver and I love each other very much. We're aware it's only been eight months since we first met, but we also know we're right for each other.'

'No, you're not. He's even older than me,' she spat.

Lily glanced at Oliver, sitting on the edge of his chair, his hat in his hands. Her heart sank. She could not blame him for looking wary.

'After everything I went through during the war, I have learnt that life is short, Mrs Sanderson,' Oliver said. 'We all need to snatch happiness when we can.'

She ignored him.

'You can't marry him, Lillian. I will explain in more detail when he has gone.' With this she departed, leaving the three of them in stunned silence.

Peter was the first to speak. He cleared his throat. 'I'm sorry about this, Mr Craig. I don't know what has got into my wife.'

Lily felt angry, and worried, and embarrassed. 'Oh come on Dad, Mum often behaves oddly.'

Oliver gave her a pained look. 'I'm sure there is a reasonable explanation for the way she feels, and hopefully, we will sort it out.'

'I hope so too,' Peter murmured.

Oliver stood up. 'The sooner I leave, the sooner the three of you can discuss this. So let me say my goodbyes.'

'Oh no, you can't go like this,' Lily wailed. Nothing had turned out the way she thought it would. 'You haven't even had a piece of the vanilla sponge I made for our celebration.'

Oliver's face cracked for a moment, but he pulled himself together again. 'We will eat a whole cake as soon as we have resolved things. Please don't see me out.' He patted Lily on the shoulder as he walked past her and shut the door behind him.

Lily sat still, tears rolling down her cheeks. Then she put her hands to her face and sobbed, wracking sobs of frustration and fear. What would happen if they could not sort this out? What would happen if Oliver decided he didn't want her after all? And why was her mother behaving like this?

'Let me find your mother,' her father said, not knowing how to console her.

He walked down the passage, shouting Ella's name. She must've been in her bedroom, because Lily heard the door open, and she muttered something to her husband. She came back to the sitting room and collapsed into the armchair opposite Lily, who pulled herself together with her mother sitting there.

'What a sorry mess you have made of everything, Lillian,' she said. 'Right from the start, I knew you should never have become involved with those people. I hoped it would fizzle out once you'd come to the end of your teaching contract with them. But oh no, now you want to marry into that family. It's beyond belief.'

Lily gaped at her mother.

'I have never wanted to tell you anything about my connection to them,' Ella continued, speaking in a monotone voice. 'There was no need.' She fiddled with the top button of her blouse. 'But now you are forcing me to.' She sighed and glanced at the door leading into the passage. 'Where is your father? He might as well hear the whole story too. I certainly don't want to repeat myself.'

'I will find him,' Lily said, getting up from her chair. She walked into the passage and called out to him. He answered from the kitchen where she found him standing over the wood stove, feeling the side of the kettle.

'I think this water is hot enough to make a pot of tea,' he mumbled, looking up at her. His face dropped when he saw how distressed she was, and he took her in his arms. She collapsed on his shoulder, sobbing again. He stroked her hair. 'There, there, Sweetheart,' he kept saying until her sobs subsided.

'I'll make the tea,' Lily said, pulling away from him. 'Mum wants to talk to both of us.'

'Good.' He took the plate with the vanilla sponge on it and headed for the sitting room.

Lily followed, setting the tray next to the cake on the coffee table. Her mother looked tense, slumped in the armchair, still fiddling with the buttons on her blouse.

'Would you like a cup of tea, Mum?'

'Yes, I think I would.'

Lily poured the tea and sat down. The cake remained uncut.

'Right now, Ella, what is going on?' Peter asked.

Ella sipped her tea and then put her cup back on its saucer. She glanced at her husband and sighed.

'You know I'm adopted, I told you that when we first met.'

'Of course.'

'We both know the Pingstones aren't your real family, Mum,' Lily said.

'They took me in when I was a tiny baby because my parents abandoned me. They abandoned me, and we have never heard from them again. Ever.'

'Sorry,' her husband said. 'It can't be easy for you, knowing this.'

'No, it's not. And it's even harder knowing why.' Her words hung in the air. Neither Peter nor Lily wanted to interrupt, but when she did not continue, Lily had to ask.

'Why Mum?'

She sighed again and looked at her hands, which were now folded in her lap. 'They ran away,' she said, but then stopped. For a moment it seemed she would not continue, but then she started again. 'They ran away because they were being investigated for the murder of Mr Anthony Craig, Oliver Craig's father.'

Lily gasped.

The room was silent.

'You've got to be joking,' Peter eventually said.

There was silence again until Ella said, 'I wish I was, but I'm not.'

'How long have you known this?' Peter asked.

'I don't know. Since I was about five or six, I think. Mum and Dad, Mr and Mrs Pingstone that is, they didn't tell me. It was one of the children, my stepbrother, Derek. He was old enough in 1905 to understand the commotion that followed Mr Craig's death. I wasn't even born, but he was old enough to have known what was happening. They lived next door to each other, you see, my actual parents and my adopted parents. Derek noticed odd things happening in their garden and gave a statement to the police.'

'Why didn't you tell me before?' Peter asked. 'All you've ever said is that they adopted you.'

'It upset me when Derek told me, and Mum, Mrs Pingstone, was angry with him. I don't think she was ever going to talk to me about it. She got all of us together, me and her other children, and told us we were never, ever to mention it again. She said that none of us knew what really happened, and we must not try to think we did. So we never spoke about it, although I knew my brothers and sisters resented me because of it.'

'Surely not. It wasn't your fault.'

'They still resented me. That's why I was so desperate to get away from home. That's why I,' she glanced at Peter. 'That's why I was pleased when I was pregnant at sixteen, and you married me. I needed to get away from the Pingstones.'

'What a shame you never told me any of this,' Peter said, a bitter edge coming into his voice. 'I would have appreciated knowing you were using me to get away from your previous life.'

Ella blushed. 'It wasn't like that. I, I……'

'Mum and Dad, please,' Lily said, but then she could not bear being in the room with either of them a moment longer. She sprang from her chair and tore out of the room, down the passage, through the front door to the gate, and along the road to her favourite granite hill; the place she fled to before, when her father's affair confused her. She scrambled up the *dwala*, panting as she got to the top. She sat down and looked out, waiting for the lovely view from this hill to soothe her. After all the rain, there was a small rock pool near where she was sitting, and she could see other pools, with the water collecting in the cracks and crevices of the huge rock. There were dark, brooding storm clouds in the north, and she concluded that more rain was heading their way later. The impending storm cast an interesting hew on the afternoon light, with the effect of making the lichen on the rocks more vibrant. Even in her despair, she appreciated the fluorescent yellows, oranges, and whites.

She sighed and strained her eyes to gaze as far north as she could. Oliver would be there somewhere, probably driving back to Brightside. Tears trickled down her cheeks again as she thought of this. He was angry, and she could not blame him. But how could she tell him what the problem was?

Chapter 24

OLIVER Craig was not as far away as Lily assumed, as she sat on her *dwala,* looking out in despair. True, he was angry and hurt, but he was not driving home to lick his wounds. The place he stopped at first, on his way back into town, was the Matopos Hotel. He drove up the hill to the hotel and remembered the first time he saw the Sanderson family, as they drove up this same hill in reverse because their old Model T Ford Tourer could not travel forwards up steep slopes. The image of the Sandersons then still made him smile, despite everything. He got out of his car, locked it, and walked up the steps to the front door. He intended having a cup of tea on a terrace overlooking the dam, but as he walked in, he changed his mind and headed for the bar instead. Julia Manning was standing behind the counter with her back to the room. Doing a quick stock take before the evening punters arrive, Oliver decided. His footfall was soft as he crossed the room, and she only heard him when he pulled out a barstool. This gave her a fright, and she gasped, putting her hand to her chest.

'Sorry,' he said, as she gave him a penetrating look. She blushed. 'Do you remember me, Oliver Craig?' he asked. 'I stayed here in April when we came for the royal visit.'

'Oh yes, of course. I was just trying to place you. How are you, Mr Craig?' As she said this, her eyes drifted to his mouth for a second. She is a sensuous woman, he acknowledged, unlike that shrew, Mrs Sanderson. He wondered if there was a link between this lady in front of him and Mrs Sanderson's odd behaviour. Maybe that Sanderson woman knew about the affair. He was about to say something brash but stopped himself. I must not be like that, he thought.

'I'm in excellent form,' he said instead. 'And, because it's Saturday afternoon and I'm driving aimlessly around the countryside, I decided to stop off at your lovely establishment and have a whisky.' Her eyes widened. 'I know it's still early, but what the hell, we only live once, eh?'

'Those are my sentiments,' she answered. 'What would you like? We have quite a range these days.'

He stared at the line of whisky bottles on the shelf behind her.

'You have a most impressive selection.'

'It's because of all the people moving to Rhodesia from Europe. Many have discovered our hotel, and come here for weekends, or even just for Saturday night dinner. If they stay Saturday night, some have sailing boats and sail on the dam on Sundays. We're busy these days, and therefore I try to keep a well-stocked bar.'

'I see you have a bottle of Johnny Walker Black Label, which I haven't had since getting back from the war, so I think I will celebrate with that, please.'

'Well, of course,' Julia said, reaching for a glass. She ran her cloth around the rim and set it down. 'What would you like with it?'

'It's not yet five o'clock, so I should have it diluted with soda. You have soda?'

'Oh yes.' She poured the drink and handed it to him. 'So what are you celebrating?' she asked

'Nothing. Life.' He gave a small laugh and downed the drink in one. 'Mm, that was good.' She smiled nervously. 'I will have one more for the road.' Her eyes widened again and her lips puckered. 'Fear not,' he said, 'this time I will sip it slowly.'

She poured a second drink, and he added extra ice.

'How is your mother?' Julia asked. 'She's such a talented artist.'

'True. She's well thank you, although things have been difficult for her recently because her studio burnt down.'

'Yes, I read about it in The Chronicle. What a terrible loss.'

'It was. A lot of her paintings went up in flames. Not to mention the loss of the studio itself. She loved that place more than anywhere else in her home. Now that it has burnt to the ground she cannot bear being near it and has sold the house.'

'Oh no. That is so sad.'

'Yes. It was my childhood home, so it's difficult for me too. But, you may be interested to hear that the new owner is going to convert it into a hotel.'

'Really?'

'Not that it will be any competition for you. It's going to be a residential hotel, for people who are awaiting the completion of their homes in the area. A lot of the new houses being built for the immigrants are behind her house; Sunrising. She does not like this, and that's another reason she wanted to sell up and move away.'

As he spoke, more customers trickled into the bar. Two couples and a lone man. He marvelled at the fact that they were all strangers. After spending his childhood and youth knowing almost everyone who crossed his path in Bulawayo, he still found it odd that now he often found himself amongst foreigners in his home town.

'I had better attend to them,' Julia said.

'Of course, don't let me keep you.'

She gave him another of her penetrating looks. 'I hope we meet again sometime. If you ever feel like a weekend near the Matopos Hills, you know where to find us.'

'Yes. I might even consider taking up sailing too,' he laughed.

He watched her as she left him to greet the new arrivals, obviously not strangers to her. He could understand Peter Sanderson's attraction; she was so unlike his ghastly wife. What a mess that family is, he decided, as he recalled the scene in their sitting room. What a shame Lily is caught up in all of it. He drained his glass and slipped out of the bar.

As he drove towards town, it rained; at first a few spots, but it soon became hard, pelting down, making it difficult to see where he was driving, even with his windscreen wipers on full. He hoped he would not meet another car, as this would mean he would have to drive off the strips of tar and onto the now muddy verge. Storms like this will help fill our dam, he hoped, wondering if it was raining hard in their catchment area. All he could see was a sky filled with heavy, black, clouds. He sighed with relief when he got to the outskirts of Bulawayo without encountering another vehicle. As he drove down the Matopos road, with the town centre visible in the distance, the rain stopped, and it brightened up. It was after six o'clock now, and the sun was low beneath the clouds, giving off a warm, glowing light. The beauty of this scene made his heart heavy again.

He stopped off at the Skittle Inn, on the corner of Fifteenth Avenue and Jameson Street, for another whisky. That would make him feel better. He had not been into the Skittle Inn since returning from Europe, and when he walked in he saw that, although the interior was the same, the clientele were different. Again he found himself in a room full of strangers, although, when he got to the end of the bar to order his drink, he recognized the proprietor from days gone by.

'I see your bar is doing well these days, Mr Dobson,' he said.

'Never better. People who work on the railways and at the new power station come in here. The Skittle Inn is booming with such an influx of new artisans and other railway personnel. Saturdays are my best night, but many drop in for a quick pint on their way home from work. A lot of them stay in boarding houses in the area, and in the Railway Hotel.'

'Well, being so close to the railway station has its perks.'

'It certainly does.' A client further down the bar distracted Mr Dobson.

'Don't let me hold you up,' Oliver said. 'I'll finish my drink and be on my way.'

He sipped his whisky, watching and listening to the surrounding banter. Some people were playing darts, others were standing or sitting around. Most of the accents were English, from what he could determine; many East Londoners he thought. What a relief it must be for them to escape that bombed-out place, and, indeed for England, to have countries its citizens could flee to. This must surely make it easier for them to rebuild.

He decided he was enjoying his pub crawl, so when he left the Skittle Inn, he weaved his way towards the Bulawayo Club. There was a sizeable crowd there too, and the nearest place he could find to park was up the hill near the High Court. There was just enough light left in the sky to show up the copper dome on the High Court building. He locked his car and sauntered back down the hill towards the Club, admiring the architecture, as he always did. He skipped up the steps, across the veranda, and through the massive wooden front door with glass panels. Cecil John Rhodes glared unblinkingly at him from his portrait above the fireplace in the wood-panelled hall. Oliver greeted the concierge, as he passed the wood and glass booth where he sat, just to the right of the front door.

'Good evening, Mr Craig,' he replied, glancing at the list on the counter in front of him. 'Are we expecting you for dinner tonight, Sir?'

Oliver could hear laughing and chatting emanating from the bar, muffled by the wooden panelling, and then louder bellows, echoing around the atrium, the open centrepiece of the building.

'No, no. I thought I would just stop in for a quick drink on my way home. Who's in the snooker room tonight?'

'Um. Messers McAllister, Greaves, Halsted, Sly, and Rushmore are there. And Sir Patrick Fletcher, too. I'm not sure who else.'

'Ah, people I know. I will see if I can join them for a quick game. Now that would be fun.'

He ambled through the atrium, stopping off at the green and white tiled lavatories on his way, and then headed towards the snooker room. It was dull, lit only by the lights underneath each of the canopies hanging above the three snooker tables. Cigarette smoke filled the air.

Bloody hell, I am going to have a cigarette tonight, he decided, ignoring his newfound resolution to stop smoking. He ordered a whisky and soda and a packet of cigarettes from the waiter who appeared at his side. Patrick Fletcher was standing at the table nearest the door and beckoned Oliver over.

'We're about to start a game. Do you want to join us?'

'I do,' Oliver said, slapping him on the back in a friendly manner.

The game carried on long enough for Oliver to sink another two whiskies, but they also ordered a large plate of sandwiches, which lined his stomach nicely, he decided.

Edward Rushmore and his brother-in-law, Mac McAllister, beat Oliver and Patrick, thanks to Oliver's lack of skill.

'Shall we have a revenge match?' Patrick asked.

'Nice of you to ask, old chap,' Oliver said, 'but I think I should call it a night.'

'You driving all the way back to Brightside?'

'No, I'll stop off at Sunrising tonight.'

'Good idea,' Patrick said. 'Do you want me to drive you there, on my way back to Umvutcha? We can come back for your car in the morning.'

'Kind of you, but no. I will head straight there now. It will be the last night I ever stay in that house, so I might as well enjoy it.'

'Sad. The end of an era,' Patrick said.

However, as Oliver turned from Selborne Avenue into Main Street, he saw an empty parking place right outside the Exchange Bar. He decided this must be an omen to stop there for one last drink. All the other parking bays, including the ones in the centre of the road, were taken, and Oliver walked into a packed bar. There were one or two familiar faces, but on the whole, strangers filled the establishment again. He looked around the smoky room and decided that he would just have one whisky.

Driving back to Sunrising was difficult, and he was pleased that he met only two cars on the way there. He parked right outside the front door, and struggled with the key, but eventually unlocked it, and staggered down the passage to his old room. The house was unfurnished now, except for a few arbitrary items, including his bed, and he fell onto it.

He did not appreciate being back at Sunrising for one last night because he was out for the count until the middle of the next morning.

When he regained consciousness, he knew his heart was heavy, but he did not know why for a moment. He had a sudden panic attack when he couldn't remember what plan he had made for Amanda, before recalling that she was staying the night with the Brookes. Good old Serena, he decided, the ever-dependable Serena. So unlike that woman in the family he believed he was so desperate to marry into just yesterday before she showed her true colours. But no, the mother might be unstable, but the daughter was lovely. Sweet Lily. Mixed up in all that drama. He could not, for the life of him, work out what it was all about.

Chapter 25

DEPENDABLE was not a word Serena would use to describe herself. No. She had given up all claim to a title like this the day she started having an affair with her brother-in-law, Graham Brooke. Despicable maybe, but not dependable. Despicable because she hated herself for what she was doing, yet she could not stop. She was utterly infatuated with him. She felt like she was thinking of him every waking second of her day, constantly planning and longing for the next time they could be alone together. It was bliss when they were together, and torture when they were apart, and worst of all when they were in the company of others and had to pretend there was nothing between them. It amazed her that no one was suspicious, but she worried about what would happen if someone were to discover their treachery. She knew it was sordid and secretive, yet it was all she wanted. And what about their future? They could not go on like this, yet she could not bear the thought of their affair ending. She was a desirable, beautiful, thirty-three year old woman, married to a man who, almost from the moment he became disabled, shunned her and pushed her away. As much as she had tried to ignore his behaviour and continue being the dutiful wife, she could no longer do so.

Of course, she kept these dark thoughts well hidden when her mother-in-law and aunt-in-law came for brunch on Sunday morning. Act natural, she kept telling herself, and she excelled at this.

She had asked Oliver to join them, expecting him to arrive mid-morning to pick up Amanda on his way back from town. But when, by eleven o clock, he had still not materialised and everyone was "dying of starvation", as her son John informed her, she walked into her husband's study to telephone Sunrising and find out what time he had left. Tim was sitting at his desk, as he almost always was during the day, and she explained to him her concern. He nodded and continued reading his paper. She did not bother to make small talk with him while she waited for the operator to put her call through. Instead, she looked out of the window, watching Amanda, John, and Bea playing with Amanda's dog on the lawn. She could hear the two old ducks talking on the veranda, discussing the final loose ends they needed to tie up before Isabella moved into Celia's house, and she knew that her two older children were mooching around in the drawing room, desperate to play a record on their gramophone when their grandmother and great aunt left. All so normal and homely, she thought, except for the fact that I am going to sneak off later to my secret spot, to be with my lover for an hour of passion.

The operator finally put her through and Gonda answered. This did not surprise her. He was back at Sunrising, doing a final clean-up and clear-out before they gave the keys to the new owner.

'Good morning Gonda. Did Mr Craig stay there last night?' she asked.

'He did madam, and he is still in bed. I have just taken him a cup of tea.'

'In bed?' She glanced at her watch. It was now ten past eleven. What was Oliver still doing in bed? He was always up with the sparrows. 'Why is Mr Craig still in bed?' she asked.

'I believe he is tired Madam and needs some rest. The gardener has stoked the boiler and he will fill the bath, and then I have prepared a light lunch for him.'

'Oh. Did he not mention that I was expecting him here for brunch at ten-thirty?'

'No Madam. I do not believe he will get back there until this evening.'

'Oh. Well, could you ask him to be kind enough to telephone me when he gets up, to tell me exactly what he wants me to do with his daughter until then.' The thought that leapt into her head was that she could not meet Graham later if she was waiting for Oliver to pick up Amanda. She dared not raise his suspicions by not being there when he came round.

'I will Madam,' Gonda said, after a pause.

She slammed down the receiver.

Tim scowled at her. 'Honestly Serena, you don't have to talk to Gonda like that. I'm sure there is a satisfactory reason why Olly is running late, and it has nothing to do with Gonda.'

'Well please, can you deal with your cousin when he telephones? Tell him to get back here as soon as possible. In the meantime, I will take care of your mother, aunt, and children. Everyone is starving, waiting for your cousin. I assume you won't be joining us for brunch?'

'No.'

'I'll send a tray in here for you. Tuppence is frying eggs. Do you want one or two?'

'One is fine, thanks.'

Tim stared at the door after Serena banged it shut. What was it with her these days? She seemed moodier than ever. He shifted in his wheelchair and tried to reposition his right leg, before focusing on his paper again. Tuppence brought his breakfast in to him a few minutes later and, as he took his first mouthful, the telephone rang. Two long rings, followed by one short. He let it repeat itself, while he swallowed his mouthful, and then picked up the receiver.

'Good morning. Sunlands, Tim Brooke speaking.'

'Good morning Mr Brooke,' said Mrs Bradshaw, the telephone operator. 'I have your cousin, Mr Craig on the line.'

'Thank you, please put him through. Morning Olly.'

'Morning Tim. Thank you Mrs Bradshaw.' They both paused, waiting to hear the click as she put down her receiver, knowing she listened in on calls as often as she could.

'What's up, Oliver? Serena expected you back for the brunch she arranged for the old girls.'

'Yes. My apologies.' His voice sounded muffled, gruff.

'You okay?'

'To be honest, no.' Tim thought he heard his voice crack as if he was about to cry.

'Can I help?'

'I doubt it. I went on pub crawl last night and I've got one hell of a headache right now.'

'That's not like you. What precipitated that? The pub crawl, I mean.'

'Bloody women,' Oliver groaned.

Tim was silent, as Oliver sniffed into the telephone.

'Sorry,' Oliver said, after a few moments. 'I'll tell you about it when I get back. I think it's the alcohol in my system that's making me emotional. And seeing this house packed up and empty. I've always loved this house and hate that Mama has now sold it. This will be the last time I'm ever here.' He sniffed again. 'Sorry, I'm going to go now. God forbid Mrs Bradshaw hears me like this. I'll see you later.' Tim heard the click on the line as Oliver put his receiver down. He returned his handset and stared at his plate of food, but then closed his knife and fork. He didn't feel like eating anymore.

How he hated being like this. Trapped in his own body. A prisoner in his own house. Useless. That's how he felt.

All of a sudden he decided he was not going to sit there all day, wondering what was going on with Oliver, waiting for him to come back. No. He would go to him. If nothing else, he was sure Oliver would appreciate having him at Sunrising when he closed the door for the last time. And besides this, he would like to look around the place once more too. That house may not have been his childhood home, like it was Oliver's, but it was still a special place for him. The history; his father building it, one of the first grand houses built in Bulawayo. What an achievement it was then. Transporting all the windows, doors, door frames, floorboards, ceiling boards, corrugated iron, roof trusses, you name it, first shipped from England to Cape Town, then transported by rail from there, when the railway lines had only just reached Bulawayo. As he sat in his wheelchair thinking about it, an overwhelming sense of loss swept through him. It now belonged to someone else. A newcomer from England. Someone who would not appreciate the history as they did.

Tuppence came back into the room to fetch his tray.

'Please find Miss Wolhunter. I need to speak to her, chop, chop.' Tim said.

A few minutes later Daphne came into his study. 'Morning Tim. Tuppence said you wanted me.'

'Yes. Would you be able to take me into town now?' Daphne swallowed, not sure how to respond. He never requested anything like this. He continued: 'I know it's a lot to ask of you on a Sunday morning, but I'm desperate to see Sunrising one last time before the new owner takes over later this week.' Daphne still said nothing. 'It could also be helpful for my cousin, who is there now. He may have some stuff we could load into my vehicle. Sorry Daphne, you probably had visions of a relaxing Sunday afternoon on your bed.'

'Well, yes,' she said. 'But I don't mind taking you. I always enjoy the drive into town. I'm just a little concerned about the roads and the river, after all the rain we had last night.'

'But you're always telling me what an experienced driver you are on rugged roads' he half-joked.

'Well, I am.'

'So a bit of mud, and maybe some water running over a low level bridge, shouldn't be a problem.'

'You're right. Let me have a quick bite to eat, and then we can go.' She glanced at her watch. 'If we leave by twelve-thirty, we should get to Sunrising by one-thirty. And I suppose we could stay there until five-ish, to get back here before dark. Will that work?'

'It will, thanks. Please ask Jesus to come here and help me prepare for the trip. He can push me to the car.'

'Right oh boss. I'll meet you outside the front door at twelve twenty-five.' Daphne saluted and left the room. He smiled after her. He doubted she would ever lose the soldierly manners she perfected when doing military service in East Africa during the war.

As they set off, they were relieved to see that the sporadic bursts of sunshine during the morning had dried the dirt roads. This made the drive from the house to the main strip road into Bulawayo easier. From there, the journey was easy, as long as they did not meet another car coming the other way. This would mean having to half pull off the road and drive with two wheels on the dirt and two wheels on the left-hand strip. They were lucky; they did not meet another car, but as the road dipped down to the low-level bridge across the Umguza River, they knew why. Water was gushing over the bridge. Daphne stopped the car and they both gazed at the scene in front of them.

'Oh well, it looks like we will have to go back,' she said.

Tim continued staring at the water. Now that he was out and about, the last thing he wanted was to go back. 'Why don't we wait a while and see if the water goes down enough for us to cross.

Daphne looked at her watch. 'Right, let's give it half an hour, and then make up our minds. Of course, I drove over many a low-level bridge in East Africa during the war.'

'I do not doubt that you have a great deal of experience with low-level bridges,' Tim laughed. 'I might have a brief nap while we wait.'

'Good idea, but first I will pick the flame lilies I see growing over there. I love flame lily flowers. I'll put them in water when we get to Sunrising. That way, they should remain fresh, and I can enjoy them in my bedroom when we return.'

She got out of the car and put a rock on the side of the road to mark the edge of the water. As the minutes ticked by they watched as the river dropped below this marker.

Half an hour later they reassessed the water level. 'You know what,' Daphne said, 'I think the water is shallow enough over the bridge now that we can proceed.' She started the car's engine.

*

Oliver pulled himself together after his early emotional breakdown. His behaviour embarrassed him, but he and his cousin were close. He knew Tim would understand, and they'd end up laughing about it like they so often did.

He packed his car to overflowing, with the last of the personal possessions piled in the box on the back and secured with a rope. They left behind a few of the bigger items of furniture which had no sentimental value. The new owner might find a use for them. Finally, at three pm they were ready to drive down the long curving driveway towards the grand old gate posts. Gonda was squashed in the passenger seat with bits and pieces all around him. At the gate, Oliver stopped the car. He wanted to look at the property one last time. The sun peeped out from a cloud, casting a warm glow over the house, but the burnt studio looked even more desolate and skeletal than ever.

Oliver sighed and climbed back into the car. 'I'm going to miss this place,' he said.

'Yes Sir,' Gonda answered. Oliver patted him on the shoulder. Sunrising had been his home for longer than Oliver's even, and he knew he felt the loss too.

'But it's for the best. My mother is no longer up to the effort needed to either demolish or rebuild the studio, and she hates seeing it like it is now. And of course I'm too busy on the farm to find the time to maintain this house.'

'Lady Brooke needs Mrs Craig at the farm now that Sir is gone,'Gonda said.

'True. And I'm sure your children will be pleased to have you there too.'

'Yes.'

Having consoled themselves that everything was turning out for the best, they drove off, through the new housing development towards the main strip road out of town. As they turned, Oliver glanced at the sky. It was dark and menacing again.

'I hope we get back before the next rainstorm,' he said. 'I might have left it a bit late, but I was waiting for the river to go down. It will have come up after all the rain last night and it takes some hours for the bridges to be accessible again.

They got to the first bridge that spanned the Umguza River on their route home, and indeed, water was trickling over it, but low enough to cross. They proceeded up the slope from the bridge and drove a further eight miles, the road winding around the low, flat-topped hills.

But as they drove down the incline to the second bridge they saw something that made both their hearts sink. A vehicle washed off the bridge, the front half submerged, the back sticking out of the water, a tree pushed up against it, creating a wave that swirled around the side of the car.

Oliver rammed his foot on the brake and they both stared at the sight in front of them. Shock turned to horror as they recognized the vehicle. It was a Buick.

'Oh my God,' Oliver murmured. 'That's Tim's car. What on earth is it doing here?'

Oliver pulled off the road, and they both got out. They ran to the edge of the bridge and looked around from there. There was no one about.

'You walk down this bank and I'll look on the opposite side,' Oliver said. He took off his socks and shoes and rolled up his trouser legs so that only his feet would get wet as he walked across the bridge. He stopped in the middle to inspect the car, opening the boot to check if Tim's wheel chair was stowed there. It was, but he could determine nothing else, with water splashing around the vehicle.

They both walked for a short while along opposite banks, but the grass was long and thick, and bushes and branches were blocking their way. Neither of them saw anything else connected to the vehicle.

After a short while, Oliver yelled across the river to Gonda.

'This is pointless. Let's get back to the farm and find out what's going on.'

After driving another three miles they spotted a dishevelled figure walking along the side of the road. It was Daphne, and Oliver's heart sank further. She burst into tears when she saw them. So unlike the war-hardened woman Oliver knew her to be. Her blouse was torn, her skirt was skew and her stockings were around her ankles. Her hair had fallen out of the neat bun she wore it in and was hanging around her face.

Oliver leapt out of the car and rushed to her side. She collapsed against him, and he grabbed hold of her to stop her from falling.

'It's too awful,' she sobbed. Oliver didn't have to ask her what had happened. He knew. 'We waited for the river to go down,' she continued. 'After about half an hour we decided it was fine. As I was driving across the bridge a tree trunk, which had fallen into the river near the bridge, came loose from whatever it was caught on and rammed into the car, pushing us off the bridge.' She sniffed and Gonda reached in his pocket, took out a clean handkerchief, and handed it to her. She took it and wiped her nose. 'I hadn't even noticed the tree before,' she said. 'Well maybe I had, but I didn't realise it had fallen right into the river, roots and all.' She began sobbing again.

Oliver asked the question he dreaded asking, the question he already knew the answer to. 'Did you have Tim with you?'

'Yes,' she moaned.

Oliver hesitated for a few moments. 'And do you know what happened to him?'

'No. I, I, I struggled to get out of the car. I, the tree was against my door and the car was filling with water. Thankfully the window was open and I pulled myself through it. I managed to move around to the other side of the car so that I could grab him, but, but he, he was no longer there.'

No one said a word.

Oliver finally broke the silence. 'You looked for him?'

'As best I could. But the water was swirling everywhere. I pulled myself along the tree, which was now against the car, and steadied myself on the bridge. I thought to swim back out, to dive down and find him, but as I slid into the water I could feel the current pulling me down, and I knew I would, I would drown if I attempted to swim out again.'

Oliver patted her back. 'Yes, it's for the best that you did not do that.'

'I, Oh God, I feel awful.'

'Let's get you back to the house. You need to dry off and have a hot cup of tea. You are in shock right now.'

Oliver and Gonda squeezed everything from the front of the car into the box in the back. Then the three of them squashed up on the front seat, Daphne wedged between Oliver and Gonda. As they drove back, she explained how Tim suddenly decided he wanted to go to town to bid one last farewell to Sunrising. Oliver's hands gripped the steering wheel ever tighter when he heard this, and he regretted more than ever his earlier emotional outburst.

They drove up the drive to Brooke House, and swung into the roundabout outside the door leading into the hall. Before Oliver even switched off the engine, a furious-looking Serena appeared at the door.

'What the heck is going on?' she said, her expression turning from anger to surprise as the three of them dragged themselves out of the car. 'Goodness Daphne, what have you been doing?'

Daphne burst into tears again.

Oliver grabbed Serena's shoulder. 'Come, let's go into Tim's study. Something terrible has happened.'

'Where is Tim?' She asked as they walked through the study door. 'I thought he was still in here.'

'Sit down,' Oliver said, slamming the door behind them. He collapsed in the armchair opposite her and told her what he knew.

When he finished, he phoned the police. They went out to the scene of the tragedy where their diving team found Tim's body, trapped on the river bed by a branch of the tree that had pushed the car off the bridge.

Chapter 26

OVER the next few days, Serena felt she was living a nightmare. Her remorse was profound, and she loathed herself. She felt nothing but shame that, while her husband had gone off to join his cousin, the only thought on her mind was how to spend a passionate hour in his brother's arms. It had not once occurred to her to check on him or attend to his needs.

From the moment she heard about Tim's death, she vowed her affair with Graham was over.

Of course, she could not confide in anyone about this. She would not even dare tell Graham. Her only option was to arrange a good send-off for Tim, in the hopes that this would ease the pain, even if by a fraction, of her children and in-laws.

She immersed herself in the funeral arrangements.

Two evenings before the event she needed to discuss the finer details of the service with Oliver. As she walked along his veranda towards his study, where she knew she would find him, she glanced through the window and saw him sitting at his desk. He was slumped in his chair, his head bowed, his fringe falling across his forehead, but this did not hide the look of despair on his face.

She knocked on the study door, and, after hearing his call, walked in.

'Hello Serena,' he said, pushing back his chair and taking his handkerchief out of his pocket to wipe his face as he stood up.

'Oh Oliver, I'm so sorry,' she said.

'I'm taking Tim's death badly,' he said, collapsing back into his chair while Serena perched herself in a chair on the opposite side of his desk. 'I'm trying to write Tim's eulogy,' he continued after a short pause. 'I have been struggling with it for days.'

'Yes, it's hard,' Serena said.

Silence spread between them until Oliver finally said: 'My biggest problem is knowing I'm responsible for his death,'

'What? Oliver, how can you think this? It wasn't your fault.'

He groaned, scraping his chair out again. 'Would you like a drink?' He pulled himself to his feet. 'I haven't told you everything.'

Serena raised her delicate eyebrows. 'What do you mean?'

'Drink?' he repeated, walking with his empty glass to the drinks tray.

'Alright, yes. I'll have a brandy and water.' He poured her drink, and refilled his glass. 'So, what are you talking about?' she asked.

'Well, Lily and I, what can I say? We have become very fond of each other. I asked her to marry me and she said yes.'

'Oh Oliver, that is good news, in amongst all this sorrow.'

'You would think so. On Saturday I visited her parents, to get their permission. I knew there would be some concern about our eighteen-year age gap, but I thought everyone would soon get over this and it would be a foregone conclusion. However, her mother became, um, animated, and said we could not marry.'

'What? Why?'

'She wouldn't say. Anyway, I got a letter from Lily yesterday, sending her condolences for Tim's death. She read about it in the

Chronicle. She was her usual sweet self, but at the end of the letter, she said her mother had explained the reason why we can't marry, and she's right, we cannot.'

'Did she tell you what this reason was?'

'No. She said she could not talk about it.'

'Why ever not?'

'She didn't explain further.'

'That's ridiculous. She owes you an explanation.'

'She doesn't think so.'

There was silence again as they both sipped their drinks.

'Why don't you go back there and speak to her face to face?'

'God, no. Her mother practically threw me out of the house on Saturday. I'm not going to put myself through that again.'

'Well, I am sorry,' Serena said.

Oliver then told her how he spent Saturday night getting drunk, only to wake up on Sunday morning feeling distraught, and how he let this slip to Tim on the telephone.

'If I had not behaved this way, he would not have had the impulse to come to Sunrising, and he would therefore still be alive.'

Serena stared ahead of her and took a swig of her brandy. Where would she start if she told Oliver about her own shameful behaviour? But she could not do this. No, she could tell no one of her treachery. Instead, all she said was, 'You are not to blame. He loved you, and you, more than anyone else in recent years, made his life worth living.'

Oliver sighed. 'Mm. I will have a hard time believing that.'

'Well, you must. You were the best friend and cousin he could ever have asked for.'

There was another long pause, broken by Oliver.

'Well anyway, what did you want to talk to me about?' he asked.

'Daphne wants to write up the order of service for the funeral, so we need to discuss it. '

'Poor girl, she also feels responsible.'

'You, me, and Daphne. We all feel we could have avoided what happened. But let us try to put this behind us for now and concentrate on giving Tim the best funeral we can?'

*

Serena considered Oliver's predicament as she drove back to Brooke House. Mrs Sanderson's behaviour seemed bizarre, and it was unreasonable that Lily had not told Oliver the reason why. There was little wonder he felt so depressed, with this on top of Tim's death. Her heart went out to him, but, as she pondered over his situation, she realized there was something she could do which may help. She could see Lily Sanderson and find out what was going on. She and Lily were friends. Surely she could coax an explanation out of her.

She parked her car in the garage and walked straight to Tim's study to use the telephone. The empty space behind his desk where he had always sat reinforced her self-loathing. She grabbed the receiver and wound the handle, crossing her fingers that Mrs Bradshaw would pick up her end quickly. She did, just as Serena was about to wind the handle again.

'My dear Mrs Brooke,' Mrs Bradshaw said, her voice dripping with sympathy. Serena could hardly bear it. If only they knew what a hypocrite I am, she thought as she answered Mrs Bradshaw. 'Good evening Mrs Bradshaw, please put me through to Umvutcha 296?'

'Umvutcha?'

'Yes, the Fletchers. I need to speak to Lady Fletcher as a matter of urgency.'

'Oh yes, but of course. Let me put you straight through.'

Serena waited a few seconds, listening to Mrs Bradshaw connecting them.

'Mrs Brooke for you Lady Fletcher,' Mrs Bradshaw said when Barbara answered. She hesitated before putting her receiver down so the two women could speak in private.

'Hello, Barbara,' Serena said. 'I have a huge favour to ask of you?'

'Oh yes?'

'I need to go to the Matopos tomorrow.'

'The Matopos? Serena, goodness, why there?'

'I can't talk about it right now, but I may be gone for most of the day, so I want to ask if you would mind coming here and helping with the last-minute preparations for the funeral.' There was a pause, and when Barbara said nothing, she continued, 'I've prepared almost everything, but of course, Tuppence will need to do all the cooking for the luncheon, and someone will have to oversee him.'

'Of course I can do this for you, dearest,' Barbara said.

Serena breathed a sigh of relief. 'Thank you. I have written the menus and, well, you know my staff and your way around my kitchen, so I'm sure you will do what is necessary.'

'Yes.'

'You are welcome to stay the night afterwards if you like. To avoid driving home, only to make the journey back early the next day.'

'Thank you. I will do that, as you need all the company you can get right now.'

Serena slept better that night and was up at dawn to prepare for her drive to the Matopos. It had not rained for three days, so she did not worry about the rivers still flooding, although she dreaded crossing the point where Tim's car had been swept off the bridge. She left Brooke House and turned onto the dust road heading to the main strip road into town. It curved around a slight incline and, as she crested it, she spotted Graham's red MG parked on the grassy verge. He was standing next to it, and she knew she could not sail by and ignore him. She pulled in behind his vehicle and got out, her heart drumming in her chest, her legs shaky. He came closer, but not too close, and for what seemed like an age they stood, staring at each other, neither of them knowing what to say.

Graham was the first to speak. 'I'm so sorry.'

Her lips puckered. She looked away. The last thing she needed was to cry.

'Me, me too,' she stammered.

'I think I'm such a heel.'

'Probably not as much of a heel as I think I am.'

'I keep trying to rationalise that your marriage was over, except in name, and after all those years in that bloody prisoner of war camp, I needed to grasp life with both hands because you never knew how much time you have.'

'Yes, but none of that makes it better,' Serena said.

'You're right.'

'Please, please, can we tell no one, absolutely no one, ever, about what we did? For the children's sake. They look up to you, you are their uncle. You and Oliver are the primary male figures in their lives now. It would devastate them if they ever found out how we betrayed their father.'

He put his hand on his chest. 'I swear, I will never tell anyone.'

'Thank you.'

'But Serena.' He looked at her. 'I have always loved you and I always will. Maybe one day, when the dust has settled.'

She thought her knees were going to buckle. 'Please Graham, we can't talk about it.'

'You're right.'

'Were you waiting for me?'

'Yes.'

'How did you guess I would be out so early?'

'It wasn't a guess. Jesus told Amen, my gardener, that the Madam was going to the Matopos early this morning, and Amen told me.'

'Of course.'

'Why on earth are you going there?' Graham couldn't help asking.

'I can't say. But I had better be going.'

She climbed back into her car, her hand still shaking as she turned the ignition key. She gave him a brief wave as she passed by, but watched him in her rear-view mirror, standing in the road, staring after her, until she turned another corner and he was no longer in sight.

It would be her punishment, their punishment, living so close to each other and having to keep up the pretence of being nothing more than brother and sister-in-law. Nothing more. And he would find someone else, she was sure. The idea of filled her with dread.

*

Serena turned into the road towards the Matopos railway siding, knowing the Native Department offices and staff houses were somewhere close. She stopped before she got to them, unsure of what to do. She had no idea which house the Sandersons lived in, and she had not told them she was coming in case they refused to meet her. She wondered now if this had been such a smart idea. What if Lily was not there?

She looked around. The dust road ahead was white-yellow in the morning sun with wide verges on both sides. The grass, cut short near the road but left to grow long further away, was waving in the breeze and the huge *dwalas* beyond were covered in bright coloured lichen of many shades. She loved the Matopos. It was a special place, but now was not the time to enjoy its unique atmosphere. She dragged herself out of her car and was about to walk towards the houses further along the road when an African man appeared from what seemed like nowhere.

'Phew, where have you come from?' she said. 'You gave me such a fright.'

'Good morning, Madam,' he replied.

'Can you tell me which house Boss Sanderson lives in?'

He pointed to the first one along the road.

'Oh good, that's easy.'

'Is Miss Lily home?'

'*Yebo*, I am their gardener, Obvious. She is there.'

'And Mrs Sanderson?'

'She is there also, but the boss has gone off on business.'

Serena was undecided. Should she go up to the house and risk Mrs Sanderson throwing her out, as she had Oliver? Or should she ask this helpful man to call Lily? She decided on the latter.

She was nervous as she watched him walk towards the house, disappearing around the back, but it did not take long for Lily to appear at the gate. She stopped when she saw Serena standing next to her car further along the road. Serena smiled and waved, praying Lily would not turn and ignore her.

Lily hesitated, then walked down the road towards Serena, looking embarrassed and self-conscious.

'Hello,' Serena said.

'Hello. Um. I'm so sorry to hear about your husband. Did you receive my letter?'

'I did, thank you.'

'How are the children?'

'Well, you can imagine. The older ones are devastated, the younger ones are too, although I think they have not yet grasped the reality of their loss.'

'Yes. It's difficult understanding the finality of death at their age,' Lily said.

Serena blanched.

'I saw in the newspaper that the funeral is tomorrow,' Lily continued.

'Yes. And that is why I have come to see you. Oliver is in a bad way. He and Tim were close. I think he needs you.' Lily opened her mouth to say something, but no words came out. 'He told me all about you,' Serena continued.

'Did he tell you we have called everything off?'

'He did, but he said he does not know why.'

Lily glanced back up the road towards her house.

'Let's go somewhere, so we can talk,' Serena said.

Lily hesitated.

'Please,' Serena said.

'Let me make some excuse to my mother. I will be back in five minutes.'

When she returned Serena suggested they went to the Matopos Hotel, where they could relax with a cup of tea.

'No!' Lily said.

'So where then?'

'There are lots of places we can go,' Lily said.

'Right. Lead me to one.'

Lily climbed into the car and instructed Serena to continue driving along the same dirt road they were on. They passed all the Native Department buildings and continued for another mile before getting to an arboretum. Lily told her to turn right once they had passed it and, after travelling another mile down this road, Lily instructed her to turn right again, onto a track Serena would never have noticed if it had not been pointed out to her. They stopped when they got to an outcrop of shady fig trees. Beyond these trees, flat rocks swept down to a pool. Thick, reeds surrounded this pool, except for the rocky places.

'My goodness, this is lovely,' Serena said. 'I have never been here.'

'This pool is seasonal, but, there's a lot of water around now after all the rain we've had.' There was silence as they both considered what the excellent rains had done to Serena's husband. 'Sorry,' Lily said.

'Let's sit on the rocks next to the pool,' Serena said. 'We can take our shoes off and paddle in it if we're hot.' They sank down and both stared into the water for a while. 'Now Lily, I'm going to ask you to please tell me what is going on and ask you to trust me to decide if things can or cannot be resolved between you and Oliver. I hate seeing him so sad.'

*

Two hours later Serena dropped Lily back at her parents' house and began the long drive back to the farm, but on her way, she stopped at the Matopos Hotel for a much-needed cup of tea. Mrs Manning asked her if she wanted lunch also, but she said a scone with her tea would be enough. She found a bench to sit on in the well maintained garden overlooking the dam.

What a ridiculous coincidence, she thought as she sat there, staring down at the murky waters of the dam. Surely Oliver would not hold Lily responsible for something that happened before even her mother was born. And Isabella? She had no idea how Isabella would take it. Celia had mentioned to Serena once, when they were talking about Anthony Craig, that Isabella took his death badly. And of course she had never remarried. Was this because she had never got over her husband's death? Would she still resent anyone connected to his death, however remotely? They would not know until she had been told. For now though, at least Serena was relieved she had convinced Lily that Oliver had a right to know what the problem was. Lily would come to the funeral the next day with her father. There was no doubt in Serena's mind that Oliver would appreciate this, however the rest of it turned out She and her father would stay in Lily's cottage and sometime, after the funeral she, Lily, must find a time to explain her predicament to Oliver.

When Serena questioned Mr Sanderson's compliance in all this, Lily said there was something the two of them needed to resolve. Lily said she had been putting it off, but she intended approaching him that evening. She was sure he would not hesitate to help her after their discussion.

After finishing her tea, Serena walked up the steps to the hotel. She wanted to speak to Barbara, to find out if there was anything they still needed in the way of food or refreshments for the next day. She found Mrs Manning on the veranda and asked her to put a call through to Brooke House, 'with the cost of this call on my bill, of course.' Serena was thankful that the operator connected her within minutes and Barbara answered the telephone. She said there were some items they could do with. They agreed Barbara would phone the order through to the Haddon and Sly grocery department so they would have a box ready for Serena to collect on her way through town.

She left the Matopos Hotel feeling like she had accomplished something useful that day, something that would help others. Her depression lifted slightly, knowing that she was at least trying to do something positive that did not revolve around her.

Chapter 27

PETER Sanderson drove his car into the clearing which, judging from the number of vehicles already there, was the designated parking place for the funeral. A man was doing his best to direct the parking in an orderly fashion. This man noticed Lily as she walked from the vehicle.

'Good morning, Madam Lily,' he said.

'Hello, Bhutu. How are you?'

'Madam. We are very sad, the Boss, he is dead.'

'Yes, I'm so sorry.'

'I suppose most people who work here know you,' her father said as they walked in the direction of the graveyard.

'Especially him,' Lily said, 'as he works in the stables, and, as I mentioned, I've developed an interest in riding.'

They walked the short distance up the dust road towards the graveyard. Although they thought they were early, mourners already crowded the place, with people squashed inside the walled perimeter. There was a bottleneck at the gate, but Peter and Lily pushed their way through and were lucky enough to find themselves a place to stand under a shady tree close to Miss Harrison's grave. Tim's grave was near his father's. Lily fought back the tears when she saw the coffin, lying next to the freshly dug earth, with his four children and Serena, who was almost unrecognizable in a long black veil covering her head, lined up alongside it. Lady Brooke stood on the opposite side of the grave with her two remaining children, the daughter Lily had only heard about, and Graham. Lady Brooke kept clutching Graham's hand. Lily looked around for Oliver, and her heart missed a beat when she saw him standing with his mother and daughter and the dogs, Eddie and Frank, next to his father's grave. They were leaning against the gravestone and looking out at the view, detached from the quiet commotion going on in the rest of the graveyard. Lily bit her lip. It took every ounce of strength not to flee from the place.

The service started with the children from the farm school singing a hymn, Mrs Tate conducting. They sang a melodious African song, accompanied only by a simple drum beat. How clever, Lily thought, asking them to sing, rather than having us attempt to sing church hymns which would carry away in the breeze. The Reverend, whose name Lily did not catch, then said some prayers and read from the Bible, after which the choir sang again and then Mr Tate said a prayer, followed by a tribute on behalf of the school children and everyone who lived and worked on the farm. Oliver stared out at the view for the entire time, but when Mr Tate finished, he moved from where he had been standing, to the foot of his cousin's grave. He took some notes from his pocket and, as he unfolded them and looked up before reading, noticed Lily and her father under the tree. A look of surprise crossed his face, and then his expression hardened and he turned back to his notes. Lily's heart sank, and she did not hear a word he said or anything else that happened for the rest of the ceremony, other than that the singing was hauntingly beautiful. When the service finished and everyone started making for the gate, Oliver appeared at her side. He nodded at her father as they went through the gate and indicated they step to the side to let everyone else pass.

'I was not expecting you here,' he said. Lily thought this was an accusation rather than an expression of gratitude, and her heart sank further. But, before either she or her father could say anything, several people came up to Oliver to give their condolences, interrupting them.

It was not until much later at the luncheon that Oliver approached Lily again.

'Sorry I was not able to talk earlier.'

'Don't worry, I can see how busy you are.'

'Thank you for your letter. You didn't mention you'd come to the funeral, so I wasn't expecting you.'

'We're going to stay the night, my father and I.'

'Ah. And your mother?'

'No, she's at home.'

'So you'll stay in your cottage?'

'Yes, and Dad can sleep on the sofa.'

'Not at all. I'll get Prince to prepare a guest room.'

She was about to resist when another well-wisher interrupted them again and led Oliver off to talk to a small group of people Lily had not met. But his offer cheered her up a little, and she looked around for someone to talk to. Anyone who was anyone in Matabeleland was there. There were many faces she did not recognize, some because they had only moved to the country in recent years.

She was thankful to spy Priscilla, chatting away in her usual buoyant way, but as soon as she saw Lily she left her companions and took Lily aside.

'Oh my word, there is something I want to discuss with you. Let's go outside. Let's go to the end of the garden so we can be alone,' she said.

Lily had not told Priscilla about any of the dramas in her life, so felt awkward now that Priscilla was desperate to confide in her.

'I'm afraid I'm losing hope with Graham,' Priscilla said, once they had settled down under a tree overlooking the river. 'I'm positive there is someone else in his life.'

'I hate to say it, but he's always been a bit of a lady's man,' Lily said.

'Yes, he is, sort of, but, well, I told myself it was an act. We saw a lot of each other, and then it stopped. Before his brother died, I kept trying to contact him, phoning him for a chat, suggesting we meet for tea, or at the swimming pool, all the things we used to do. But he always had an excuse.'

'Maybe he's busy with his air charter. That could be what is taking up his time.'

'No. I've made some inquiries about it, with someone else who's in the flying world. From what I gathered, he has not been busy.'

'Well, you can't force these things.'

'Of course not. I'd just love to know who this other person is. It's not you, by any chance?'

Lily blushed. 'Honestly, Priscilla, you are crazy.'

'Okay good, I needed to know.' She hesitated, fiddling with a piece of grass. 'Of course there is always Oliver. I do enjoy his company, and there is something romantic about him. I was looking at him earlier when he was giving his eulogy and thinking how attractive he is.'

Lily stared at her. 'Oh dear Priscilla, I don't know how to say this?'

'What do you mean?'

'I feel silly telling you now, but well, we, Oliver and I, we have become close.'

'What? You?' Priscilla stared hard at Lily, her eyes wide. 'Well, how about that?' she eventually said. 'Who would ever have believed it?'

Lily looked down. Her face crumpled and her shoulders heaved as she began to sob.

This shocked Priscilla even more. 'Gosh, Lily, what's the matter? I thought you would be happy. Well as happy as anyone can be under the circumstances, with his cousin dying and all of that.'

'Oh Priscilla. Everything is such a mess,' Lily wept.

'Lily, you aren't making any sense. What's going on?'

'I can't tell you right now. I would if I could, but it's too complicated.'

It took Lily a while to calm down, and, when she did, her face was red, her eyes swollen and the last thing she wanted was to go back to the wake.

'Would you mind finding my father and asking him to take me back to Brightside? I'm really, really sorry, but I can't stay here anymore.'

'Of course. I'm sorry too that I caused you such distress, even though I have no idea why.'

'It's not you, I promise. I will tell you all about it another time.'

Lily had pulled herself together by the time her father found her, although she still did not want to return to the wake, so the two of them walked around the side of the house, down the drive and along the dirt road to where they had parked their car. They drove back to Brightside in silence and when they got to Lily's cottage, she said she needed to lie down because she had developed an excruciating headache.

'You do that, poor girl,' her father said, disturbed that she was so emotional She wasn't often like this, only recently, and he could hardly blame her after what they had discovered. 'I will go for a wander and then relax on your veranda. Nice little place this is. Don't worry about me.'

Prince appeared at the garden gate and came across the lawn.

'Good afternoon, Miss Lily and Sir.' he said. 'Mr Oliver said I must show you to your room when you get here, Sir.'

'Even better,' Mr Sanderson said with obvious relief. He was not at all sure how to fill his afternoon, but, at least now he could have a rest on his bed once he'd finished his "wander". 'You sleep as long as you like,' he called, as he followed Prince through the gate.

Without meaning to, Lily took him at his word and only woke in the early hours of the following morning, confused and not sure where she was. Her surroundings were dark and silent, except for the whine of a mosquito. Then she remembered everything and her stomach tightened. She fumbled for the light and switched it on, looking at her wristwatch with horror. How could she have slept so long? What would the Craigs think of her, disappearing like that? And how would her father have coped with them by himself? She flopped back onto her pillows and tossed and turned until dawn, worrying about what had happened while she slept. Her agitation was not helped by the mosquito, which persisted on flying close to the bed, its whining piercing the otherwise soundless night. But when it was silent, she imagined it biting her, so she flapped her hands in an attempt to bat it away, resulting in the whole rigmarole starting again.

Finally, at five, she arose and crept to the kitchen to make herself a cup of tea. She prayed she would not meet anyone while she waited for the kettle to boil on the wood stove. She was relieved that this didn't happen and she crept back to her room with the tray, setting it on the metal table in the middle of the veranda. She poured herself a cup of tea and sat there for a long time watching the day slowly come alive, wondering what it would have in store for her,

Nothing that she had hoped for, as it turned out.

Her father appeared at the garden gate at seven and came over to her when he saw her sitting on the veranda. He looked fresh and relaxed, his hair combed, a touch of shaving foam in his ear.

'I'm afraid I can't offer you a cup of tea, Dad. I finished the pot I made earlier as I've been sitting here since before dawn.'

His brow furrowed, but he forced a smile. 'That's alright. Prince brought a tea tray to my room earlier.'

'I'm sorry I didn't reappear last night. I could hardly believe it when I woke up and discovered the time. It was after three in the morning.'

'Mm. I came to see how you were before dinner. I crept into the sitting room but your bedroom curtains were drawn and I could hear you snoring, so I decided it was best to leave you.'

'Me snoring?'

'Oh yes.'

They shared a brief smile.

'Well, my apologies again that I left you to fend for yourself.' She hesitated. 'So, what happened?'

'Mrs Craig returned from the wake early evening, and the two of us had dinner together.' He lit a cigarette and inhaled, gazing out at the garden. Lily stared at him, willing him to continue: 'I'm afraid Oliver did not come home,' he said.

Lily's heart skipped a beat. 'What do you mean?'

'Just that. He disappeared, telling no one where he was going. Well, no one that we know of, at any rate.'

There was a long pause until Lily asked: 'And what about Amanda?'

'Mrs Craig said she was staying with her cousins at the other house.'

'I suppose that makes sense. The younger ones will be better for having her around.'

'That's what Mrs Craig said.'

'I'm sure Oliver told Serena where he was going,' Lily said.

'Hopefully. But we didn't want to worry her last night by phoning to ask.'

'Oh dear Dad. And there I was, hoping to talk to him today.'

'Yes.' He paused. 'I told Mrs Craig about your mother's connection to them.'

'Dad!'

'Wasn't that one reason we came here?'

'I suppose so. What did she say?'

'It surprised her at first. It was the last thing she expected.'

'Like all of us.'

'Yes.'

'Was she upset by this revelation?'

He dropped his cigarette butt onto the floor and stubbed it out with his shoe, kicking it into the jasmine growing up the pillar next to him. 'Not in the least.'

'It's just that she's been alone all these years because of, well, because her husband died so young. It can't have been easy for her.'

'No, but she's very philosophical about everything. We had a lengthy chat. She said she struggled for a long time after he died, but it was many years ago, and life has been good to her since then. I'll tell you all about our conversation on the way home.'

'So we're leaving now?'

'We'll have breakfast and then go. Mrs Craig said she wouldn't be up in time to see us before we depart.' He looked at his watch. 'I'll meet you in the dining room in half an hour. That should give you enough time to change and pack.'

'Yes, Dad.'

But Lily remained on the veranda for a while longer, mustering up the strength to get on with these routine tasks. She noticed a lizard sunning itself near the wall and watched a frog squeeze out from where it had been lurking under a pot plant. Lucky reptiles, she thought. They can stay here. They don't have to pack up and leave. She had loved living in this cottage, she had loved teaching the children. But most of all, she had loved Oliver, the life he led and what he represented. She hated the idea of not being a part of it.

She dragged herself to her feet and walked into the cottage, glad she had not taken her big suitcase when she left at the beginning of the school holidays. At least she could pack everything into it and not leave anything behind.

She decided she would ask Priscilla if she could take over the teaching post. Priscilla would love that.

But the thought made her heart sink.

As Lily and her father were finishing breakfast, Isabella appeared at the dining-room door. She was wearing her dressing gown, her long grey hair scuffed back with a hairband. Lily had never seen her with her hair down. Something must've ruffled her, to come rushing over to them like this.

'Good morning Lily, Mr Sanderson,' Isabella said, waving a piece of paper in the air. 'Thank goodness you haven't left yet. I hurried here as soon as I'd finished reading this, afraid I would miss you. It's from Oliver. He says he has gone away for a short time. He says he and Tim had planned to go north together sometime soon, to look at a piece of land they were thinking of buying in the Gwayi River Valley. The man selling this land was at the funeral and invited Oliver to go back with him afterwards and Oliver took up his invitation. He's struggling with Tim's death, and he hopes that going away and keeping busy will help him.'

'Of course,' Peter said.

'I didn't know about any of this last night when we were talking,' Isabella continued. 'Apparently he came back here to pack and left this note with Agnes. But Agnes sent it to Celia's house, thinking I would sleep there last night. The staff only returned the note this morning.' She paused. 'Oliver apologises to you both for leaving. He said he wanted to speak to you, but Agnes told him you were both sleeping and he did not want to disturb you.'

Lily could feel her face turning as hot as fire. How could she have done such a thing? What must he think? She wanted to kick herself for falling asleep the way she had. But it was too late now. She had lost her opportunity to explain everything to him.

Chapter 28

AS Lily considered her dilemma over the next few days, it became ever more apparent that her mother was wrong. She loved Oliver and Oliver loved her, why should something that happened before either of them were born come between them? In her mind she went over and over her father's account of his conversation with Mrs Craig, and how reasonable she had been. Surely Oliver would be the same? But how to discuss this with him? She was half-crazy with vexation, not knowing how and when she could see him again. It did not help that she had nothing to do while she was in the Matopos except having driving lessons with her father.

Priscilla had left for the Victoria Falls the day after the funeral, not giving Lily a chance to give her more details about what had caused her breakdown. A small part of her was glad of this. She had changed her mind about wanting to tell Priscilla the teaching position at Brightside was now available.

Lily decided to discuss everything with her mother. She told her about Mrs Craig's response to her revelations and, although Ella listened, she refused to talk about it further.

Then, a week after the funeral, a letter arrived for her mother. Ella and Lily were sitting at the breakfast table and Ella let out a small gasp of surprise when she opened the envelope and saw who it was from. Lily watched as she read the letter, her lips twitching, her brow furrowing. When she finished she looked at Lily, her face white, her mouth tight.

'What is it, Mum?'

'It's from Mrs Craig.' She handed a single sheet of paper to Lily, who cringed when she saw Mrs Craig's name printed in flamboyant letters at the top of the page. Would her mother use this as another example of the Craig's snobbishness? She glanced at her mother, but her face appeared to have softened.

My dear Mrs Sanderson, Lily read.

I was more sad than shocked when your husband explained your background because he told me you have struggled with this heavy burden since you were a young girl. I am quite mortified that this is the case, and, if I had known it before, I would have tried to put your mind at rest.

Although I knew Mr and Mrs Brown left their daughter in the care of the Pingstones, it never once occurred to me she may have felt uneasy in their home. I wish now I had done my utmost to assure her, and the whole Pingstone family, that no one should associate her with my husband's unexplained death.

Please accept my deepest apology that I never thought to check on you and make sure you knew this.

I came to terms with my fate many years ago and believe that if the Browns did have anything to do with my husband's demise, it was an accident rather than a malicious act.

I realize now, in my old age, that I have had opportunities many people living here have not had. Your mother came to Africa looking for a better life and it must have frustrated her that things did not go the way she expected. As such, I feel sympathy that she did not have the life she had hoped for, and that she could not raise you in a happy home, which I am sure is what she would have wanted.

So please, Mrs Sanderson, I implore you to stop being hard on yourself over something you had no control..

I hope we will meet again one day under happier circumstances.

Yours sincerely

Isabella Craig

Lily stared at the letter for a long time, amazed that Mrs Craig had taken the time to sit down and write it. She felt a surge of affection for her. She peered at her mother, but could not read her thoughts and decided it was better to say as little as possible. Lily was elated by the letter and did not want her mother to spoil the good will it contained. So all she said was: 'Well, that was nice of her to write to you, Mum,' and then picked up her dirty breakfast plate and took it to the kitchen.

But she could not stop thinking about the letter, and, as she did, an idea took shape. She would take matters into her own hands and contact Oliver. She would ask for them to meet so they could discuss everything in person. She would not wait in the hopes he contacted her first. He was in mourning, but, if she intended on being his wife one day, she needed to console him, not stay away and pray that things between them would miraculously improve.

If she had her driver's licence she would drive back to Brightside to see him, but, as she did not, the next best thing was to telephone.

She did not want to make this telephone call in front of either of her parents, so had to wait for the house to be empty. However, her mother went nowhere over the next few days, pottering around the house and garden, always within earshot of the telephone. Finally, when Lily wanted to scream with frustration, her mother said she needed to go to town to buy groceries. And even better, her father said he had business to do in town also, so he would take her the next day.

'Would you like to come too?' he asked Lily. 'We could have lunch at that new restaurant, the Kingfisher. I hear it's very pleasant.'

'No thanks, Dad. I will stay here tomorrow,' Lily said as nonchalantly as possible, hiding her relief that she would have the house and telephone to herself at last.

The Sandersons left just after seven the next morning but Lily waited until eight-thirty to phone Brightside. She hoped Oliver would be having his breakfast by then. She knew his routine. He always left the house early to check on everything around the farm, returning for breakfast after eight.

Her stomach felt as if an invisible band was squeezing it as she waited for Mrs Bradshaw to put her call through and then listened to the ringing on the other side of the line.

'Hellooooo. This is Brightside, and I am Prince speaking,' Lily heard above the beating of her heart.

'I have a, um, a Prince on the line,' Mrs Bradshaw said.

'Thank you, I'll speak to him.' Lily said and then paused until she heard Mrs Bradshaw put her receiver down. Oliver had warned her about Mrs Bradshaw's tendency to eavesdrop on telephone calls.

'Hello Prince. It is Miss Lily here. Please can I speak to Mr Craig?'

'Hello Miss Lily. Mr Craig, he is not here.'

'Oh, is he still out on the farm?'

'No. He will be in the Victoria Falls today, Madam.'

This news struck Lily like a slap. 'Why, why is he there, Prince?' she spluttered, but even as the words were coming out of her mouth she knew it was a silly question, so she followed it up with: 'Do you know when he is coming back?'

'Christmas, I am sure, Madam.'

'Christmas?' Her head spun. Today was the seventeenth of December. That was a whole eight days away. She wouldn't be able to intrude on his Christmas if she hadn't sorted things out before then. She had to do it now. She would go mad if she waited until after Christmas, or, worse still, the following year.

Lily heard murmuring on the other end of the line, followed by Isabella's voice. 'Oh Lily, I am so pleased you phoned. How are you?'

'I'm fine, thank you. And you?'

'Improving, slowly. But I am afraid Oliver is still not home.'

'Yes, Prince told me.'

'Apparently a few months ago he and Tim planned to go on a safari to Wankie National Park, followed by a trip to the Victoria Falls.'

'Oh.'

'He decided that, as he was near there anyway, looking at that land he's thinking of buying, he might as well follow through with their plans, in memory of dear Tim.'

'Yes, of course.' Lily said, even though she was not at all sure about this.

'It will do him a world of good, I think. He arrived at Robins' Camp a few days ago. My old friend Herbert Robins left his farm and home to Wankie National Park when he died, and they've converted it into a camp and named it after him. Did you know that?'

'No,' Lily murmured.

'It was a very generous gesture on his part. We visited him there years ago, the Brooke family and Oliver and I, when Herbert was still alive and Oliver and Tim were small boys. Graham hadn't even been born then. There were lions roaming around every night, and Oliver and Tim found it immensely exciting.'

Lily had never been on a safari, although they had to be careful of lions when they lived in Nyamandhlovu, but she didn't tell Mrs Craig any of this. She was too busy wondering how she would meet Oliver again when he was traipsing around the countryside.

'If he has not changed his mind since we spoke last week,' Isabella continued, 'he should leave for the Victoria Falls this morning. The road from Robins' place will be rough, but once he gets to the main strip road, it should be easy going. He will stay at the Victoria Falls Hotel for the rest of the week, before starting his trek home.'

'Right, well thank you for letting me know.'

'Don't worry about Amanda,' Isabella said. 'She and I are making the most of being together while he is away. I am all for him going on this expedition, as I know it will help him come to terms with his cousin's death.' She paused. 'Is there anything I can help you with in his absence, Lily dear?'

'No thank you Mrs Craig.'

'Well, I am looking forward to seeing you again soon.'

'Thank you, Mrs Craig.'

Lily put the phone down, her head reeling. It had not occurred to her that Oliver would still be away. She made herself a cup of tea and walked into the garden, finding a rock to sit on, resigning herself to a bleak future. She felt both hopeless and helpless as she watched Obvious weeding the rockery in their back garden, the rockery that blocked their old long drop from view.

But as she sat there, an alternative plan took shape in her mind. She would follow him to the Victoria Falls, a place she had never been to before. Priscilla was always telling her she should come and stay when she was there, and this was what she would do now; catch the train that very night if possible. She glanced at her wrist watch. It was nine-thirty. The train left the Matopos siding at noon. This would give her plenty of time to get to Bulawayo and then catch the night train to the Victoria Falls.

She sprang from her rock and ran into the house to put a telephone call through to Priscilla.

*

The train journey from Bulawayo to Victoria Falls went without incident. The conductor showed Lily to a four-berth compartment, but only a Miss Ellis shared it with her. Miss Ellis, who told Lily to call her Louise, was travelling to Northern Rhodesia to spend the holidays with her family on their tobacco farm near Livingstone. The two girls enjoyed dinner together in the dining carriage and then settled back in the compartment for the night. Two bunks, on opposite sides of the compartment, had been made up with crisp white sheets and scratchy blankets with the **RR** emblem on them. The rhythm of the wheels on the tracks soon sent them both to sleep, but it ended up being a long night because the train stopped and started at every siding along the way, waking them up each time it did. However, as they sat in the dining carriage the next morning, eating their toast and marmalade and looking out at the clear dawn sky, streaked with yellow and orange across the blue, Lily felt a surge of excitement. Even if Oliver did not want to meet her, she was glad she had come.

Her only concern was that she had not spoken to her parents before she left, although she had left them a note telling them what she was doing and promising she would be home before Christmas.

Priscilla was at the station to meet Lily, and after bidding Louise goodbye, they rushed off in Priscilla's parents' Hudson Terraplane, Priscilla driving.

'So you passed your driving test before me,' Lily said. 'I'm determined to get my license before the new term starts though.'

'Do. It makes all the difference not having to rely on others for transport,' Priscilla said. She leant over and squeezed Lily's hand. 'But Lily, you were in such a bad way when I last saw you. It worried me. I'm so glad you are here now.'

'Thank you, Priscilla. As soon as we're settled at your parents' house, I will tell you the whole story. I think it will surprise you.'

*

Once Lily finished explaining everything to Priscilla, she wrote Oliver a note, telling him she was in the Victoria Falls and asking if they could meet at the David Livingstone statue that evening at five. If this was not convenient, then tomorrow morning at nine. She and Priscilla decided it was best not to give Oliver her contact address or number, in case he wrote back saying no. They thought there would be less chance of him standing Lily up if he knew she was waiting for him. Lily did not know where the David Livingstone statue was, but Priscilla assured her it was the best place to meet someone. It overlooked the part of the waterfall known as Devil's Cataract, and, if their conversation did not go well, at least they had something glorious to stare at, far enough from the rushing water that they could talk above the roar, but noisy enough to prevent any uneasy silences. Lily laughed at Priscilla's reasoning.

Once the letter was written, Priscilla drove to the Victoria Falls Hotel to drop it off at the reception while Lily stayed at her parents' house. When she returned she told Lily how splendid the hotel was and hoped Oliver would invite them both for tea there once they had sorted everything out between them. Lily was grateful Priscilla no longer harboured any romantic thoughts for Oliver, her only focus being on getting the two of them together again.

At four o'clock she drove Lily down to the waterfall, saying it would soothe her nerves to gaze at it while she waited for Oliver to arrive. They hoped Oliver would bring Lily back to her parents' house later, but Priscilla said she would drive back to the car park at six, where Lily would wait if Oliver did not turn up.

'I'm crossing my fingers that doesn't happen,' Priscilla said as Lily prepared to climb out of the car. She pointed to the path Lily needed to walk down to get to the statue. The noise of the water was apparent as soon as she stepped out of the car, but became more muffled as she entered what Priscilla called the "rain forest". A duiker ran across her path, making her jump. She peered into the thick vegetation for fear of there being any more wild animals and was relieved she saw none. The thunder from the mighty Zambezi River became ever louder as she proceeded down the path, through the shadowy forest of human-sized ferns and palms under a canopy of tall, shady trees which thinned out to reveal the rushing, gushing river. Lily gasped in wonder at the sight of it, as she saw the statue of David Livingstone. Underneath it, sitting on a bench near the statue's feet, Oliver. Her heart skipped a beat. He looked boyish in khaki shorts and shirt, his thick hair wet.

He was early, like her.

She stood, wondering what to do when he looked around and saw her, and his face gradually creased into a smile. She ran to him as he stood up and pulled her into his arms, kissing her slowly and deliberately on the mouth. Passion shot through her and she gasped, opening her lips under his. She felt the sharpness of his thin body, and a melting warmth flowed through her veins, depriving her of strength. Feeling her falter, he tightened his arms to support her as she buried her face in his shoulder, relishing the softness of the skin on his neck, breathing in his warm, musky smell.

'I can't believe you came,' he whispered into her ear. 'I would never have expected you to do something like this.'

'I had to sort everything out. I couldn't wait for you to come home.'

He kissed her again and stroked her hair, which was damp from the spray and curlier than ever. 'Well, I'm honoured that you made such an effort.'

She pulled away and stared into his eyes. 'We spoke to your mother, and she told us that my mother's background has nothing to do with me.'

'Exactly,' Oliver said. 'She mentioned it on the telephone, and I agree, it's something that must never come between us ever again.'

'Never, ever,' Lily said

Oliver sat down on the bench again and pulled Lily next to him, holding her hand tightly in his. 'Let's relax here for a while and enjoy the view while we chat. The Falls are too wide for us to walk their length now, but we can come back tomorrow.

'That would be lovely,' Lily said, nestling as close to him as she could.

Oliver put his arms around her shoulders. 'I'm so pleased you are here, dearest Lily. I will remember how you came to find me like this for the rest of my life.'

'That makes it worthwhile then,' she smiled.

They were silent for a while, listening to the muffled roar, relishing being together again. 'It means so much that you are seeing this amazing sight for the first time with me,' Oliver eventually said: 'The Victoria Falls has a particular significance for my mother and me.' He rubbed her arm as he spoke.

'Oh, yes?' she asked, staring up at him.

'My mother fell in love with Thomas Baines' paintings of the Victoria Falls when she was a little girl. His paintings ignited her interest in Africa, and her desire to paint African scenes. It was because of this that she came to Africa, back in 1900, and that's why this country is now our home. The sight before us is quite superb, isn't it? I can see why it inspired her so.'

Lily tore her eyes from Oliver's face and looked at the scene in front of them. The cascading mass of water, the island beyond filled with tall palm trees, and the deepest gorge she had even seen. A curtain of water and spray blanked one side of this gorge while a carpet of grass and ferns covered the other. Lily pushed her hand deeper into Oliver's and leaned her head against his shoulder as she savoured the wave of happiness which swept through her.

THE END

Acknowledgements

I would first like to acknowledge my huge appreciation to Margaret Montgomery. Margaret and I shared a friendship of nearly forty years and together we shared many meals, cups of tea and coffee, and glasses of gin and wine. She was one of the first people to read "Sunrising" and this inspired her to talk about her life in Southern Rhodesia in the 1930s and 1940s. I decided to write about this time period because of what she told me about the visit by the British Royal Family in 1947, and how, because her father was the Matopos District Native Commissioner, their house had to be renovated for the Royal Family to briefly use. Margaret also told me about her teacher training days at college in Grahamstown and then returning to Bulawayo and living in a boarding house near the power station in Lobengula Street. Margaret was a mine of information about holidays to Beira, tea dances at the Grand Hotel, and what it was like to be a young teacher in Bulawayo in the 1940s. Without her I would not have been able to write a story set in this era.

Unfortunately, just as I was finishing the "The Sun is Bright" and editing my manuscript, Margaret died at the grand old age of 93. I will always be sad that I was unable to read my story to her. I know she would have found it amusing, although I must hasten to add that her father did not behave like Mr Sanderson.

The second person I need to acknowledge for giving me a wonderful insight into World War II in North Africa and Italy is my grandad, Harry Carver. Grandad died in 1989, but the year before, he sat down with a tape recorder and spoke about joining an armoured division in Egypt at the beginning of the war, fighting in the desert, being captured in Libya and shipped to Italy where he was marched from one prisoner of war camp to another until he escaped and had to spend the next year in hiding, before climbing the Alps into Switzerland. All the war time flashbacks I have written about in "The Sun is Bright" are based on his experiences.

Other people I need to thank for helping me write about this era are: Pete Abbot, for explaining how dams were built in the 1940s; Ian Brown for clarifying what servicemen from Southern Rhodesia may have experienced during WW2 and deciding what my character Graham could do after resigning from the RAF; and Bruce Beckley for selecting the cars my characters should drive.

Next, my thanks to the 'first readers" of the story; my parents, Christopher and Moira Carver, my brother, Michael Carver, and my book club friends, Lisa Kaufman and Tina Booth. On their valuable recommendations I shortened the opening scenes and lengthened the ending.

A huge thank you also to the people who proof read the book; first Frances Randell and Karen Vincent, and then Sarah Bowman, Maureen Van Der Horn and Lyn Rawlins who read the final drafts and still found many errors.

Finally I would like to thank the people involved with the cover. Frankie Kay, for the beautiful background photograph of the Matobo on the front, Duncan Watson for designing the cover, Gavin Stephens for the photograph of the Aloe aculeate, and Frances Randell for the lovely photograph of my Staffordshire bull terrier on the back cover.

I would not have been able to produce this book without the help of all these people.

More about Cyrene Mission

I chose the title of this book partly because of what took place at Cyrene Mission from 1940 to 1947.

Cyrene Mission is near Bulawayo on the Plumtree Road, and the Reverend Ned Paterson was the mission priest during this time. He trained at the London School of Art before moving to Rhodesia, where he taught art to boys and young men at Cyrene Mission. He and these young artists created stunning paintings, as well as murals on the walls of the mission chapel. Cyrene was a casualty of the war of independence and the chapel was badly burnt. However, it was rebuilt with a new roof and the murals were repainted in the 1970s, so the legacy the original artists instigated is still apparent today.

There is more to the story than just this though.

In 1947 a number of the Cyrene paintings were sent to England and somehow they went missing, only to be found again in 2020 in a disused church in London. An exhibition of these beautiful works of art was held in London later in 2020 and the name of the exhibition was THE STARS ARE BRIGHT. Around this time, the curators of the exhibition asked my friend Frances and me (amongst others) to go to Cyrene and see what condition the murals were in. Not bad, as it turned out. I was also intrigued to discover that the Reverend Peterson's first wife died when they lived at Cyrene, and she is buried in the small graveyard behind the chapel.

I like to mix fact with fiction in my novels, so when I discovered what took place at Cyrene Mission in the 1940s, I had to weave it into my story.

The curators of the exhibition are publishing a book about the Cyrene Mission artists and their work.

The Sunrising Series

The Sunrising Series depicts the lives of fictional families, the Craigs and the Brookes and their relationship with Africa and the people who they mix with there, from the time the first generation arrived as pioneers at the beginning of the twentieth century to the modern era. There is a forty year gap between the books, and each is a standalone story.

Real life events and experiences are mixed with fiction to reveal the evolving interpersonal and socio-economic landscape as the country moves from a British colony to an independent African country. The first two books in the series are set in colonial times while the second two, to be published in 2023 and 2025, will focus on life in the country after independence

About the author

Susan Hubert was born and has lived in Zimbabwe all her life.

She has an English and Psychology degree from the University of Kwazulu Natal in South Africa, with Mathematics as a minor.

She taught Mathematics for 16 years at high schools in Bulawayo, Zimbabwe, before retiring so she could spend more time with her husband, who was working as a professor of Equine Surgery at Louisiana State University and then Colorado State University. It was during this time she started writing.

When she was back home in Zimbabwe she tutored Mathematics and looked after her husband's herd of cattle.

She now lives full time with her husband on a farm just outside Bulawayo, where they are establishing a pecan plantation. She has one son, Jack Allard.

Learn more on Facebook: Susan Hubert – Author

Made in United States
Orlando, FL
30 November 2025